Andrew Sarkady

ever-life

The C.P.T. Incident

SOUL FIRE
PRESS

an imprint of
Christopher Matthews Publishing
Bozeman, Montana

W9-CJS-876

What readers have said about *Ever-Life*

"Sarkady invites the reader on a curious journey through his futuristic world in which he crafts a captivating story of technology, discovery, and power."
—J. Swartz

"This is a wonderful story and a global thriller, like no other I've read. It's a Pandora's Box filled with hope and questions."
—A. Rittenhouse

"I could picture everything like it was a movie, adventure, science fiction, lots of fun and very thought provoking! I liked the way the love story weaves in, too. It has something for everyone."
—K. Maitzen

"I was very intrigued by the characters and held captive by the storyline.
—L. Ward

"A real page turner. I have fallen in love with this author's work and have read several of his books"
—D. Wolford

Ever-Life: The C.P.T. Incident is Book I of the *Ever-Life Series*
Book II: *Ever-Life: Time Trust*
is available from bookstores, online and from
Christopher Matthews Publishing
http://christophermatthewspub.com

Ever-Life: The C.P.T. Incident

Editor: Jeremy Soldevilla
Cover design: Armen Kojoyian
Interior illustrations: Andrew Sarkady
Typeface: Georgia

Paperback ISBN 9781938985638
ebook ISBN 9781938985645

Published by
Soul Fire Press

An imprint of
CHRISTOPHER MATTHEWS PUBLISHING
http://christophermatthewspub.com
Bozeman, Montana

Printed in the United States of America

Acknowledgements

There are those without whose encouragement, I never would have finished this labor of love. It is with the utmost sincerity and affection that I thank my close loved ones and family for supporting me.

To all my children and grandchildren, thank you for giving my life meaning and hope, and, in the end, for a reason to write. And hi, Mom and Dad—thank you! I know you are watching.

Finally, thank you, Karen and Jeremy, for your undying patience and support during rewrites and the final edits.

Table of Contents

Hope and Love abide with all who believe.
May we all believe in the future
Many people write books to tell a story they imagine.
That is fiction today. But, what if someone writes
a true story that hasn't happened yet?

PREFACE

I HAVE HEARD IT SAID that everyone has at least one book in them. In my case, yes, I was compelled to write this. My story is quite an exciting one, really. I am simply an ordinary man, having no scientific or medical background; but I am the world's first real time-traveler. The purpose of my recounting all that happened was to get it out of my head, and it did haunt me until I finished.

I know, you're thinking, here we go; what kind of idiot would believe that statement? I don't blame you. I wrote this to relieve my mind, and as a record for my family and those loved ones who inspired me to do so, even without knowing they did. But, I want to be clear. This is in no way a technical or medical manual explaining any methodology. It is no more than the information given to me through a process I experienced. It's all written from headset sessions. So, if curiosity is truly irresistible, perhaps you will read on, enjoy and be driven to study what is truly the strangest, most exciting tale I couldn't forget.

First, to be precise, I was abducted into the future three times and came back twice. The people there told me it is only possible to travel into the past. Actually, as I understand the way it works, all the events I recount here did happen in their past, so from their perspective, I guess that is correct. They have what they call headsets, quite remarkable little devices. Some fit like old hearing aids, while others fit like police swat-team communicators. Each one carries knowledge in the form of data, recorded up to the moment you put one on. When they activate it, your brain's chemistry alters, and you upload any or all information of whatever the subject inquiry is. That is how I was able to recall the events.

My recollection is the journey of several people who became involved in each other's lives because of a remarkable discovery and a threat posed to it by the actions of a power hungry billionaire. It all began in the year 2999, when Dr. Jack Sheldon, Head of Research at the Brock/Swanson Medical Complex was taken to a hospital emergency room. Some time before that, he had discovered something that would change everything, a wonderful medical secret—C.P.T., Chemical Personality Transfer, which he had prepared to introduce to the public that very week. At the same time, billionaire Marion Brock plotted and stopped at nothing to get Jack's secret.

However, unknown to Brock or anyone on Earth's surface, deep below the Complex was a futuristic health-base, Ever-Life, and its leaders wanted Jack's secret too. A catastrophic event occurred, from the conflict between Ever-Life and the Brock Empire, which triggered my time travel to the future.

The following is the written recall of the events from the first headset session given to me.

CHAPTER 1

RISEN

IT WAS 1:59 A.M. Nurse Angela Esposito sat in her office, leaning on her elbows and stared at the medical display monitor for Room 309. She could not stop thinking about the events of the last several hours. Three straight green lines beeped across the black screen from left to right with no vital signs indicated, no heart, no brain and no blood pressure activity. Angie typed her security code into the computer and stood up, putting a two-inch blue vial into her pocket. She turned, picked up a food tray and walked briskly to Room 309. As she opened the door, her eyes popped wide open. She dropped the tray and screamed. Jack Sheldon was sitting upright on the gurney pulling off the adhesive tabs, intravenous hook ups and bandages as if they were annoying insects.

Angela barely regained her composure as Jack sniffed the air, oblivious to the hospital surroundings. He shook his head and looked down at himself.

"Jesus! What is this? And that smell! What is so rotten?" As he blinked and squinted, the blur cleared, and he did a side-to-side scan around the room. Then, he looked keenly at the nurse. "Who are you? Where the hell am I?"

In that instant, Angie reacted with raw emotion, not as a trained nurse. She turned and ran out of the room shaking and repeating, "Holy shit! You're supposed to be dead; you're supposed to be dead!"

◈❦◈

Angie Esposito was the security nurse in charge of the special Focus Ward on the third floor of Andrews Hospital. The hospital was one of 15 buildings housed on the highly secure 600-acre campus of the Brock/Swanson Medical Complex. The Complex, located in Arden City, was some 75 miles south of Albuquerque, New Mexico, in a desert landscape west of White Sands.

Andrews itself was unique. Unlike any other building, it towered 10 floors above ground and had an elaborate underground construction six stories below. Like all staff, Angie went through a comprehensive training and security clearance. She was a petite 5'2" black haired beauty, a sharp, quick thinker, loyal, dedicated and over-experienced for her age. She completed her undergraduate studies in Chicago, graduating with highest honors. She had a good friend and mentor in Dr. Mathew Bellos, Chief of Hospital. He took her under his wing 16 years ago, after her mother died. Bellos supported her financially, and coached her through her residency, medical Master's degree and several private tours. He brought her to Andrews specifically for the lonely specialized position on Focus Ward.

Angie performed many secure tasks for Dr. B., over the years, but she never prepared herself, in any way, for what she just saw, a man rise from the dead.

◈❦◈

By the time the 32-year-old nurse reached the bathroom, she gasped for air thinking, *This just isn't me, get a hold of yourself girl!* She sat on the floor cheek to bowl, motionless. After several minutes, she felt sufficiently in control to get up and race down the stairs to the nurse's lounge on the second floor.

Everything started when she received the priority email earlier in the evening:

Time: 10:25 p.m., U.S.A. Mountain Time

 Andrews Hospital

To: Angela Esposito>Focus Ward

From: M. J. Bellos, Chief of Hospital>001-001

Subject: Immediate Security Priority 01-Response Required 001-Code AO-25646

I authorize you to check immediately the security attachments describing Protocol 060 for specific instructions regarding emergency arrival of expired bodies resulting from multiple auto accident at 10:15 p.m. Patient 004 will be delivered to Focus Ward, Room 309. You are to monitor all vital signs and chart a matrix for review, by 'me only'. At precisely 2 a.m., you are to personally deliver a food tray to Room 309 and inject vial 134 [from Focus security station box 1120-password, 2fy947t] into the subject's right carotid artery. Memorize and delete this mailing.

Mathew J. Bellos

Chief of Hospital, Brock/Swanson Labs

Security 01-Code AO-25642

At the time, Angie thought, *So odd, bodies, monitor—how do I monitor the dead? This isn't the morgue. Somebody is screwing with me. Why take the food tray? Why inject the syringe? But, the email was from the Chief, himself . . . whatever . . . doing anything for Dr. B. is an adventure.*

So, at precisely 2 a.m., with her food tray in hand, she walked briskly to Room 309.

᠙᠂ᡝᠣᠣᠽᡝᡪᠣᡵ

When the door to the second floor nurses' lounge flew open and slammed against the wall it was obvious to the small group near the coffee machine that something was very wrong. Every head turned in shock to see a terrified, young, tearful face crying with no discernible voice, "H-Help me, for God's sake."

Barb Sawyer, floor supervisor, moved quickly to the girl, but Angie pushed her away and ran to the opposite side of the room, panting, "He was dead, he was dead . . . Shit!"

Suddenly faint, she fell forward, and two nurses caught her, Barb Sawyer, 45-year old with five years of experience at Andrews, and Ralph Walker, 34-year old Princeton graduate, who started at the hospital a year ago. They carefully laid her on the floor, and Barb laid her head down on a small pillow.

"Hey, easy, Angie; it's me, Ralphy."

Barb looked around at the group and spoke in a soft whisper, "Angie, tell us what happened. It's going to be all right."

"I don't know. He was in pieces. They reattached his limbs in surgery. I still don't know why they bothered. The only bones that weren't broken were in his hands." She looked up at Barb, gasping, "I got the email; his remains came to Focus Ward with no vital signs. I took the tray in, right on time. He just sat up. He looked like a bloody monster, but, my God, he was alive." Angie squeezed Barb's wrist. "It can't be him...they must have switched bodies. That's not Jack Sheldon in 309!" She began to hyperventilate. "But, why? How could they do that? I had sensors hooked up all over him. Honestly, he was dead."

Barb motioned toward the cooler. "Give me water here . . . all of you may leave. We have this. Give her some breathing space, will you? Ralph, get Dr. Bellos for me, please? We need him here stat!"

CHAPTER 2

RACHEL

RACHEL SHELDON HELD HER HEAD IN HER HANDS as she slumped in a cold hard ER-1 room chair at Andrews Hospital. She gathered herself, trying to gain her composure. It seemed like everything was happening so fast, but taking so long. There was so much to think about; images of their lives popped in and out of her head.

When her phone rang earlier, around 11:15 p.m., she had been dozing in her favorite lounge on the screened porch, waiting for the garage door to open signaling Jack's arrival. The two had built a wonderful life together over the years.

They'd met in Maryland, where Rachel was working her first real job in microbiology as a new team member under Jack. He was a young director of government operations responsible for developing new vaccines for unpopular illnesses referred to as 'orphan diseases'. Their first meeting never would have happened, except on that night, during a routine procedure in front of five other experts, Jack's overwhelming presence caused her to make a mistake so obvious that he had to write her up. Ten 'write-ups' and you were fired. 'Write-ups' were posted at the central station for any and all to see.

The next day, Rachel was devastated to see her name was first on the list. She went to see Jack, hoping to corner him after his presentation lecture to funding gurus on 'Brain Function and Control-Through Chemistry'. She sat swelling with anger outside of the banquet room. As the doors opened, she pushed and shoved her way through the exiting crowd. When she found him, they argued in front of everyone for a good 45 minutes.

The rest was mad microbiological love. They became the most famous success team known at the agency, having discovered a record number of medical cures. They were married the next January, and Rachel gave birth to their only son, Brian, in November of the next year. Brian graduated Georgetown University Law, and he became the personal apprentice to Marion Brock, philanthropic billionaire and co-founder of the Brock/Swanson Research Complex.

During the Complex's construction, Jack and Rachel built their dream home on 70 acres, conveniently located 10 miles from Andrews. Their beautiful swimming pool and botanic garden centered within a U-shaped, stone four-bedroom ranch where they managed 15-20 horses at a time. They had three working ranch hands and a full-time housekeeper. In the basement of the house, they furnished a completely self-sufficient private laboratory with state of the art equipment so Jack could continue home research. Over the years, they and their research teams were responsible for a stunning 30 medical breakthroughs, pioneered and patented with their long time partner, Dr. Mathew Bellos.

Rachel was an attractive 44-year-old woman. She had medium blonde hair sprinkled with just a tad gray here and there. When she smiled, the creases around her eyes spoke of many happy times. She was 5'2" tall and had a strikingly beautiful figure.

Jack had a buff-like appearance, even at the age of 46, standing six feet tall. His olive complexion fooled most into thinking he was Italian rather than French. He had a magnetic demeanor and the looks to match. His full head of hair was graying at the temples, and there was no mistaking that smile or curt staunch look when he was concentrating or guiding his team. Years ago, Jack's young talents brought him the highest achievements tenured at Johns Hopkins University. His career soared after receiving awards in genetic analysis during those government contract years. Eventually, his expertise brought him to Brock /Swanson as the Head of Research. He and Rachel were the quintessential couple, and they had all the amenities befitting their extraordinary expertise.

It was hours ago that Rachel awoke at home from her cell phone ringing.

"Hello?"

"Mrs. Sheldon?"

"Yes."

"This is Ron Sandry at Andrews Hospital. I'm sorry to call at this hour, especially to tell you this."

"What's wrong?"

"It's Mr. Sheldon, ma'am. He was in a car accident. It's bad, Mrs. Sheldon; you had better come. I really don't know what to say. Dr. Bellos told me to call you. He is with him now. That's all I know."

Rachel felt her heart and mind race. "How bad?"Her hand shook so that she almost dropped the phone. "Is he alive? I'm on my way. Where should I go?"

"Doctor said you should go to ground floor ER-1. He will be there as soon as he can. I'm sorry, I can't tell you anymore than that."

It was 2;30 a.m.; Rachel paced in the private room. Three different doctors spoke to her in the last two hours, but they gave her no definitive news. Jack was in isolation surgery. That's all they said. Rachel tried to think. *Accept Jack's possible death? Even if he lives, life will be so different. What would he want me to do? Matt, I need you! Where the hell is he?*

She didn't want to fathom any of this. Still, somehow, she had ingrained within her the Pollyanna notion that all would be okay . . . *There has to be something. Maybe what we have done in our work could help. After all, honey, we cured the common cold and proved the impossible possible, right? Hmm, Rachel, think, damn it!*

She pushed the nurse's call button, but there was no reply and no one came. Finally, she went to the bed and lay down, hoping to drift into sleep.

CHAPTER 3

NURSES' LOUNGE

BEFORE RALPH WALKER COULD PAGE HIM, Dr. Mathew Bellos walked into the nurses lounge. Bellos was 52-years-old, 6' tall and 185 pounds. He was average to describe, but impressive at first sight. He was a complicated man, well-educated, extremely talented and creative and with a background to envy. Most of all, he was a visionary and persuasive. One of his ancestors worked with Jonas Salk researching the Polio vaccine.

After his parents died in New Mexico, young Bellos moved to Washington, D.C., and earned master's degrees in both genetic analysis and organic chemistry. Two years later, he received his Ph.D. in political philosophy. The Washington elite welcomed his expertise and commanding presence. His published work, Viruses to Recover Life, made Bellos popular worldwide. Now, at Brock/Swanson, Mathew Bellos reigned as Chief of Andrews Hospital. The buck stopped with him. Over recent years, he mentored and hired many of the hospital staff.

Tonight, during the horrific early morning hours, news spread quickly throughout the Complex about Dr. Jack Sheldon's arrival. Overall, in the hospital's hierarchy, the entire staff thought of Jack, Rachel and Bellos as 'the big three'. However, only a select few knew Sheldon's injuries were fatal.

The moment Bellos entered the nurses lounge, he went to Angie and the two doctors holding her. Her face changed when she saw him.

"Dr. Bellos, I'm so glad you're here. Listen to me. I was in Focus 309. I did everything you instructed. He was . . . "

Bellos placed his forefinger to his lips and smiled. "Shush, it's okay." He embraced and lifted her. She noticed that he applied unusual pressure to her upper arms, guiding her out of the lounge toward a security guard. Bellos spoke firmly but quietly, "Please take Ms. Angie to my office and stay with her until I get there. Give her anything she'd like. If she is hungry, order from the kitchen. Let her relax. I will be there as soon as I can . . . and give her privacy. Wait outside."

Angie looked confused. At the same time, Barb Sawyer stepped in front of Dr. Bellos and whispered to him, trying to recount the story's bits and pieces, but Bellos interrupted, "Barb, you didn't hear anything but the ravings of an emotionally unstable woman. Unfortunately, Angie has had a problem lately, of which I have just become aware. She has allegedly been abusing her access to the private prescriptions on Focus Ward. It's a very sad, highly secure issue because of the particular hallucinogenic involved. So, we didn't have this conversation . . . we have invested a lot here and we need her. I need to get her through this as quietly as possible, and make her rehabilitation work. Are you with me here? I will handle this."

"Yes, of course. She seemed stressed, yes, emotional, yes; but, believe me, she was coherent. Look, Dr. Bellos, there are so many things I don't know about your precious Focus Ward; but, I know people, and she wasn't on drugs."

"Well, I hope you don't make me pull rank. I've told you more than I should already." Bellos turned to walk away, and then he stopped, turned back and put his hand affectionately on Barb's shoulder. "We have bigger problems, Barb. Please, work with me here. I have to go. Use that talent of yours to calm these people. Let them know this is a special security situation. Nothing goes beyond this room, all right?"

Sawyer was a professional, loyal trooper, yet always the skeptic. She blinked and nodded, "Right."

Bellos paused again, as though he just had an epiphany and looked deeply into her eyes. "You've been here five years and have a great record, Barb. You know more than most about everything here, don't you?"

"I like to think I'm up to date."

"Well, until we sort this out, I am reassigning you. You are the only other person I trust, who has the qualifications and experience to oversee Focus Ward. Report to me at 4 p.m. sharp, this afternoon, to my 10th floor office. Meantime, check your computer and read all the 'redirect security protocols' involved. We will discuss your specific duties and access codes at that time. Please be prepared to perform on a 24/7 basis."

It was close to 3 a.m. when Bellos sped off to the elevator. Barb Sawyer stood in shock at the door, watching Angie and the guard, disappear down the hallway.

CHAPTER 4

TOTAL RECALL

AS DR. BELLOS ENTERED the elevator and pushed ER-1, he couldn't help thinking about his history with Rachel and Jack. Their first meeting took place while they all worked at V.I.R.A.I.D.—Viral Infection Research and Internal Development. At that time, it was a U. S. Defense Department sub-contracting company. Jack and Rachel's team were researching a new military concept. The premise was that too much testosterone and adrenaline caused over-aggression, which was the basis for military behavior. Their objective was to suppress these two chemicals in the body by deploying a gaseous contagion during combat. Rachel and Jack isolated and defined formulas, which, if proven correct, would prevent the human body from secreting these hormones within 10 seconds. One exposure covered 100 square yards. If they succeeded, the target troops could not fight . . . no fighting, no war. That effort was the foundation upon which Jack would later define his 'chemical personality controllers'.

At that same time, young Dr. Bellos' team was researching dormant virus' reactions to various stimuli. A virus can lay dormant for thousands of years, and then, with proper stimuli, it can become active-alive, again. His research team progressed to re-activate not only several viruses, but also some rare bacteria. Eventually, Bellos hoped to create a practical use for his findings, like transporting donor organs or limbs without the need of refrigeration. Later, Bellos would hypothesize that death itself was an illness, and the cure lay in the viral world.

Jack and Rachel were attending a three-day V.I.R.A.I.D. convention, and Mathew Bellos was the keynote speaker. What he said profoundly moved them, so they finagled a meeting with him, and, after finding out they had so much in common, the three bonded. They became unmatchable research team leaders.

Bellos' mind drifted as he rode in the hospital elevator. He thought about how it all seemed so convoluted now. Jack's C.P.T. discovery changed everything. Recently, Bellos had become embroiled with it all. He thought back to his life changing morning years ago on May 12 . . .

It was shortly after he began working at Brock/Swanson. Bellos was enjoying coffee and a croissant at the small café, Gus' Coffee in Arden, New Mexico. Focused in a brief moment of relief about getting away from the East Coast political arena, he noticed a rather stiff looking man sit down at the table next to him. Although dressed in jeans and a sweatshirt, the man was obviously not from the Southwest. At first glance, he reminded Bellos of the FBI types within the Washington, D.C. cliques. The man made no eye contact; however, after five minutes or so, he got up and dropped an issue of the local Arden Gazette onto Dr. B.'s table. Bellos looked at the man with some confusion, as the man nodded and then quickly walked to his car and sped off. Bellos noticed a part of a Post-it note wedged in the newspaper that read:

Mathew Bellos: You have been chosen for a high purpose. We want you as our ally in the struggle to preserve and better humanity. It is urgent you phone me @ . . .

There was a small iconic signature stamped at the bottom, which looked like an old Christian fish symbol with a dollar sign before it. Questions haunted him on and off all day. That evening, in the privacy of his office study, Bellos made the phone call that would change his priorities completely.

A voice answered, "Bridger here . . . "

Bellos froze for a second. "Yes, I am Dr. Mathew Bellos. Ah, one of your people approached me this morning and asked me to call this number."

"Oh, yes, Dr. Bellos, that wasn't one of my people, that was me. I am Tom Bridger. I apologize for the cloak and dagger. We can never be sure of our response rate from first encounters. When you learn about our organization, you'll understand."

Bellos was hardly interested. "I called because the cryptic method you used haunted me, but frankly, I'm not interested in solicitations of any kind, thank you."

"Dr. Bellos, we are on the verge of making one of the most important announcements in the history of medicine; perhaps even the most important announcement in all history, but we need you. I am not exaggerating in any way."

"I really don't have any idea what you are talking about."

"Doctor, why do we become medical researchers? Why do we fight disease? What is your goal in medicine? Please, I cannot discuss this over the phone. I assure you, I am sincere. We must meet. It will not just change your life; you will fulfill your destiny."

"This is a ridiculous conversation. I am not going to commit myself to some drama that sounds like a scam to me. Good bye."

As Bellos pulled the phone away from his ear, he heard, "Doctor, your father and great grandfather were one of us. We are your family."

Bellos pushed the phone back against his ear.

"Doctor, please, I know your history. We have to meet. Doctor Bellos, are you there?"

"Yes, I am here."

"I can't say anymore; anyone could be listening, you know that. Believe me, I am not a fake. Will you meet me at the same café, tomorrow morning, say at 7:15? Come on, Doc."

"Hmm, if this is so damn important and secret, why the café; why out in the open?"

"Because we know it's secure. We own it, and the surrounding five stores on each side of the street. We don't own the airways however, or the phone lines."

"Oh . . . " Leery of it all and with a slight grin, Dr. B. hung up the phone and sat back bewildered.

The next morning, as Bellos walked to the café, he studied his hometown street as if for the first time. Usually, there was a line stretching out the door to buy morning sweets and hot drinks; but that morning, as Bellos approached, only one single person sat at an outside table.

"Good morning, Doctor . . . " Bridger extended his hand.

"Good morning."

"Please, have a seat. I hope you don't mind, I bought you an espresso and donut."

"Thank you. Now tell me why I'm here?"

"I am Tom Bridger, a recruiter, so to speak. I represent an organization, which has been in existence for a very long time, millennia, actually, by your standards. Please, excuse me if I seem uneasy. You see, I know how what I'm about to say will sound."

Bridger smiled and took a deep breath before explaining, "We have been involved in, and continue to influence, most modern countries' medical and political systems. Medical advancement is our purpose and politics is the vehicle we use to fund ourselves. The civilized world all over the globe has prospered, using our medical discoveries. Anyway, you'll learn as you go."

"What?" Bellos sat looking a bit annoyed.

"The thing is; it's only been within the last 800 years that things have become really interesting. We are the richest, most advanced research organization on the planet. I am authorized to tell you that we are on the verge of announcing the greatest of discoveries. It will be the answer to why we all got into medicine."

Bellos' eyes widened and he said cynically, "Really, I got into medical research to combat disease and improve the human condition. What question or answer are you talking about?"

Bridger did not react. He just smirked and said, "We have followed your career and those of your close colleagues for some time. We need your help, and you need us. This is the end of a 10,000-year-old journey, and the beginning of a new era for all humankind. Doctor; this is not some Hollywood nonsense or CIA undercover plot to overthrow a country."

"Well, it sounds like wild science fiction bullshit to me."

"Perhaps, but it isn't." Bridger took an envelope out of his rear pant pocket. "Here, this is for you. There is a letter of instruction in there. We crossed out some words, for security purposes, but you will get the gist. There is also an airplane ticket. Only one person has authorization to explain more, and he awaits your arrival."

Bellos unfolded the papers and looked through them.

"My instructions are to ask that you read the first page now and the rest on the plane."

Bellos shook his head in disbelief, as he pulled a wad of money from the envelope."

"Oh yes, there's also $200,000, a bit of petty cash. You keep that whether you go or not. If your answer is no, give me the paperwork back. That's it, Doc. Now or never, no more talk until you reach destination."

Bellos looked at Bridger and rolled his eyes. "Jesus, this is insane."

Twelve hours later that same day, Mathew Bellos reached the front stairs of the United States Capital building in Washington, D.C. He spent some time sitting on the concrete stairs, overlooking the downtown campus, and reflecting about his past there. The streets were unusually quiet for that time of day. Nevertheless, as instructed, he stood by the curb at 7:30 p.m., waiting for a white stretch limousine to pick him up. Bellos scrutinized every vehicle that passed. After several minutes, he felt a hand on the back of his shoulder and heard a soft baritone voice, "Good evening, Doctor. Thank you for being so punctual."

As Bellos turned around, he looked up to see a distinguished tall, white-haired man, around 60 in age, standing before him wearing gray plastic rimmed glasses. "Good evening, I am Mathew Bellos."

"Yes, I know, I am Gordon Swanson. I must apologize for all the mystery, but our history, our purpose and success are beyond security, as you understand it. I promise, I will explain everything."

A white limousine pulled up to the curb; the driver got out and opened the back door. Swanson gestured politely to Bellos. "Please, Doctor, come; we will talk."

It was a cabin fit for a king. Bellos had never seen any vehicle like this, and he studied everything inside. Swanson simply uttered two words, "Master secured." As Bellos listened to clicks and flinched at the blinking lights, the two side door windows became 3-D monitors and pivoted around in front of them. Each one displayed video with unfamiliar languages.

"I activated security protocols; that's all."

At the same time, a small, sleek automatic drink dispenser rose up from the floor and made two perfect martinis. "Here, Mathew, you will want this."

The driver made a U-turn and sped off. Bellos couldn't help but start. "Look, Mr. Swanson . . . "

"It's just Swanson."

"Yes, well; Mr. Bridger told me a few things that certainly would interest anyone. He was very persuasive. And the money . . . well . . . thank you, but . . . but, I have many questions."

Swanson turned from looking out the window at the night sky. "I'm here to answer your questions and determine if you are truly suitable for our organization—our society, really. You see, Mathew, we have monitored you and two of your colleagues for quite some time. We know you have what we want, and we are certain we can provide you with all that you need."

"What exactly does that mean? Your man Bridger said the same thing. I have no idea what you are talking about."

Swanson turned to view the Washington Monument. "Did you know, Doctor, it's been said that at the time of its construction, this city was designed to impress and outshine all other cities in the world? That is one reason we finally settled a key post underground here."

Bellos was anything but impressed. "Yes, the city is beautiful, basic American history. Wait a minute. What did you say about underground?"

"You could say we have been 10,000 years in the making. Did Bridger tell you how old we are?"

"Not really, that I remember."

"Our organization has outlasted most cultures on the planet. We research and develop medical breakthroughs to preserve and improve humanity. Our new campus is nearly complete in the southwestern United States, quite close to where you grew up; and we are recruiting. Ours is a society of sorts, but not a democracy. It is, well, a sort of monarchy, in your terms. We have only one absolute authority, one person, responsible for all matters and everyone."

"We call that a dictatorship."

"Far from it, actually; having authority and responsibility is quite different from exerting power over people, an argument for another day. Regardless, today it happens to be a man. There have been women, famous women, who have been great leaders. It is truly amazing, when I think about how many people live on Earth's surface serving us, dutifully working double lives. They research for some country and for us. It is through their loyalty and commitment that we have been so successful for so long."

"Sounds like treason; we're not at war; that's absurd. All of us with half a brain know standard ethics, not to mention signing non-disclosure pledges."

"I suppose," said Swanson. "Ah yes, non-disclosure pledges, those are the documents that grant government and corporate dictatorships power over people. Your corporations are insecure institutions surviving by competing. They all require control to assure profit, management by fear. Unlike them, neither do we hold creativity captive, nor do we blackmail our employees. We are completely secure. Let us say, for example, a corporate researcher discovers something quite stunning. By signing non-disclosure, one is bound legally not to share the information. Whatever it is could remain hidden, unknown for years, even decades. Eventually, at some time in the future, your global communication media would find out and announce it. Then, all of a sudden, it's news out of the closet. Within days, at most weeks, it becomes a standard across the globe, right? That's when we all benefit, right? Think of what we do as shortening the whole timeline. We do not cheat or steal profits. We expedite discoveries to the public, and of course, we share in the wealth, when we can. Actually, as it turns out, we help grow corporate and government profits faster. You will understand as you go."

"Wait a minute. Let me understand this. So, you are recruiting; why would I consider such a thing? You say you built here underground, during the 1800s, when the city as we know it was constructed, right? Look, I hope you did not spend this money and time to give me a history or economic lesson."

"Actually, Mathew, I brought you here for many lessons, and to show you something that will change you. We are at a turning point of deciding whether to . . . " Swanson paused and stared at Bellos. "You see, Mathew, one of your colleagues is in the process of refining a medical hypothesis, which, if proven true, or more specifically, if the wrong people get a hold of it, well, chaos, frankly, may result. For the first time in our history, we have to decide whether to assist or stop it. All this is quite contrary to our usual involvements . . . and you are a big part of it. You have contributed, you see. I know you don't understand your part in this, yet; but, even your viral research over the years has components that, when put together with your colleague's data; well, the potential medical wonders for the future are unmistakable, and unavoidable to us. Although you two brilliant scientific minds have worked separately, you both have stumbled onto what we discovered, refined, and kept silent for well over 3,500 years by your timeline. We certainly didn't expect this from any surface researcher. I neither exaggerate nor mock you in any way. If nothing else, the $200,000 petty cash was to impress upon you that what I tell you is not to be taken lightly."

"My timeline? What do you mean by that?" Bellos scratched his head. "Why are you afraid of this 'hypothesis' you speak of?"

"Because it could threaten the balance of life on the planet, my boy; I wish I could give you all the knowledge right now; but, please, do try to have more ear than mouth."

Bellos rolled his eyes, and then he swallowed the martini in one gulp. "What is this secret that you and Bridger speak of anyway?"

"Well, as you said, first things first. It seems the more I say, the angrier you become. I wish to educate you, not sour you. Patience, Doctor, patience," Swanson smirked. "Perhaps you'd like another martini?"

"No."

"Frankly, when I think about it from your point of view, it is very spooky and cryptic. I will give you that. I wouldn't want to listen to me, either; but it is worth it. It is well worth it."

The limo rounded Madison Street and turned into an alley. Swanson took out his key fob and pushed a button. "Mr. Mike, are we ready?"

"Yes, sir, we are here."

Suddenly, Bellos felt the front of the car nosedive, as if they were on a rollercoaster.

Bellos felt his stomach in his throat. "Whoa! What is that?"

The car circled down and around to the right, twisting and turning into the dark.

"It's all right, Doctor." Swanson held tightly onto the door handle himself. "We have buildings below just about a mile or so away now. There are ramps like this throughout the city. All of them wind around like the tentacles of an octopus, eventually leading back to its head. You are going to love it. Now, the new campus I spoke of will be much more in the open, completely different, of course; but then, security will be of a different type altogether. Ah, progress, I love it. Relax, Doctor, only a few more minutes. Everything is ready for you."

"I don't even know this place and you're already describing a new one . . . ready for me? What a headache. I don't get this one bit, not one bit."

Gordon Swanson grinned as the car sped through a dark one-lane tunnel. After a few minutes, the tunnel opened up to a wide, brightly lighted area several miles in diameter. Bellos stared in wonder at the beautiful wild flowers that filled the fields and the unfamiliar trees all around the perimeter.

"How is this possible? Where is the sun?"

In the distance, Bellos could see what looked like an immense structure cut out of the surrounding rock. "What is that? It's glowing."

"That is our destination."

Finally, the car stopped at an entrance, and the two men walked up several stairs, beneath a sculpted rock canopy. The underside displayed frescos worthy of Rafael and Michelangelo. Bellos strained his neck studying it all. "Are we at the ancient Venetian in Las Vegas?"

"Not quite. Come. Beautiful, isn't it? And this is just a side entrance. Wait until you see the main foyer."

Everything seemed bathed in an unfamiliar, comfortable light. However, Bellos could see no source—no lamps of any kind. They walked some 20 yards in and stood at the bottom of another staircase. Bellos noticed an etching in the rock above a double doorway at the top. It looked like the outline of a huge fish.

"Mr. Swanson, what does that mean? Bridger stamped it on a note to me, when we first met."

"Eye catching isn't it . . . tweaked your interest, eh?"

"Well, yes."

"It is part of an old character alphabet that existed for who knows how long. As you know, in any language, words or phrases connote several meanings. I like to think of that in particular as 'thesauretical'."

"What language is that? It looks like an old Christian fish with a U.S. dollar sign in its mouth."

Swanson squinted, cocking his head to one side. "Yes, it does; very perceptive . . . think back, long ago, when cell phones first became the rage. 'Texting' was not even a word in the English language. Over the years, certain icons or expressions become acceptable colloquialisms. Even down here that happens. Regardless, literally translated in English that means, 'Money comes from God'." Swanson raised his eyebrows with a grin. "We do have Christians here, too. Of course, that may mean something different to you, as time goes by."

Bellos shook his head in complete frustration. The two stepped up the deep maroon, paisley-carpeted stairs; and at the top, a strangely dressed guard greeted them. He stood in front of two beautifully carved and lacquered 15-foot by 11-foot double doors. Bellos stared at his strange outfit. "Are we in ancient Rome?"

"No," Swanson giggled, "although the Vatican's Swiss Guard uniforms did have a similar pantaloon look. Except, of course, we, on the other hand, keep up with our latest state of the art weaponry. You won't see his kind of sidearm anywhere on the surface. It fires a simple burst of air, which will knock you out, up to 50 yards away."

"Air?"

"Yes, it's technical."

They entered and the guard shut the doors.

"This way, Doctor; it's late and we have a full schedule. I hope you slept on the plane. After we talk, you have to be processed, tested and remember quite a lot."

"You're going to test me?"

"Not the way you think, my friend."

They walked across what looked like a one hundred-foot long library. Bellos marveled at the medical reference books on the shelves, printed in many different languages. He stopped at one point and took a book off a shelf. "*Polio Diaries* by Jonas Salk. How did you get this? This is original penmanship. He died back in 1995, right?"

"Centuries ago; that was a gift to us, resulting from an unfortunate political negotiation, I'm sorry to say. This way. Shall we continue?"

Swanson gestured to the other end of the room. Bellos put the book back on the shelf and they walked to another set of doors.

"Come in. Welcome to my endless hallway. I am rather embarrassed that I am a bit nervous. People here will tell you, I never seem nervous . . . "

"Imagine that," Bellos chimed.

"Yes, well, this way. I should also tell you that involvement with us is for life, Doctor. Every life here benefits from the omniscience of the whole. However, like anything else, none of it works without trust, you know? I like to think we are one reason mankind is at the top of the food chain, hah . . . "

"And that means?"

"In the final analysis, it is the genetics of it all that brought us to you. It is you, Mathew . . . " Swanson gently touched his sleeve. "What I said before is certainly true. Your colleague is going to discover something profound; but, he will want us as much as I need you."

"Sir, you talk in riddles."

"Sorry, this is my first and only time doing this," Swanson paused, looking Bellos squarely in the eye. "You see, I am not just recruiting . . . in fact, I am Great Grand Master, Gordon G.

Swanson. In our vernacular, the population refers to me as 'GGM' . . . I run this place, lead it, if you will. I represent all the lives here. And, I am recruiting you to replace me, to help me decide if some of our very important information should be made public to the surface."

"What?" Bellos said. "Are you Masons?"

Swanson lifted one eyebrow. "No, although several terms they use may have originated from us, neither great, nor grandmaster came from them. And, just for the record, I think you may be asking 'what?' quite a lot . . . come to think of it; so did I."

"This is a mistake; really," said Bellos rolling his eyes and shaking his head.

"No, Doctor, it is not!" Swanson squeezed his shoulder. "It's no mistake. I need you. We all need you. Come, I will try to explain as much as I can, within what time we have." They began walking again. "Now pay attention. Here, in our world, we measure a lifetime in genetic terms rather than in time cycle terms. That is to say, we measure age and general health as it relates to individual DNA or gene structure, depending . . . "

"I know how important good health is," Bellos said. "I am a doctor."

"Well, we certainly use concepts of physics, time, economics and politics; but, we have concentrated our cultural strategies with different frames of reference. You see, we isolated, defined, and started applying the human genome to diagnose illness several thousand years ago.

"This is a crazy dream."

"Hardly, listen; on the surface you measure everything as it relates to rotations of the Earth around the sun. You use what you call textbooks in schools, based on historical data—Newton, Darwin, Einstein and Hawking; so many people up there you worship, not just within religions, and so many years of schooling . . . the point is that you are just now beginning real medical research, in-depth miniaturization and the use of genetics."

"I hate to disappoint you, but we all know Newton, Einstein and Darwin. I studied modern man's boom in discovery. It began pushing limits with the space race, back in the 1960s. That alone started generating tremendous strides in miniaturization. Our people continued for centuries making great discoveries—transplants, artificial limbs, skin grafts, venom vaccines. New research is endless."

"Yes, well that's right. Do not think I am belittling your accomplishments or culture. Quite the contrary, I just wanted you to know that we were where you are now, millennia ago. Imagine this; our children learn and understand courses of study like quantum theory, organic chemistry and genetic analysis at the primary school level. When we tried to get you going on it, you burned witches. The mind can be a very bad enemy, Mathew."

"So the $200,000 was payment for listening to this fantasy?"

"No, my point is, down here we do not see the sun; we use other frames of reference as time controls and guideposts to improve learning and progress."

"What are you talking about?"

"We are a health-based society. Sometimes we borrow things from the surface, and then we give discoveries back to you, as payment—as medical science advancements, you see. However, we are at a point now where I will need your help specifically. I am going to help you for starters, and show you exactly what I mean. We will answer all your questions; and make no mistake—you will flood me with them."

"Hah, you haven't answered one yet. I have no idea what all this is about . . . what about you, your health . . . is there something wrong with you?"

"Yes, hmm, in my case, I do have a specific genetic issue. I have a flaw that develops later in life. It is sort of an 'orphan's genetic disease'. I must address it. However, I have to do so with and through you. Your family does not have genetic flaws. In fact, you are quite gifted, genetically. On the other hand, my condition has no cure, yet."

A small smile appeared on Swanson's lips. "Given our way of measuring time down here, and my condition, I must choose my successor now, and that's that. There is no committee, no vote. I am sole authority. Our laws state that my successor may be of any background, but there are other specific rules. We have studied the genetic codes of all the candidates within the entire global community, both up there and down here. Of all people on the planet, you are the only one, who can fill this position."

"Pardon me; that is crap. This is all bullshit! I can't believe anyone would fall for this. If I knew how to leave, I would. But frankly, I have no idea how to get out of here."

"Mathew, please, your reaction is quite understandable. Just come with me. I have something to show you."

They walked down another long, winding corridor that reminded Bellos of a church cathedral. He was in awe, and stopped to study several oil paintings, sculptures, and mosaics that lined the walls.

"Are these all originals? Who the hell are you guys?"

"Leonardo donated that one. Beautiful, isn't it? Look here. This Islamic mosaic is from the Second Crusade. One thing we are not, Doctor, is fake. Everything in any of our facilities across the globe is authentic . . . nothing made by old Hollywood."

"Hmm, you sound like Bridger."

"Don't get me wrong; I love movies, especially the ones from its golden age. We watch them throughout our colonies. I envy that talent, the classics, superheroes, cowboys. God, do you remember that old, old musical dancer, Fred Astaire? And there was a librarian . . . what was his name? I know it was so long ago, but he was an adventurer of sorts. He fell in love with a vampire. I just love those creatures. Years ago, Bridger said I looked like a vampire. Sometimes I think I should have had his blood sucked dry, hah. Anyway, you have to love what Hollywood 'was' in those days."

Swanson slowed and gestured to the right. They stopped in front of white, ornately carved wooden door. This time Swanson pulled his fob out and waved it in front of the door lock. Then, with both hands, he turned the golden knob and pulled. "I hate this door."

Slowly, the heavy door opened, leading into a stark white sterile room that looked surprisingly like one on Focus Ward back at Andrews Hospital.

With that image and the ding of the elevator, Mathew Bellos was shocked back to the reality of present day and the ER-1, where Rachel Sheldon waited for the word she dreaded about Jack.

CHAPTER 5

BELLOS AND RACHEL

IT WAS 3 A.M. WHEN BELLOS EXITED the elevator. Rachel Sheldon lingered in a dream-state, on the hospital bed in a private room of the ER-1. She had so many thoughts; their last cup of coffee together; his bad joke that made her force a giggle and such a satisfying evening of loving intimacy. Jack left them both laughing . . . then, Rachel heard the door squeak; she opened her eyes and Mathew Bellos entered the room.

"Matt, thank God." She rose and embraced him like a brother.

"Rachel, I'm so sorry. I've been working on Jack."

"Tell me, for God's sake!"

Bellos held her, and then he led her to the bed. "Rachel, the surgical team and I have been working non-stop on Jack since he arrived at 11 p.m. He was in a horrible car accident, honey. I can give you details, but the point is . . . Rach, he died."

Bellos drew her to him as she broke down. "No! God, no . . . he has to be all right. I know it! You told me they were doing everything possible. I know this place, damn it!" Rachel grabbed his hospital coat lapels. "There's no way he died."

Bellos took her wrists gently. "He didn't suffer, Rach, but he died. There was no indication he regained consciousness. He didn't feel a thing. I am so sorry."

"I want to see him!" Rachel turned pale white in disbelief. "I have to, damn it; so I know he's really gone . . . please?"

Then she fell limp in his arms, shaking and sobbing. Bellos sat her on the bed and they both cried. He received several beeps on his cell phone; however, he only took one call. After a time, Rachel gathered herself and listened.

"Rach, please stay here, for a while at least. I want to monitor you, then I will take you home myself. We can talk about everything in detail, when you are up to it. Please. You have a lot to take in. Here, take this, it's just a mild sedative, doctor's orders. I want you to rest here, just a little while. I have to go; but I will be back shortly. If you need anything, call me. Do you have a phone?"

She took hers out. "Oh shit, it's dead."

"Here, take this." He gave her Angie's. "I'm only a click away."

Rachel nodded and took the pill. Bellos turned, exited the room and walked down the hall to the private elevator. He pushed three, to Focus Ward, and the elevator moved up against his feet. After only a second looking at his reflection in the bezel, he wiped his red eyes and pushed the red stop button.

CHAPTER 6

THE BIG TOUR

THE ELEVATOR STOPPED AGAIN, and in a flash, Mathew Bellos recalled every detail of that first time he met Great Grand Master Gordon Swanson. With a hint of a smile, he thought, *What a first night that was. My heavens, sir, that hallway! I did think it was some movie's endless vampire castle . . . those doorways; wow, so impressive . . . hell, I am still impressed . . . Alice, your 'looking glass' was nothing.*

Bellos could see it all so clearly in his mind's eye. He had so many questions then. *What a virgin I was. That was truly a night to remember.*

It really all began when Swanson opened the heavy door in that hallway. Bellos stepped into a bright pristine chamber. The room was an elegant, reflective, pearl white light, yet unexpectedly easy on the eyes. At first, Dr. B. was not sure where the walls began and the ceiling or floor started. The room was 20 feet wide, by 30 feet long, by 15 feet high and oval shaped. A large beveled glass fireplace was at the far end. Two white Santa Claus patterned high back Victorian chairs faced each other, one on each side of the blazing fire. Directly facing the fire was a cream-colored, plush looking, leather couch. On each side of the couch sat ornately carved, white wooden lacquered end tables, each with a glowing 15-inch lamp on it, shaped like an obelisk. Above the fireplace was that iconic fish, etched out of a beautiful purple and white geodic stone, measuring at least six feet long by two feet high. Each wall had window clusters, five feet long by three feet high; but, rather than being completely transparent, each pane had a colorful scene of celestial constellations, meticulously cut in stained glass. The oddest thing was that each window looked like light was shining into the room from outside. However, Bellos had no idea how, since the room was far below the surface and he could see no evidence of a source outside the room. Even more curious, he studied the light glowing from the obelisks on the tables. Again, there was no bulb or filament, yet each lamp radiated a full spectrum of light without causing discomfort or eye damage.

"But that's impossible," Bellos whispered to himself.

He turned and marveled at the ornately carved wall-to-wall bookshelves and the exquisite drop leaf tables against the walls at each end of the room. All the books were the same size, bound in an iridescent pearl white leather. Each had embossed on their binding a set of three different letters in gold leaf.

For some reason, Bellos hadn't noticed at first, but suddenly, there were three men and a woman sitting on the furniture, who stood up smiling to greet him. Each person held what looked like a wine glass filled with a white sparkling liquid that was clearly not milk or champagne. Bellos smiled and continued studying the room as Swanson introduced him, "Good evening ,everyone. I trust you all have been enjoying yourselves so far . . . "

Each person looked at the other and spoke in unison, "Yes, thank you."

Swanson tapped Dr. B. on the shoulder and said to the others, "I am proud to introduce all of you to someone I hope you will get to know quite well. This is Dr. Mathew Bellos . . .

Dr. Bellos, this is Professor Jonathan Witt, Lionel Benton, and Dr. Andrew Pine."

Bellos bowed with a respectful smile. "How do you do?"

Then he quickly focused on the woman to the left of Dr. Pine, ignoring Swanson's voice. He could not believe his eyes. As he started to move toward her, Swanson gently grabbed his arm and interrupted the moment, "I think you two know each other, if I'm not mistaken. Dr. Bellos, you remember Ms. Carla, do you not?"

Their eyes fixed on each other. Swanson smiled politely and said, "Before you get too carried away, Doctor . . . "

Actually, before either of them could reach out and touch one another, Swanson pulled Bellos to the right.

" . . . Mathew, may I present the last in this evening's introductions."

Bellos was even more shocked, if that was possible.

"Dad . . . DAD?"

"Sonny?"

Richard Bellos and his wife died 10 years ago. At that moment, Dr. B. felt emotions he never knew he had.

"Dad, it's you. Is it really you? How?"

"Yes, Mathew! It is really me. It's a miracle!"

They grabbed one another, embraced, and Richard gestured toward Swanson. "Our friend, here, I have no idea how or why, but I'm so happy. Son, you're so grown."

After a moment, Bellos noticed something else; flickering lights. The other people in the room began to pulsate. Their images sparkled like a strobe light. Bellos and Richard froze. Carla and the other three men wiggled, blurred, and vanished. Bellos did a double take and then looked back at his father. They both looked at Swanson in complete amazement.

"Mr. Swanson," Richard said. "What just happened? We were all talking together. I only left to use the bathroom. They were as real as you or me. Professor Witt poured the drinks."

"Have a seat, gentlemen. I am sorry about Carla, Mathew. There is much both of you must learn. Our ways take time to understand. Unfortunately, you have to learn quickly. I want you to remember three important facts from this." Swanson looked at Richard. "One is that we have the capability to give a person rebirth. Two is that you, Mathew, have a destiny with your daughter . . . Believe me, both you and your father are real, but the others I introduced to you here were solid holograms, programmed transport models. I suppose you could say it is a sci-fi sort of thing. Regardless, today is a very special day. Richard, there is a very good reason you both are reunited. Let's take a breath and celebrate that. Mathew; I told you I had many things to show you. Your father is the first. Trust me; there is nothing to fear at all. I am going to give you two a chance to catch up a bit. Press the red button on that table twice when you are ready. The first push will take you off privacy, and I will answer the second."

Bellos was speechless. He looked at his dad in utter amazement and asked, "Wait, what is the third thing? You said there were three facts you wanted us to remember."

"Oh, yes," Swanson winked, "the third is, we can make people disappear."

With those words, GGM Gordon Swanson turned and left the room. Mathew and Richard Bellos sat, cried, and talked for about 15 minutes before considering the call button.

"Son, I know this place, somehow. I just know it. As strange as this may sound, I sense there is nothing we should fear. This is all so right; weird, isn't it?"

"They told me you worked for them."

Richard sat back on the couch. "Maybe I did. The more I study, the more I remember. I need to think and organize my thoughts."

"Just take it slow; one step at a time. We should find out as much as we can."

"Well then, I guess we better get started."

Richard pushed the button on the table twice. It squeaked, and Swanson appeared in minutes.

"Yes, you do need to take it slow, Dr. Richard. That is what we used to call you. I trust you two had a good, but much too brief visit. Here, Dr. R., drink this. It's medicinal."

Swanson handed him a wine glass.

"It certainly doesn't taste medicinal. It's delicious."

"Would you two care to take a short tour with me? I think you will find things here more than interesting."

Mathew nodded, "Yes, I guess. That's why we are here, right?"

"Well, as I told you, you are here because I am recruiting you to be my replacement. Actually, I am recruiting you both. Richard, it will come back to you. You just need time and a little help. Please, follow me."

The three walked out the far back side of the room, through a glass door and onto an outside half hallway with a guardrail. As they stared over the railing, the newcomers were shocked and amazed at what they saw. It was a vertical cavern, at least a quarter-mile in diameter, extending too far down to see the bottom. They saw round glass-like walking tubes, with no visible support, crisscrossing the chasm like spokes on a bicycle wheel every 300 feet or so, down. The circumference of the chasm was tiered with levels resembling the sides of glass skyscrapers. In addition, there were tunnels every so often, 30 feet wide, going deep into the earth.

"Jesus, it looks like a Christmas tree, only hollow instead of wood," said Bellos.

They looked up, and the top of the cavern was at least a mile high, but there was no opening. Instead, it looked like a gigantic round beveled glass window, similar in design to the ones on the walls in the room they'd just left. The patterns reflected gorgeous colors.

Bellos tapped his dad's shoulder. "Look at that. How is it possible? There is no round glass structure anywhere in D.C. up there, and the light shining through cannot be coming from the sun. My watch says 9 p.m."

"Frankly, I have no idea," said Richard. " My question is; where is all this light coming from down here? Look at the rock walls. None of this can be sunlight. It is a lot to take in. I just don't remember."

Bellos counted 30 tier levels downward that he could see. "Mr. Swanson, we don't see any lights or wires? How is all this possible?"

"It's quite something, really, isn't it? Let's walk."

They followed him holding onto the railing, looking in wonder at everything. After some 50 feet, Swanson stopped and turned to them.

"I know you have many questions; so I'll start by saying that all of this, everything you see and much more, started many thousands of years ago, when the 'first ones', as we call them, discovered the underground, in what you know today as Northeastern Asia. They also found a new different life form deep below. What you are looking at, the light itself, is what they found, first. They are alive and far too many to count. They live in a variety of sizes and shapes here. I suppose, at this stage of their life, they could be far distant cousins to deep-sea creatures that self-generate light in the dark, miles below the ocean's surface. However, I have to say, these are far more interesting. The fact is, all this light you see is trillions of microscopic life forms. The strange part is that they all feed off darkness itself, and whatever else the earth's core expels. They don't require sunlight, they would die in it . . . But, that is not all they do. They also filter our air. They metabolize in almost the opposite way of plant life on the surface. One by-product of their feces is light; quite mind blowing, actually; and remarkably, there is no odor at all. In fact, their light sterilizes everything. Figure that one out, Mathew, hmm. So, we live in an environment that cleans itself and filters our air for us. This whole place is germ free."

Bellos replied, "So, wait; the light destroys them and then they die, no?

"No, this is not sunlight. It is made up of different photonic, or particle components. Nevertheless, it all happens in much less than a flicker, a millisecond. It is dark; they eat, metabolize and live, reproduce, give off light and die. Their offspring grow, and so on, then it happens all over again. Our science engineers tell me it is just very technical. I see it as very simple. Scientists get far too detailed, don't you agree? While the whole process actually happens as pulses, it is so fast that we see it as steady light. Their ability to propagate is utterly amazing. None of us has ever been able to calculate their numbers. While very few evolve beyond this stage, some do develop into much more complex beings; very intelligent to be sure, compared to what you see here at the microscopic level. Now, come."

Bellos was intense with interest. "I could spend a lifetime studying this alone." He grabbed Swanson's shoulder. "Look, I'm sorry. We are so grateful, but, the 'first ones', who were the 'first ones'?"

Swanson stopped, turned and extended his arm over the chasm. "This world is unlike the one on surface Earth. Actually, there are countless levels and much life, reaching miles below.

Eons ago, somewhere in Northeast Asia, where cold was mother and father to all life, there lived a simple people, a tribe starving. They decided to look for food elsewhere. They climbed never before known high mountains. Unfortunately, there was a great and horrible earthquake. The earth opened and everyone fell, deep underground. Eventually, over eons, those mountains became flatlands without evidence of the original quake. Anyway, roughly half of the tribe survived. They were the 'first ones'. In the beginning, as they explored the cave structures underground, water was easy. It melted off the mountains and drained into the caverns. After a time, the deeper they went, they found underground rivers strangely abundant with life. The light that you see all around you is just one of many discoveries they made. There was no way up, only onward; so, they had to create and develop from the unknown that mystery and opportunity offered; much like your pioneers, yet so different in many ways . . . the deeper and darker they went, the more stable the light and environment became.

"They found enormous chasms, of indescribable beauty. These organisms not only lighted the caves, but also generated a mean temperature of 65 degrees, and they purified the air. The people endured, prevailed, and began to prosper. They bypassed much of what the surface cultures went through. They survived without much of the worry and pressure of the surface world. They had the advantage of this life form's ability to provide basic utility. Food was plentiful, unlike on earth's surface where man had to be on guard to seek out basic life-giving essentials, and up there, man migrated to conquer real estate, build social order, industrialize, politicize; stress, stress, stress himself. Within the subterranean culture, the human mind matured quicker, bypassing man's tendency on the surface to make war. Don't get me wrong, I don't mean your ancestors were all bad. Your culture discovered so much from conflict. As you pointed out, Mathew, look at your race to space. Why, out of that alone came so many things—miniaturizations, medical applications, vaccines, Nanite research and the electronics explosion. However, your history tells us that even that just generated political gain to sidestep a Soviet war. War has been the most profitable venture of surface humanity. Otherwise, you would have never discovered the many facets of the atom, itself. And let us admit it—out of your wars grew your knowledge of physics' wonderful quantum theory. No, it has not been all bad, just considerably slower and mucky, at times. Of course, you did have to propagate to replace all those you killed; all that information and learning you destroyed in each being, not to mention the repetitive effort to re-teach the children—quite a waste of time when you think about it, no?"

Bellos and Richard remained speechless.

"Richard, do try and remember. The truth is, Mathew, we have never made war down here; nor have we had any conflict between us like humans have on the surface. We bypassed all that, like your freeways bypass the congestion of inner city traffic. We have answered many questions, which you are only now starting to research, because we got around things that still stand in your way. We learned to respect life much sooner. We found the issues of hunger, utility, ethics, morals and curiosity itself are all issues of healthcare; improving the human condition. With good health comes progress in all aspects of life.

"Today, your people and mine may start to come together. You see, we have been working for a very long time on 'eternal life'. These microscopic life forms, over millennia, have been a basis for our discovering many new and wondrous things; things you must learn.

"Sorry, I can be a bit long-winded at times." Swanson studied the doctor's expression. "Then again, consider this; by the time we did go to the surface, we preferred our own way of life. We invited very few of you from up there to partake in our culture. I will be honest. Over the years, of those who chose to venture up, you would most certainly know if I told you. They were wrong, thinking they could bring any of what we have to the surface . . . ."

Bellos raised an eyebrow in question, and Swanson looked sternly at him.

" . . . You killed them, Doctor. You killed every single person in history that ever let it be known they had our secret of life to share with you."

Then he backed off and took a breath.

"Anyway, over centuries, we developed a recruiting system for only 'special people' on the surface to join us. It is a genetic formula. Today, there has to be a damn good genetic reason if we approach anyone on the surface. Of course, you will fill in many gaps as time passes; but way back then, there were very few ways up, and that in itself was a potent driver to prosper down here, don't you think? Come through here. Follow me."

Bellos hung on every word. "Wait a minute; are you saying no one has ever stayed topside? Come on; what you are describing is a bit too Shangri-La-ish . . . utopian. I don't believe it."

Swanson smiled. "Oh, yes, *Shangri-La*; I read that book a very long time ago, and I saw the original movie, Ronald Coleman starred, I believe. But that took place in the Himalayas. I can tell you this. Way before you started assassinating our ambassadors, before humans up there recorded our time, there were dinosaurs, and then the Ice Age. The weather alone kept us down here.

"However, here is the big thing, Doctors. We discovered that once you give people light, oxygen and food—basic needs—they seem to sense their self-worth sooner. They do not get lazy, as your pompous ass media purport. Every person naturally develops his or her individual talents and skills, which is what has driven our culture to surpass the surface in so many ways. We are far from utopian. We are just different."

Swanson stopped talking and faced them both. "Another thing; you grew up with time cycles as your frame of reference for all behavior. We do not have anything like that. You have day and night. Face it; you have 'habitualized' your lives into cyclic behaviors. You only allow yourselves to produce or achieve when 'they' tell you to . . . and do not get me started on who the they is, of where you live. Let us agree that it's your culture . . . "

Bellos looked like he was going to argue, so Swanson gestured him to stop.

"And yes, we know the cycles of work that you live by have become necessary for you. As I said, we do not see sunlight. It is relative, I suppose; but topside is certainly different from down here. I do not judge; live and let live, I say. You know, war and let war. Besides, even today, no one floods the Mongolian tundra with tourism. So, our people kept on with life; and, just when you don't expect it, life gives you wonder. These life forms have been below here long before anything was on the surface. They evolved, too. Today, they are much more than the basis for our light, food, oxygen and transportation—a lot more. We owe them so much."

"Transportation?" Richard looked as if he remembered something.

"Yes," Swanson said. "That's right; remember? Our transportation is based on magnetic energy. Frankly, down here a lot is. As some of these microscopic creatures grow, their metabolism changes and they are able to utilize the earth's inner magnetic forces to move."

47

Richard interrupted, "Wait. It is a bit fuzzy, but I do remember something. Adult creatures . . . they are called Carrier-Units, right? They travel fast, deep within the earth, across the globe, right?"

"Hmm . . . ?" Bellos raised an eyebrow. "Dad, you mean like the Asian speed trains, all across the Far East?"

Swanson looked at them both with a grin and said, "Not exactly, my boy; these Carrier-Units are much faster and far more maneuverable than a train or plane. I assure you, there are certainly no train rails of any kind down here."

He continued, "Now it is true that, like in some surface vehicles, we use petroleum-based materials for many applications, just not for transportation. We refine oil differently down here. Any by-products end up as food for these creatures, rather than toxic waste. Look you two; you are the only new ones I have brought here in a very long time. You two will know what very few here know, and that is for a very good reason."

"Oh, and what is that?" said Bellos.

"Whatever I've told you is true, gentlemen, and there is something else. We are not just a small group of outcasts or a sect of some sort. This is not an isolated community. We are a global society. You are surface inhabitants, and we are sub-surface."

"Global? You mean you live under all of us?" Bellos snapped.

"Yes; as I said, we are a planetary society, but subterranean. We even have settlements deep below the great oceans. Think about that. The barometric pressures alone should keep you wondering. Regardless, our transport system is far too travel-friendly and efficient for you or anyone from above to comprehend."

"Well, you are right about that, because I have no idea what you mean. I'm completely confused," said Bellos.

"Doctor, I don't expect you to understand everything I say right now, but I do expect you to remember most of it. If your cultures up there knew we were down here, and how extensive we inhabit their planet, they would panic. That is the nature of your upbringing, fear of the unknown; you are all afraid of someone or something taking what you think belongs to you. Too many of you view cooperation as more of a concept or goal, rather than a way of life. Little by little, we help change that."

"You know, Mr. Swanson, I'm beginning to think you may have some anger management issues," Bellos said with a smirk.

Swanson grinned. "Yes, well, perhaps, to a degree; but, unfortunately, we have to postpone this part of our conversation anyway. We three are on a timetable. You, me, your father; we are not like most others here. We have been chosen; cryptic term, I know, but frankly, I'm done with the seminar for now. Please, follow me."

"What does all that mean, for God's sake?" Bellos snapped.

Swanson moved to his left, reaching for the glass door. "It means I brought you here for one purpose, Doctors, and I have told you what that is already. Now, let us begin."

Swanson opened the glass door and led the two into what Bellos thought was a gigantic, pristine warehouse. In one direction were enclosed modular rooms, one next to the other like show booths in a large convention hall. In another direction, there was some sort of clean room manufacturing operation. Bellos turned to see what looked like an enormous laboratory setting with futuristic medical equipment. Above many tables, there were stunning colorful holograms of organs, torsos, legs, even full moving human bodies. The entire area was beautifully carpeted, tastefully decorated and, of course, the lighting was the same as throughout the chasm.

"Mr. Swanson," Bellos said, "exactly how big is this place anyway?"

"As big as the surface, inner Earth is really much bigger," Swanson giggled. "Sorry; my mind wandered. This area is roughly 25,000 square feet, I think."

"In either case, though, what's the population? How many people are here?"

"Mathew, you are way ahead of yourself. Please focus; try to pay attention to what I present; and, do try to stay calm. We all have much to discuss. Save it for later. Remember, first things first. Agreed? Good."

As they walked awestruck through the expansive area, a man and a woman greeted the GGM.

"Good morning, GGM; and good morning to you, sirs."

Each wore white fabric lab coats, which just did not look right to Bellos.

"Dad, is there something about their coats?"

"I do believe they are glowing?"

"Dr. Bellos, Richard, this is Dr. LuAnne Rather, and Dr. Andrew Pine, whom you met earlier."

"Hello again, sir," Richard smiled and shook his hand. "I hope you are a real person now."

"I'm leaving you two here for a bit," Swanson said. "You are in good hands. When you are done, you can push the fob I gave you. I will return to pick you up. Please, be as attentive as you can."

He smiled and walked out the door at the far end of the area.

"Well, we should get started. You may call me LuAnne, or Dr. LuAnne, if you like."

Dr. Andrew fidgeted a bit and said, "W-welcome to 'Eh-Ever-Life' one- Lab-202 . . . um . . . W-we are 'care holders' and 'group examiners' . . . um . . . W-we are going t-to . . . "

"Oh for God's sake, Andy," LuAnne interrupted. "You two must be buzzing with questions by now. If we let you ask, we wouldn't accomplish a thing today, and it is critical that you two give us a few minutes; so, if it's all right with you?"

Bellos and Richard shrugged.

"All right then; to start with, Andy and I are 'care holders' of this lab section. We manage and perform special advanced medical procedures within the worldwide Ever-Life umbrella. Please follow me."

"Ever-Life umbrella?" questioned Richard.

Dr. LuAnne smiled. "Yes, in fact, in the entire world, you are the first today. I am sorry. Don't be too shocked. The program is quite reliable and always evolving. It started roughly 8000 years ago. Hmm, how do I put this?"

Bellos interrupted as they walked, "Can you tell me something, Doctor?"

"If I can, certainly . . . "

"Well, Mr. Swanson said you all were global. Does everyone speak English?"

"Yes, as a matter of fact, as far as I know, we all speak pretty much every used language. It is fundamental. We are all able to share and learn knowledge between us. Master Swanson could give you details on that though."

"But, how do you learn it all?"

Dr. Andrew looked at Bellos and grinned. "You will see."

"Come . . . this way," Dr. LuAnne said. "Please, try not to let your mind wander too much. Over there, that area—that is OGD—Organ, Growth and Donate."

"Can we go over there?" asked Richard. "It looks familiar."

LuAnne gently urged them onward. "Later, if time permits, yes, of course. This Ever-Life facility consists of about 25,000 square feet of atomic, viral, cellular and final function organic growth. We research, evaluate and apply all manner of genetic biochemistry-microbiology to improve and extend life. We have records of all known life dating back approximately 500million years. I know that must sound fantastic, but we utilize our data banks of genetic indexing to grow almost anything. Over there, we seed cells of a specific recipient, and then we grow partial or complete organs. Then, we implant; quite basic here, really."

"Well," Bellos bragged, "we have researched and successfully grown various body parts. Some have been used in cosmetic, kidney, liver and some heart applications. And we can attach limbs given certain circumstances."

"Yes, we know, Doctor. Here, that kind of thing has been standard for a long time. We can supply the needs of any person or animal. We even use insect DNA, when appropriate. Genetics and miniaturization have been the foundation of all our work for millennia."

Bellos could not be quiet. "You mean you transplant organs at will?"

"Yes of course; we do most micro, cell or tissue transplants or transfers daily, hourly. We have eliminated most genetic mistakes, diseases and certainly most common ailments, as well as organ failures."

Bellos took a deep breath and shook his head, looking at everything. "Incredible, just incredible; what is the lifespan here? How do you perform heart transplants? What are all those holograms? . . . Can I just ask you about your coats? Are they glowing?"

"Our coats?" LuAnne laughed. "Why, yes; no, not really. I suppose, to you they glow, but not to us. We are used to the light. Everything here gives off light. We do not see the glow anymore. Do you, Andy?"

"Um, nope . . . "

"You see, our coats are white too; so I'm sure that enhances the effect. Anyway, I am sure you have hundreds of questions, but try to let me finish. We also grow organs within a body, human or otherwise; but it is more than that. You see, we can even grow a complete body; again, based on compatible genetics, of course. Here, genetics is everything. Growing organs isn't that difficult once you have gone through our iterations."

"My God!" Richard said. "How is that possible? Is that what I am?"

The two men listened in wonder.

"Our GGM has briefed us about you two; so, we are authorized to say the following: We do grow bodies, but they are not clones, as I understand you would describe. We grow both males and females; however, unlike cloning efforts on the surface, ours have a complete DNA sequence. Although we can also alter the DNA, in certain structural chains, we cannot duplicate a person's memory. Therefore, we have to accelerate the 'newborn's' learning process. That is what we are going to do here, with your father. He is your father, complete in every detail physically; but, he has memory voids, and . . . "

She looked at Richard.

"I'm afraid, as far as we know, you always will. So, one of the things we do here is endeavor to fill some of those voids. That is why you are here today. Will you help us, son of Dr. Richard Bellos? It's completely painless; I assure you."

Mathew looked at the doctors and his father.

"Why, yes; I'll do anything. But how will my father get all the other memories he needs?"

"Follow me. In here, I'll show you."

"Mathew," said his father, "I do keep having memory flashes of being part of all this; but, they are fragments. It is so strange. Some things are clear, but others are so vague. They come and go."

"That is a good start," LuAnne said. "Dr. Bellos, you sit here, and Dr. Richard, you here, facing your son. Here are headsets for you. Just place them on comfortably."

"See, our worlds aren't that different," Bellos said. "I have a pair like this at home."

"Now relax, you two. Listen; you are not in a surface experimental hospital. This is not an experiment at all. It's a procedure, and a painless one at that. So, are we ready?"

The two took a deep breath, and Dr. LuAnne touched their shoulders.

"I realize this may appear futuristic to you both, but it's really simple, principally. You, Dr. Bellos have many memories of your father. These headsets will allow your mind to talk to your father's mind, and he will remember what you say. That's it. He will have filled in many memories he wants, but does not have right now. Does that make any sense to you?"

Bellos nodded and asked, "What if we learn something neither of us wants the other to know? Is Dad going to know everything I know, and vice versa?"

"No. Think of it as a computer program. There are limits. We are building your father's memories. He already knows about you. It is remarkable programming, how and what information transfers. The ability to do this depends on brain DNA; again, genetics."

They all looked at each other, and then Bellos said, "What about his past memories of this place, and the rest of his life?"

"Memory has to be transferred in stages, Doctor. This is only the first session. Richard, you will be back several times."

Mathew and his father looked eye to eye. Dr. LuAnne stood between them. With her arms outstretched, she looked like the letter 'T'. Then, the two men felt her fingers lightly tap their headsets.

"Okay, that's it, gentlemen. You can give me the headsets back." She giggled. "I told you, you wouldn't feel anything."

"I don't understand," Bellos said.

"Doctors," Dr. Andrew offered. "Can you feel a thought? And remember, light isn't the fastest thing, thought is."

"Not when I have a headache," Bellos chuckled.

"So, now what? What's different in me, then?" Richard asked.

"I don't know. You should remember something you didn't before. That's all we have for you two today," Dr. Lu said. "I hope we didn't frighten you."

They all heard a buzz from Dr. LuAnne's waist.

"Oops, that's me. I have to answer it. You two should really page the GGM now. You see that doorway over there?" She pointed opposite from the way they entered. "Yes, there. That's 'Knofer' reception for this Ever-Life section. The GGM will meet you there."

"*Knofer*?" said Bellos. "What's that?"

"It's just a term we use a lot here, 'Knofer' [know-fer] . . . thank you, gentlemen. I am afraid we must part for the time being. Goodbye for now."

Bellos and Richard turned and walked to the doorway filled with amazement. Bellos pushed the fob in his pocket and, by the time they reached reception, GGM Gordon Swanson walked in.

"Hello, lads. I trust you had a fascinating visit. Do you have any questions?"

He rolled his eyes and snickered as he opened the exit door. Bellos and his dad both started talking at the same time. Swanson raised his arms, as though he were stopping traffic. "All right, one at a time, please! I know it is all a bit overwhelming. Let us get a bite to eat; and, Richard needs a drink. We'll go across the center scope there, to the food post and talk."

"I don't know where to begin," Bellos said. "Okay, first, about those gadgets there, on your belt. So many people are talking into them. They project holograms, too. What is a Knofer?"

"Hah; well, you pick up quickly, Mathew. Here, look at this."

Swanson handed him the small object.

"Actually, Knofer is a universal term, implying knowledge. But mostly, it refers to what you are holding."

"It reminds me of old cell phones on the surface."

"Well, I suppose you could say it is a ten thousandth generation cell phone."

Bellos examined it closely. It was a dull, silver gray color; oval, with an inner transparent body that swiveled on a blind axis. One end curved up a tad, if one laid it on a table.

"Very comfortable to the touch; it's almost weightless, isn't it?"

There were no numbers or buttons anywhere on it; just a few small unrecognizable characters, and what looked like a tiny red lens, not quite at one end.

"I give up," said Bellos, turning it over. "How does it work?"

They stopped just long enough for Swanson to take the Knofer, place it in front of his mouth and say, "GGM-001."

After it ticked, Swanson handed it back to Bellos.

"Would you like to know something? About something? Anything? Go ahead, ask. Speak into it, there."

"You are kidding?"

"You can ask it any question. That one has a record of most relevant knowledge."

"Relevant knowledge, what does that mean?"

"Use it as a communicator; receive and project any image; dictate or create a task for it to perform; here, let me have it."

Swanson spoke into it, "By authority of GGM-001-21839, this Knofer transfers to Dr. Mathew J. Bellos . . . there. Now it is yours. Hold it up. Look at the red dot and say your name."

Bellos did.

"There. It is done. By my authorization and your looking into it, you have transferred all facts that you know into your Knofer. Now, you own that one. You need it anyway. The security is quite reliable. I see no reason to dally with some things. Now let's eat. This way. Oh, and all Knofers are defensive weapon capable; in your case, not activated yet."

Bellos scratched his head. "What? But what is it made of? Does it only respond to voice commands? How do I work it? I see now why you said, I'd be asking 'what' a lot. And what are you going to use now? Where's yours?"

"Mine is right here." Swanson pulled out two more from his pocket and gave one to Richard as well.

"As I told you two, we are on a time schedule. You both have a briefing about all Knofers in one hour. Don't forget to ask all your questions then. Come on, we need food."

It was years ago when that all took place, and now Bellos snapped out of it in the Andrews elevator.

"Well, break's over."

He pushed three again, and the elevator started up to Focus Ward.

CHAPTER 7

ANGIE'S DISCOVERY

ANGELA ESPOSITO AND THE GUARD walked out of the elevator to Dr. Mathew Bellos' office on the 10th floor of Andrews Hospital. They stopped just outside his door, and Angela mimicked a cough, spitting the rest of tranquilizer pill that Dr. B. gave her onto her sleeve. She looked at the guard and wiped her mouth.

"So this is it, right? Should I be honored, or am I in real trouble here?"

"You are just fine," he said.

Once inside, the two stood looking down two steps into an oval shaped living room approximately 30 feet by 20 feet.

"I will be right outside, Miss, if you need me. Dr. Bellos said you may order anything you like from the kitchen."

"Thank you."

Angie smiled as he closed the door behind him. She turned and studied the remarkable room. The floors were immaculate dark teak wood, partially covered with a large oval Persian rug. In all the years she had worked at Andrews, she never went into Bellos' office, although she did visit his home outside the Complex frequently. She noticed the walls were a color-coordinated subdued beige and green with just a hint of gold shine that sparkled. The furniture was a combination of dark green leather and mahogany wood, carved meticulously with unrecognizable characters. There were masterful oil paintings hanging on the walls and bookshelves lined the two hallways that extended out from the main room. Angie stepped down from the foyer turning and studying every sight. The walls seemed to curve up from the floor to a round dome oculus made of beveled and stained glass. Outside of it, there were strategically placed lamps that shined in to illuminate the glass designs of the four seasons. For a moment, she felt as if there was a touch of church in Bellos' heart. Captivated by everything, she studied the oil paintings, remembering her college classes in art history and the trips abroad she had taken at Dr. B.'s expense.

"Manet? This painting is an original by Edourd Manet . . . Renoir, Matisse, They are spectacular . . . this is not just an office, is it, Doc? How did you get all this stuff? And security cameras in every corner . . . not much privacy . . . "

Between the two hallways and the front foyer, there was an unmistakable floor to ceiling glass bookcase.

"Jesus, these are priceless . . . medical reference books."

She opened the cabinet and thumbed through several.

"English, French, Latin, Greek, even Hebrew; and that's Aramaic, I think, Chinese? I should have gotten my college textbooks here. This looks like Egyptian; or South American Indian symbols . . . who can read this stuff?"

One of the back bindings on the top shelf caught her eye. It seemed to glow.

"What the heck is that?"

There were only three letters on its back binding, *J.A.S.* She found a stepstool in the corner, and, even standing on her tiptoes, Angie barely could reach under the book to cause it to fall on the floor. The book had a beautiful pearl white leather binding with shiny, large gold embossed lettering on the front cover. It simply read *John Avuar Sheldon.* She picked it up, took it to the couch, and opened it to the front page.

"It feels brand new. I wonder what 'DP-111249' means?"

Just then, she heard the front door lock click. She had just enough time to shove the book behind her. The guard opened the door and asked, "Are you okay, Miss? I heard a thump. I thought you may have fallen."

"Yes, I'm fine; thanks. I tripped and hit the table, looking around at all of this. I'm sorry."

"Please, be careful. Can I do anything for you?"

"Um, yes, as a matter of fact. I need several things from my purse."

"I'm sorry, Miss. I cannot leave. I can call someone to get it for you."

"That would be great. Can you get in touch with Nurse Ralph Walker? He is staff on floor two. If you would, ask him to go to my nurse locker 203, he knows where it is. Ask him to bring me my large gray bag."

"Yes, Miss."

He smiled and shut the door. Angie picked up the book again, stood up and walked back into the hallway to find a private spot to read. She did not turn on lights, trying to keep out of the security camera's vision. She intended only to glance into each room, as she passed by; but the first one was the doctor's bedroom and she couldn't resist. Behind the large bed was a magnificent bay window overlooking the hospital atrium. His suite was enormous and had an adjacent bath with a sunken tub and power rain shower. Thoughts raced through her mind, It all seems so comfortable, somehow, beautiful carvings in the bedposts. *They look like those Egyptian/American Indian symbols; but it's more than that; its déjà vu.*

Then, she noticed a couple of photographs on the night table and wall. *That's me; that's me in middle school; and that's my medical school graduation. Dr. B, you were there, but why are these pictures here, like this?*

Puzzled and anxious, she walked out. Through the next door, she found a completely furnished research laboratory.

This has more equipment than most of the research sections in the Complex.

Directly across the hall from the lab was a computer room containing three suspended, large, paper-thin, transparent monitors and four L-shaped computers, sitting on a wrap around wooden desk . . . the same carvings as on his bed; fascinating . . .

One item on the desk was a solid gold paperweight, a gold tone fish, standing on its tail with a dollar sign coming out of its mouth. The statue had a strange word etched on its base, *Allenfar.*

Each computer monitor displayed video and an audio tape tracing across the bottom of the screen. Each tape showed a different international time zone and displayed a different language. Two tapes were running characters that looked like the symbols carved in the desk and bed.

Angie moved on down the hall. In a second bathroom, there was just enough moonlight to sit on the commode, open the book, and read. There was no copyright or publisher on the first pages. Page 5 just began:

"The following is a duplication record of subject J.A.S. instructed by Ever-Life examiners 10362 and 10365, Lab-202, Level-red 6, this day-3635996.46."

After 10 pages, she began to skim, but by page 50, she whispered to herself, "My God, maybe that was Jack Sheldon in 309."

As her eyes wandered, she saw a security camera in the ceiling's corner behind the sink. *Dr. B., you watch yourself in the bathroom? This is not happening . . . I know what I saw and heard tonight on Focus Ward. Shit, what should I do? I have to tell someone. The person in 309 did look like Jack Sheldon, one of the big three—Bellos, Jack, and Rachel . . . Rachel . . . .*

She looked up from the book.

. . . His wife; she is a doctor; she has to know something. I have to get out of here.

Angie went out to the oval room. She put the book back on the shelf, got a glass of water, and sat on the couch, pondering. "I need Ralphy. I know I can trust him. I know he will help; if not, then what?"

She looked up; she fixed on a door in the front foyer that she hadn't noticed before, but it was an elevator.

Curiously, she walked over, pushed a button next to it on the wall, and the door slid open. "Why, Dr. B., your own private elevator. According to this panel, there are 16 floors to the hospital. Everyone knows there are only 10."

She pushed number one on the panel, but nothing happened. She pushed repeatedly, nothing.

"Damn! Maybe Ralphy can fiddle with this thing. He is good with electrical stuff."

Angie walked out and took the white book again.

"The hell with it. What are they going to do? Dr. B. said to give me anything I want."

So, she took a breath and began reading from page one.

CHAPTER 8

RACHEL AND JACK

ONLY THOSE WHO HAVE LOST TRUE LOVE can begin to imagine the emotions that flooded Rachel Sheldon. She awoke in ER-1 shaking, not knowing how much time had passed, with an overwhelming sense that she must get home.

After calling and paging Bellos several times, she decided to drive the 10 miles to their ranch, but she wasn't prepared for the uncontrollable body shakes and tears that flooded her. Add to that, she was still under the effects of the sedative Bellos gave her, so, to say the least, it was a difficult drive. When she finally arrived, she sat in the driveway; sweating, staring at nothing, thinking . . . *I rushed home to what?*

She made it to the couch in their living room, sank into the cushions and closed her eyes. Then, as if something unreal propelled her, she exploded off the couch and ran through the house searching and gathering photos of family history. With her arms full and carrying three old albums, she dumped it all on the living room coffee table and sat to catch her breath. Then she made piles and tearfully studied each photo.

That's Jack and I in our downstairs lab. What are you doing, silly?

This is one from the banquet, when we got the second check for the new funding from Marion. What a night . . . a lot of money, Jack. We never did finish the details of all that.

She squinted and looked again. "My God, who is that in the background? It can't be! That has to be a mistake."

She put the one picture aside and began rearranging others. She found three more. "I must be going mad."

She left the rest in piles and studied the four closely. Two were from Jack's cell phone, one was from Rachel's, and one was from Marion Brock's camera. She ran to the bedroom and got their old family computer pad. It seemed hours for the damn thing to start. It only took her five minutes to screen, upload and enhance the four photos. There it was no question.

Oh, my God, it is Jack . . . you are there, and there, in the same photo twice . . . why didn't I notice this before? You clearly appear twice in each of these. It has to be double exposure.

Rachel Sheldon had four undergraduate degrees, two Master's degrees, and she received her Ph.D. in microbiological processing. On this day, at this time, in this intensity, she needed to bring every intellectual wherewithal she possessed to make any sense of this. She began again slowly trying to reconstruct some terribly odd puzzle, and it was looking like a nightmare of impossibilities. She picked up the computer and studied each of the pictures with a magnifying glass.

"Jack, what's happened? This can't be right, for God's sake!"

She stood up and paced the room. "Shit! Jack, your research . . . "

She ran to the downstairs lab and muddled through his desk and files. She found his manuscript.

"It has new pages, a lot of new pages . . . Christ!"

As she opened the book, she thought back to when he first told her about it . . .

Jack had first created his theory decades ago. However, it was not until March of the first year they met, that Jack shared his work with Rachel. They became so intimate, so fast, he trusted her with all of it. She had stopped by Jack's lab to find him puttering with a microscope and writing feverishly.

"Hi, Hon; it is 7:30 p.m. I thought you would have hit me up for dinner by now.

"Hi . . . I was going to . . . just give me a minute."

"Whatcha doin?" She said with a flirty smirk. "Something I can help you with, Doctor; hmm?"

Jack smiled, looked up and squinted.

"Yes, you can tell me what you think. But, and I mean this, only if you are willing to be serious. Then, I promise dinner and whatever you want."

"Hmm, sounds like I'll pull out the chaps 'n hat for you, baby . . . woo-hoo, cowboy!"

They grinned at each other, and then Rachel changed her tone. "Fine, what is it?"

"Something I've had on my mind since I was a boy, really. It is the reason I got into medicine. We all have our pets, and this is mine. I would like you to know about it; see what you really think."

"Okay; but why the mystery?"

"I'm just possessive about it, and haven't shared this with anyone."

"In that case, I am flattered, darlin'."

"Okay, well, you know how we all talked in college about the Universe and life. You remember those days?"

"Yes, of course, I do. My first real love was Ben Verona. He was so macho and smart, philosophically speaking. He knew all the theories of the time about the Universe. Oh my, but, Ben Verona . . . just his name, I mean, no, sorry."

Jack giggled. "All right, just listen to me. When I'm done, then, you can do what you do."

He could not help rolling his eyes. "I've been playing with my pet on a regular basis all these years, you know.

"Very funny . . . "

"My fundamental notion has always been that the unique human personality is a single chemical cocktail. It's the sum total of impulses acquired from our senses and our genetics. As we grow, memories may or may not be recalled; but, in either case, they are permanently recorded, never lost; hence our individuality, our unique quality. They make us who we are."

Rachel cocked her head and winked. "Impressive, if I wanted psycho babble. What's your point?"

"To extend life."

"Hah, that's what we all want as doctors, my love."

"If you want me to explain, be serious."

"Fine, our personality is one great chemical cocktail, go on."

"Unique, honey, unique cocktail, and I am trying to summarize . . . didn't you ever wonder why several people can look at the same event and when they recall it, no two people remember it the same way. That's why courtroom dramas need more than one witness, understand?"

"Uhuh, really, really interesting . . . "

"Anyway, our memories—our personality, is stored as a chemical cocktail in our brain. Most of us think our mind is an unlimited hard drive, inputting from our senses like a computer does with its programs. But, it's not just our senses that contribute to our unique personality; our mind also records all genetic information, which is received from our cells. The brain remembers how each cell functions and then it instructs and directs those needs, so everything runs smoothly, correctly. The brain has to remember and process what the trillions of cells send to it every millisecond. Understand?"

"Yes DEAR, I UNDERSTAND! I thought you were summarizing. Huh, you sound like a textbook. We are doctors,

Jack; I don't think people care much about this, unless they're sick."

"Just follow me. Cells communicate by sending synaptic impulses from one to the other. Electrical impulses transmit through and with our chemistry. We remember, unconsciously, what each cell reports, upgrading that memory just as we input new sensations—taste, touch, etc."

"Oh sure, Jack, everyone will understand that; and why would they want to? So, you're saying I'm a glass containing one hell of a mixed drink," Rachel giggled.

"Yes, sort of; but where is it, and what is the drink? Are you a screwdriver, or a bloody mary? They taste very different. Listen, Rach, I think I can define which drink you are and then extract the mix, so to speak. I have found a way to move the mix to a different glass, or at least take it out and then put it back in; assuming there is a genetic match . . . "

"Okay, Dr. Bartender Frankenstein, ooh . . . Jack, honey, are you serious about this? I mean . . . "

"Listen to me, the brain is a mechanism that does nothing more than send and receive electrical or chemical impulses. Whether it is a body function, choice behavior or thought, every action requires a synaptic signal. That signal is an instruction, directed to and then by our memory; and, our memory is a record—a library of knowledge, stored in the physical brain as a chemical cocktail. As we add learning, the mixture changes, yes; but it is always there in the same place. The challenge is to define the mix and, if we can, we can extract it—move it."

"Jack, sweetie, let's say I play along. How do you define the mix?"

"Well, first, fundamentally by reading and studying the electrical and chemical signals—the synaptic exchanges. I had to create a synaptic alphabet. Frankly, I started with something like the old Morse code, and then it evolved from neurology, to physics, and back to chemistry. Anyway, I did create the new language. Finally, I translated that synaptic language into understandable chemistry."

"Morse code was used in the 1800s, a very long time ago. They were telegraph taps—dots and dashes, SOS . . . I don't think so. But, let's say you did this. Where exactly is the language stored? And even if you found it—our personality— how do you obtain it and extract it? How do you know you got it all and not just a portion? For Christ's sake, Jack, honey, come on . . . "

Jack had been trying to explain in the simplest of terms, but it was not going well. So, while he listened to Rachel's critique, he walked to his desk, pulled out a 2-inch thick manuscript from the bottom drawer and handed it to her. Rachel raised her eyebrows and opened it to the first page.

"*C.P.T.—Chemical Personality Transfer* . . . you wrote this?"

"You know me, babe. My presentations are not stage worthy all the time, so read. That is my journal and findings, the complete text of hypothesis, equations, final formulas and results. It's everything. I believe that it speaks to all your microbiologic questions. Just read a little and then tell me what you think."

Rachel opened it to the middle and read a page. After a minute, she looked at Jack and flipped to the front of the book again. She sat down at his desk and, after five minutes she said, "Honey, can you get me some coffee and a donut, please? Then, get lost for a while, okay?"

Jack smiled and did as instructed. He went back to his microscope and writing at the lab table. Rachel was mesmerized and after a half hour or so, Jack mumbled to himself, "I haven't heard her say nothing this long, since I met her."

Finally, she called to him, "You found where it is? Jack, okay, you write here, 'any bodily function, whether cellular or thought, requires an impulse—a synaptic signal, to and from the brain. The mind instantaneously sends a directive to the hypothalamus, our brain factory that makes peptides' . . . okay, then you say, 'these peptides are manufactured, as cells or thoughts demand' . . . okay, reading on . . . 'Then, they are instantly sent to direct or instruct function or behavior. At the same time, our mind imprints that directive and the resulting behavior in a library of the brain, for reference . . . '"

Rachel stopped and looked at Jack. "Here. Yes, here it is . . . 'The library is constantly in a state of change from learning, but it stores the memory of the directive and the result in the same place. Our behavior, our memory, is our personality in total. Although ever evolving, it is that record—that library— of repetitive impulses' . . . and then you say . . . "

"Jeez," Jack interrupted, "it sounds exactly like what I told you in the first place, hmm."

Rachel continued. "To quote you, Jack, 'I have located the primary personality vial to be 3.33 by 1.25 centimeters, and positioned .134 millimeters around the hypothalamus partially covering the hippocampus gland, tangent to the Pons . . . '"

"Pretty technical, huh?"

"You further say, 'It's such an integral part of the cerebral cortex and cerebellum, it can't be defined until one hour after death.' Jack, you sound like Descartes in old college philosophy. Are you trying to physically define the soul?"

"I suppose you could take it that way; but, there are no physical limits to the personality, only to the chemistry. I am not a philosopher talking about singular self-awareness. Don't be confused, babe; chemistry is tangible; but how big is an idea, remember? It is the link between quantum physics and microbiology that enables us to define this chemistry . . . honey, it's 9:30. . . don't you think it's time for a good meal?"

Rachel sat with her head still in the book and replied, "So what? You started this. It's Friday, and we can do whatever I want, you said."

She waved him off, in her aloof way, and read feverishly. After a while, she blurted out, "Jack, look at me! I can't believe this. Your equations and calculations— the physics and the biology are solid. Are you serious? The implications are staggering. Even the results you have so far mean that, if you are right, we could define, isolate, and contain a person's personality chemistry. If we do that, and, considering recent medical breakthrough, am I right?, we could transfer a terminally ill person into a healthy body."

Jack grinned and walked across the room, around the desk and sat on it, facing her. "That's why I love you so, babe; you are way ahead of me sometimes. Of course, it is a bit more complicated, but it only took you two hours to get what it took me years to understand; and you haven't read it all. Look at you."

Rachel looked up at Jack with love, so excited. "I see most of the proofs are good and solid. Others could use some work; but, yes, I think . . . huh, I agree."

Jack nudged her, and their eyes locked. "I love you, Rachel. I did from the first minute, the first argument. I can't picture doing this, or anything else, in my life, without you, honey."

With those words and a tear, Jack reached down and opened the top drawer of his desk. There, glistening, was a radiant 1.5-carat diamond ring. Jack took the ring out and he held her left hand gently. As he moved off the desk to her side, he knelt down, positioning himself slightly between her legs.

"Rachel Anne Tomas, will you marry me? I love you so. Please be mine through all the good, bad, happy and hard times?"

Rachel's eyes filled with tears as Jack put the ring on her finger.

"Who knows, Rach; maybe together we can make everyone else's time here better too, forever?"

"Oh my, Jack; oh yes, my love, my only . . . ."

Jack brought her close and, as he rose, they embraced and kissed, holding each other in a oneness that would last beyond their understanding at that moment.

Then, the moment was now again and Rachel was at home in the lab, remembering her night of horror. She looked at Jack's manuscript and flipped through it . . . *This is so much thicker . . . .* she turned to the new pages in the back. "Holy shit, Jack, we never discussed any of this . . . there's got to be some results here, some proof."

Then it hit her, *I have to see Jack . . . Brian, Brian, Brian. I haven't talked to Brian about anything.*

Rachel picked up her cell phone and dialed her son. The call automatically forwarded to the Brock building in Bethesda, Maryland. Marion Brock had one rule above all others . . . speak person to person. Except at his private home, there were no long, tedious message services anywhere throughout his multibillion-dollar empire. Rather a secretary always answered every incoming number. "Good morning, Brock building, may I help you?"

"Yes, my name is Rachel Sheldon. I am Brian Sheldon's mother. I am trying to reach him. It is a family emergency. I must speak to him right away."

"Just a moment, Mrs. Sheldon . . . "

Rachel sat exhausted.

"Hello, Mrs. Sheldon. Thank you for waiting. Mr. Brian Sheldon is out of town on a security matter with Mr. Brock. I will contact Mr. Brock and have your son call you as soon as possible. Can you give me time to do that? I will call you back, if that's okay with you?"

"That's fine. I appreciate it."

Rachel hung up the phone.

CHAPTER 9

BROCK'S VISIT

BACK IN FOCUS WARD ROOM 309, after Nurse Angie's exit, Jack Sheldon sat aching, confused, and unwashed. He had massive memory loss, and, in many ways, he was literally a grown child. Moving slowly off the gurney, he shuffled to the bathroom shaking and sat on the toilet, looking with welcome at the shower stall before him. It hurt relieving himself, but he noticed the ugly scar he had from a chainsaw accident years ago was completely gone. He felt physically rejuvenated somehow, but confused, with brief seconds of complete disorientation. He stepped into the shower examining his bloody body. There were no scars, sutures, cuts or bruises anywhere. When he twisted the shower knobs, to turn on the water, he exploded in pain. Although normal and unnoticeable, to Jack, the turns were deafening, stinging high pitched squeaks. He grabbed his head in pain, and the rush of water magnified his sense that someone was stabbing into his ears with ice picks. It only lasted a few seconds; but he almost fell over. Thank God for his quick reaction, grabbing the handicap guardrail. He kept his balance, and began washing off the stench and dried blood.

My mind . . . what the hell happened? Rachel . . . we were home. I left . . . I was going to nightshift— special duty . . . no, it was a meeting with Bruke. No . . . Brock . . . and Brian . . . BRIAN, my son . . . oh, my God, Brian.

Then he clenched his ears again, *The pain, the pain, Christ! I can't think. What the hell is that?*

Jack grabbed the towel, stuffed the ends over his ears, and crouched in the corner, unable to move.

The sound was coming from the corridor outside his room. Strange, too, because Room 309 was lead-lined and locked to prevent any security breach.

Voices . . . so loud; am I going mad?

In fact, it was a single voice. Barb Sawyer was merely whispering to herself as she entered the ward from far down the hallway. "Angie, what were you talking about? There has got to be a reasonable explanation?"

After Bellos ordered her reassignment, Barb decided to visit Focus Ward and see if anything Angie said made sense. She was roughly 50 feet away and around a corner from Jack's room, when she saw two men come out of Angie's office and walk toward her. Both were wearing tailored suits, so she shifted to automatic manners. The older of the two looked in his mid-50s and he commanded a second look from any woman. The other was a much younger college-age looking man.

"Good evening, Barb. I am Marion Brock. This is Brian Sheldon, Jack Sheldon's son. I hope we haven't arrived at too inconvenient a time?"

"Hello . . . "

"I hope you recognize my name, at least. I remember you from the award ceremony two years ago. I would never forget a pretty, smart lady like you."

"How do you do, Mr. Brock. You have quite a memory. You shocked me, being here like this. Can I help you?"

With a slight smile, Brock replied, "Well, we have been monitoring Brian's dad from another location; and, suddenly, all the readings went dead. So, we came directly here to try to check with the ward nurse. No one has been here since we arrived. The vital monitors read nothing. Naturally, I am concerned, not to mention Brian. We have been in that office unable to communicate with any hospital staff. They keep quite good security up here. Neither the landline phones nor wireless are working; and we found out the hard way all the entrances, exits and room doors are locked. How can we find out exactly what is going on; and we would like to see Dr. Sheldon."

"I see. I am a bit confused about how you were monitoring the doctor, but . . . first; let me say how sorry I am that this has happened to you, both. You must be quite frustrated. I will help in any way I can. You see, the nurse who normally is here has taken ill. I have been assigned to the ward, now; but I will not have authority for the floor until redirect, scheduled for 4 p.m., this afternoon. Until then, I can let you out and show you to Dr. Bellos' office, if that would help. I'm sure he can explain the entire matter."

"I appreciate that, I really do. Maybe it would be best if, as your boss, so to speak, we have a little chat before going to see anyone. Have you ever seen one of these?"

Brock handed her a badge she had seen only once before at Andrews, from Dr. Bellos.

"That is my authorization for the Complex, just to be clear, and to let you know you are free to talk about anything without fear of reprisal in anyway, all right?"

She turned the badge over and examined both sides.

"Please verify it before reacting. That is security protocol," Brock added.

The three walked back into Angie's office. Barb plugged the badge through the clearance verifier and typed her code into the computer. The monitor brought up a picture of Marion Brock and his complete security clearance. With relief and a sigh, she sat back and looked at the two men. "It has been a night, one I will never forget, sir."

Brock stood up and placed his hand on her shoulder. "I can imagine. Now, can you tell us, what is Dr. Sheldon's condition?"

"I really don't know. I was coming up here to check. I assumed the room doors would be open. I, like you, have never been in here. No one really knows the actual security measures up here, no one except the ward nurse and Dr. Bellos. I am supposed to be indoctrinated this afternoon. So far, I know the basic protocol to get in, but that is all. By the way, how did you two get through security?"

"Well, not to make too light of it; but, I showed my badge, the guard punched six numbers on the keypad, and the door opened. Do you have access from this computer to the ER or the surgical records from earlier this evening?"

"Only if I enter the proper codes, which I won't have until, as I said, redirect at 4 p.m. All medical information is stored immediately in a separate, secure hard drive, which can only be accessed by code. Patient records are retained differently than anything else in the Complex."

"Hmm," Brock took a deep breath. "Please, then we should start with what happened tonight, as you know it. Let's talk in the office."

The three walked back to Angie's office and closed the door.

Jack Sheldon crouched in the shower, painfully listening, wet, and mystified. He shouted repeatedly, "Anyone who's out there . . . stop it! Please?" To him, the conversation became unbearable noise, too much input too soon, and he blacked out.

Brock and Brian sat down with Barb, and before she uttered more than two sentences, Brock interrupted her, "Barb, is there a comfortable waiting room on this floor?"

"Why yes, at the opposite end of the hallway, where I came in."

Brock turned to Brian. "I need a few moments with Barb here, alone. Would you mind waiting for me? I won't be long. Please try to be patient, son. We will get to the bottom of this; I just need to speak to Barb about some highly secure hospital matters. You understand . . . "

Brian frowned, but he did not say anything. He just turned around and walked out the door to the waiting room.

Brock gestured to Barb. "Please, continue, and feel free that the buck stops here. You have nothing to fear."

Brian Sheldon walked one slow step at a time, quietly turning each doorknob he passed. Everyone was locked. He had an overwhelming sense that his father needed him. *My God, the doors; there are no numbers. Where is Room 309? Where's Dad?*

Barb Sawyer resumed her story. Brock listened intently and then questioned, "Barb, do you know what time the car accident happened, exactly?"

"Between 10:15 and 10:30 p.m. I think the report said."

"Okay, do you know the members of the surgical team who worked on Dr. Sheldon?"

"Dr. Bellos, I'm sure; then there is our Chief of Surgery—a new hire, and an anesthesiologist, along with two nurses and one back up doctor."

"Do you know where they all are now?"

"No, it's been a busy night."

Brock appeared perplexed somehow. He stood up and paced, pensively whispering to himself, "Holy shit, Jack . . . again? I am going to find you."

Then he sat down and listened to Barb finish. She didn't take long, and for Brock, it all fit. He pretended to focus on what she was saying.

"I know the whole thing sounds so bizarre, sir. So, I came here to find . . . I don't know what . . . something to verify what she said."

"Barb, you were able to get in here. Can we get out?"

"Yes, I have the passcode, but protocol says I may not disclose it for any reason to anyone. And all passcodes register immediately with the guard station for final clearance."

Brock smiled. "Of course, and I would never request you breach protocol. But, I'd like you to go now and take Brian with you. It's only natural that he tried to see his father. I am sure you won't have an issue with the guard."

"But what about you? Hospital security says you can't be here. I don't know if you can get out, once I go. The guard already knows you are here. If you don't have the correct security code to leave . . . "

"I'll be fine. The important thing right now is to get you and Brian safely off this ward. Something is going on, and whatever it is, it started here. Until we all know for sure it's not contagious, I want you two out of harm's way."

"Yes, I didn't think of that."

Brock got up and gently reached for Sawyer's shoulders. "Barb, after you get out, take Brian to my flat. It's in the Fargo building on the southwest corner of the campus, just until we know what we are dealing with . . .

"But, sir, I can't possibly do that. I have to prepare for my redirect meeting at four."

"Hmm, yes, of course, you must . . . "

Brock stepped beside Barb and out the office door.

"Follow me."

They walked quickly down the hall and into the waiting room where young Sheldon sat nervously.

"Hello, Brian, that wasn't too long, was it? Um, I know this is all very difficult for you. But, I need you to listen and trust me. There are things going on that I have to get to the bottom of, right now. That means you need to follow my instructions, all right?"

At first, Brian seemed oblivious and inattentive.

"Brian, are you with me here?" Brock shook him slightly.

"Am I with you? My father is somewhere on this floor, and I'm going to find him, damn it! No! I am not with you."

"Brian, listen to me. Your father has been working in secret with me for months. You are my private attaché, right now. My policy is not to discuss security affairs with new employees; I couldn't tell you. I can't explain it all to you here right now; we don't have time. Will you just trust me, son?"

Brian was livid, but composed himself and said, "Okay, fine; but hear me, Mr. Brock, I don't give two shits if you are my boss or have billions, or if you are God himself. I will find my dad, you got it?"

"Yes, son, I do . . . now listen and remember. This is a key to the Fargo building's main entrance. It's on the southwest corner of the campus. This one is my front door key and security remote. Push 145 to clear the security and 541 to engage it, understand? I need you to go to my flat and wait for my call. Will you do that? . . . BRIAN?"

"Yes. I've got it. Fine, I will."

Brock turned to Barb. "Young lady, will you trust me with one more thing?"

"Yes?" She looked at him, with hopeful affection.

"Good, after you get out of the meeting with Dr. Bellos, call me on 111-145, can you remember that?"

"Yes, of course . . . "

Brock looked at them both, "Now, go."

He walked them to the ward door and studied closely, while Barb pushed six keys on the exit keypad. The door clicked and Barb pulled it open. She and Brian walked through, and down the corridor to the elevator. As the ward door closed, Brian turned around and saw Brock walking back to Angie's office.

When he got there, Brock sat down again in front of the computer. Only this time, Barb had not logged off, so, he had access to everything except the patient records and the room door locks. He typed in his own security protocol, and two additional windows appeared on screen—a phone face instant messenger and his control module—to communicate with his personal worldwide network. He called his secretary, who informed him of all incoming messages, including Rachel Sheldon's call to Brian. Then, he called and talked with his Chief of Staff, Rash InVoy. InVoy was Brock's top security advisor. He was a small framed man of East Indian descent and, although he stood only 5'3", his ridged, military-like facial expression commanded respect. His resumé included Special Advisor and Council to the Soviet President, Special Security Council to the President of the United States, mercenary for hire during the terrorist wars; and also, surprisingly, he spent four years as Special Envoy to his Eminence Pope James X. Brock hired InVoy four years ago to manage his worldwide communications and his security network.

"Rash, good morning; or is it afternoon there?"

"It's almost noon, sir; good morning."

"I need an update on security matter C.P.T."

"Yes, sir, Cloak-Six was eliminated earlier this evening, as instructed. Primary-One should be there with you. Have you recovered vials?"

"Not yet; there has been a glitch with the girl. Primary-One is here, but I haven't found him. What is the shelf life of a vial? How long do we have?"

"We don't know, exactly, but the techs say perhaps a day or two, if that."

"Where are the other vials?"

"Sir, I beg your pardon, but this line is not secure. Our computer has identified a virus and tracking mode. I strongly advise you cease communication immediately and leave where you are. Do you copy?"

"Yes, damn!" Brock disconnected the protocol and shut down the computer. "Damn, damn you, Jack!"

He got up, walked down the hallway to the exit door and pushed 122607 on the keypad, duplicating Barb's input. The door unlocked and he walked out to the elevator. When he reached the first floor, the doors opened and a security guard, dressed in what looked like military garb, blocked his exit.

"Sir, excuse me."

Brock waved what he thought was his free pass-badge in front of the guard; but the guard just said, "I'm sorry, sir; please come with me. There has been a breach on floor three. We must follow procedure. I know you understand."

"Just a minute! Do you know who I am, boy? Look at that badge. I am not going anywhere but out. Step aside!"

Brock tried to walk around the guard; but, with one quick smooth grip, the guard took Brock by his arm and yanked him to the wall.

"I'm sorry, sir; if you don't cooperate, you will be detained by force. Please walk in front of me toward the blinking light."

"All right, fine; no need for violence."

Brock brushed himself off, and the guard escorted him down the corridor to a small elevator. They entered, and the sergeant pushed red-6 on the panel. Brock was anything but cooperative.

"Where the hell are we going? It feels like we're going down to the left. That's impossible?"

The guard stood silent, fully armed with a strange weapon Brock had never seen.

"What kind of special ops are you, anyway? Do you realize you work for me? I am Marion Brock! My name is on the marquee. I built this place. Jesus! Are you deaf, you dipshit?"

Brock turned red-faced and looked like he was going to explode.

CHAPTER 10

TAKEN

NURSE RALPH WALKER MET ANGELA ESPOSITO in Chicago, during their undergraduate years. Ralph was visiting his father,who was City Council member for the 5th district, over a Christmas break. The two students had quite a mutual attraction for one another then, almost 10 years ago. Now at Andrews, they renewed their old friendship without the romance.

The guard outside Bellos' office did exactly what he promised Angie and paged Ralph Walker. No response recorded on his talker; but, within 10 minutes of the page, Ralph appeared at the office door.

"Hello, I'm Ralph Walker. I heard your page."

"Mr. Walker, yes, thank you; but I thought you would call me back. Ms. Angie asked me if I would relay a request to you."

"Of course, I'll do anything. But, honestly, I came to see her."

"I'm not sure that's possible. Dr. Bellos was very specific about instructions."

"I see . . . " Ralph looked worried and then said, "Please, consider this. I would only be a few minutes, and, confidentially, you see, she and I are really more than just friends. No one knows it, but we are engaged to be married, secretly, of course. So, keep that between us, will you? I really need to be with her. She needs me, you know?"

"Hold on just a minute." The guard turned and walked several steps away. He cupped his talker closely, in front of his mouth, and spoke. A minute later, he returned to Ralph. "Mr. Walker, I can give you 10 minutes."

The guard opened the door, and Ralph walked in. There was Angie, reading on the couch. When their eyes met, Angie jumped up and ran to his open arms.

"Ralphy; I'm so happy to see you. How did you get in here?"

"I had to use the, 'we are engaged' story. Frankly, it's the first time it ever worked . . . Jesus, what is going on, anyway?"

"We have no time. Look here, next to this door, it's an elevator. I can't get it to work. You have to believe me. We have to get out of here and . . . and get to Dr. Sheldon."

"What? Why?"

"I mean Rachel Sheldon, Dr. Sheldon's wife. I don't even know where they live . . . so much to do . . . please, Ralphy? You have to trust me on this. I swear on our past. I swear."

"Sure, of course. Elevator eh . . . "

They walked in and Ralph studied everything.

"Look at the panel, Ralph. It has 16 floors. Am I crazy? The hospital only has 10 . . . can you get this thing moving?"

"I don't know . . . it looks a little strange. There are no screw holes anywhere; and all the material has a give to it. Feel it."

"It's warm, soft; sort of like, like skin."

"Yeah, how the hell was it built? Everything in here is unfamiliar, when you really look at it. Look around out there, see if you can find a crowbar, something to pry this panel off."

Angie ran out and through all the rooms looking for anything to help. She found a metal back scratcher, which had a sharp fork-like edge, and brought it to Ralph.

"Well, that didn't work . . . I just don't see any way to pry this bezel off. What the heck is this stuff?"

"What about the wall panels?"

They both examined the corners, ceiling, and floor.

"Angie, I'm beginning to understand why this is in plain sight. There is nothing in here that I am familiar with. Nothing is screwed down or snapped on, and there are no wires anywhere . . . I can't even make out what the material is. So; what are we looking at, kiddo?"

As they stood wondering, the front door of Bellos' office opened and the guard peeked in. "Hello? Ms. Angie? Nurse Walker? Hello?"

At the same time, the elevator door quickly slid shut, a security protocol; but it trapped the couple inside.

"Holy shit; now what?"

"Look at the door, Ralph."

The small room illuminated; and the elevator door became transparent.

"What the hell?"

The couple watched in disbelief, as the guard walked down the foyer stairs into the oval room, searching everywhere. "Ms. Angie? Mr. Walker?"

"Hey! Over here, in here!" Angie and Ralph shouted and pounded on the door. They could see the guard reach for his talker, but he couldn't hear or see them.

"Dr. Bellos, I'm in your office. I don't know how, sir, but they are not here; they are gone."

"You are sure?"

"Yes, sir."

"I'll take care of it. You may get back to your regular duties."

When the call came into Bellos' talker, he was in ER-1 with Rachel Sheldon. He answered the call quickly and hung up from

the guard. Then he whispered strange words into it . . .
"Kshieldun, Klevilun; Exhish Tuneel forktune; Childene un,
Klevelsesh-Unitem Bellos Echvator'; Exish-Enubill tuke Tuneel-
forktune . . . Shield one, level one; exit 14 with my child to level
red 6 immediately!"

Then he quietly clipped his Knofer back into his hip holster
and returned to consoling Rachel about Jack's death.

At that same moment, Angie had touched the elevator panel,
leaning so her body weight forced her right hand to palm over
the numbers on the bezel. The elevator moved and she flinched.
"Ralph, do you feel that?"

"Yes. Look out the door. We are going down . . . Shit!"

The elevator made absolutely no sound of any kind. They
barely saw the guard exit the room, as the bottom of the front
door closed behind him. Both of them leaned back against the
wall and watched.

"I hope this is what you wanted, luv?"

Then, they both startled again. The entire elevator changed
and became transparent. Unbelievably, Angie and Ralph could
see outside the hospital. It was as though they were floating
down, moving suspended in space.

"Angie, what the hell is going on? Isn't that the parking lot?"

"I think so . . . "

They stood transfixed.

"Ralph, look, up at the stars; so beautiful."

The ride took several minutes, and when they stopped, the
elevator changed back to an opaque white. After a few more
seconds, a door slid open from the opposite wall. They stepped
out into a lighted rock cave, while behind them, the elevator
became part of the tunnel's wall, undetectable.

"Cute trick; now where are we? What are we into, kiddo?"

"I think it is a tunnel, Ralph. Look at that, though. Is the rock glowing?"

They looked at each other and then started to walk, holding hands tightly. Ralph began jogging and pulling Angie in the only direction before them. After 100 yards or so, the tunnel became dark. They could see an opening ahead and they walked out, into the moonlight.

"Jesus, luv, look at that sky. By the way, this is not the parking lot."

"This is wrong, Ralph. It's just desert."

Always prepared, Ralph pulled out his trusty key chain with a flashlight and compass.

"Okay, according to this, we go that way. We should see the hospital in no time. Angie, are you with me here?"

"Yes, I guess. This is undoubtedly the strangest night of my life."

They began jogging. After several minutes, Ralph checked his compass.

"Ralph, look, street lights. Where the heck are we? Let's try flagging down a car, maybe get to a police station."

Two, three, four, vehicles passed, but no one stopped.

"Well, babe, it's 3:30 in the morning. Even if there is another car, nobody is going to pick up hitchhikers at this time of night."

"Really, Mr. Smarty, I remember college. You are so wrong."

Angie did a few sexy poses in front of the next two cars. After about 15 more minutes of walking and seeing nothing, Angie saw headlights. "Look, Ralph! Look! They are slowing down." Angie started jumping and hugging Ralph. "They are slowing, Ralphy. We're saved!"

A dark blue van slowed and stopped right beside the two, and the side door slid open. It all happened so fast, Ralph had no time to react. There were a total of three men and a woman inside. Two men with hoods jumped out very quickly. They forced the two nurses apart. While one man pushed Ralph to the ground, another grabbed Angie's arms and turned her into the van's doorway. The third man, behind her, put a black hood over her head. The first two then grabbed her on each side and swung her into the van. The last man slid the door shut and the van sped off. It was a total of 10 seconds and they were gone, leaving Ralph lying on the roadside in disbelief. He looked up to see dust, and the van, a quarter-mile away.

"You bastards; you fucking bastards!"

He was alone, with only the streetlights and nothing but sand in sight.

"What the f . . . ?"

As Ralph started to walk in the direction the van disappeared, he could hear a cell phone ringing. He followed its sound, found the phone, and pushed the round blinking button.

"Hello, hello; who is this? Please don't hang up."

"I'm not going to hang up," the voice said. "Just walk a mile in the opposite direction, back to the Complex. Good luck. If I were you, I would get back to the hospital as soon as I could. You don't want to miss any of this, do you?"

The phone went dead and Ralph stood with his mouth open.

"What the hell is going on? This is the strangest night of my life."

Chapter 11

Money Talks

MARION BROCK WAS MORE than a successful billionaire philanthropist, although that would be enough for most. He had all the characteristics of a man of stature and power, not to mention six mansions in four countries and worldwide contacts in top financial circles. He was not a self-made man; rather, he inherited millions and many family businesses, all of which made up the global Brock Empire. The Brock name was known as the 'billionaire's billionaire' for generations. However, to his credit, he also held several lobbyist positions in Washington, D.C., managing that effort with a staff of Ivy League lawyers and future state and federal judicial candidates. As part of his own investment portfolio, years ago, he diversified into medical related and high-tech markets; and he was the single credit carrier and financier committed to the completion of the Brock/Swanson Complex in Arden, New Mexico.

It was Gordon Swanson, who initially introduced Brock to Mathew Bellos and Jack Sheldon at one of the Complex's fundraisers. After Bellos gave his stunning presentation, 'The Cure for the Common Cold', Brock negotiated with Swanson and the board of directors that he alone would pay to finish the campus in the American southwest. Impressively, he wrote a single check for the last 15 percent of all construction costs; and he committed to pay for updating to the newest computer software and hardware annually. In return, the Complex would provide him with a personal 3000-square foot, three-bedroom suite on the sixth floor of the Fargo building, which lay in the remote area of the campus' 600-acre landscape. In addition, his name would appear first on the Complex's advertising marquees. His only other proviso was that he never be directly involved with the personnel working on the campus. They would know him by his name only. Any communication from them would have to be in writing, and only come from Dr. Mathew Bellos, Chief of Hospital, or Dr. Jack Sheldon, Chief of Research. Frankly, Brock just liked Jack.

He was brilliant all right; however, his financial partner, Gordon Swanson, never trusted him. Swanson knew the family history. Brock had become a classic venture capitalist, and thought of Swanson as an old school monarchical type—an un-American conservative. Swanson, so it appeared, could accomplish most anything without money. Brock could never find any information, or more importantly, dirt on Swanson. Conversely, Swanson knew every move Brock made, primarily because he had developed such a skilled network of connections within most of Brock's worldwide conglomerates. Nevertheless, Brock had billions and an insatiable hunger for power and greed. Theirs was a sour mix. The name Brock/Swanson was the only voluntary sharing they did. Brock always considered Swanson a minor player, an irritating buzzing fly. Swanson saw Brock's involvement with the Complex as another way to monitor his activities.

After the new campus was completed, Dr. Jack Sheldon continued to work on his pet theory, C.P.T. However, with a child and years behind them, Rachel Sheldon relinquished the urgent demands of career, and moved naturally into managing the couple's domestic affairs. The ranch's needs, finances, and raising Brian were more than enough to fill her day. As the years passed, she distanced herself from Jack's proofs. Eventually, she rarely visited the Complex at all, going occasionally to special annual functions.

It was early last January, when Jack first put it all together. He was studying one Saturday afternoon in their home laboratory and, quite unexpectedly, he surprised himself. Like an artist feverishly painting one subject and in a mistake of the brush, he sees something more beautiful than he could have ever painted intentionally, at 4:55 p.m. on January 12, the secret was his alone. "My God, this will change everything." Jack sat staring at his notes.

$$\oint_{J} {}^{n}_{1}Y \sum_{\propto}^{\sim} \lim_{n \to \infty} \left(7 + \frac{\pounds}{n}\right)^{n} xe^{-x^2} \triangleq$$

"I've got to tell Rach . . . " He paced back and forth. "No . . . on second thought, not until I make it real, no doubts."

He sat back down, talking to himself, "I have to extract and inject into the same DNA; I can't get around that. So, it has to be me. Okay, I'll need two major pieces of equipment; and I need money."

After much pondering, he wrote the proposal requisition and submitted it for budget approval the next day. Dr. Bellos received the request and studied it for three full nights. It vaguely reminded him of his own hypothesis that viral-based life could 'cure' death. He approached Jack the following evening after hours in Research Lab 23, Facility Four.

"Hey, you, how are you? I need to talk to you about your requisition 81114; it's a lot of money."

"Yes, it is. I thought you might be curious."

"More than curious. You and I have known each other a long time. This kind of money has to be approved by the board. I can get us a meeting with one of the big guys to discuss it, if you're game."

"Of course, who?"

"Gordon Swanson, himself; I've arranged for you, me and him to dine Saturday night."

Jack got up and hugged Matt. "My friend, this is a long time coming for me. I owe you one."

"Have you told Rach anything?"

"Nope; I want to surprise her, when everything's right."

"So be it . . . we have reservations at Café Cher, 8 p.m., sharp. I'll meet you in the lobby."

Saturday night, Jack and Matt sat in the foyer of Santa Fe's only French restaurant. "Well, my friend, are you really ready for this?"

"I know you can't know this, Matt. I've been theorizing, hypothesizing, formulating and testing for over four decades about this. I really don't know if I'm ready. But, I know one thing . . . "

"What's that?"

" . . . I know that I have to see this through, no matter how it ends. I am going to see this through."

Bellos put his hand on Jack's shoulder. "I can't know what you know here, buddy. We never talked about it, but I can support you, and I do."

They both happened to look toward the entryway, as the revolving front door swiveled and the tall unmistakable frame of Gordon Swanson walked in. He saw the two immediately, walked over and smiled. "Good evening, Mathew."

"Good evening, sir. You know Jack Sheldon, Chief of Research at the Complex."

Swanson extended his hand. "Yes, hi, Jack . . . too bad we only see each other during special occasions. I've always wanted to get to know you better."

"Thank you. I'm speechless."

"I trust that will not be the case tonight. Come, let's sit, eat and talk. I'm most interested in hearing what you have to say."

The maître d' led the three to a small, cozy room, with only one table, and began serving them like kings. Gordon Swanson took the lead and got right to the point.

"So, Jack; you and the Complex's research team have made quite a name for us all in the quest to improve the human condition. I am here because the recent request is intriguing, but it is devoid in some aspects. I want to understand the exact objectives of the equipment you need . . . sort of fill in the blanks, if you don't mind?"

"Jack," said Matt, "the descriptions of what you need are very precise and specific, detailed and reasonable. On the other hand, your justifications are, in many respects, let's say . . . not as specific. We think we know why you are asking for the equipment, but you don't spell it out. You are talking about reanimating a life, aren't you? I'm not misreading your implications, am I? You can't keep this secret to those you trust enough to ask for this kind of backing."

Then Bellos sat back, and wiped his mouth with a napkin. All three were silent until Jack spoke.

"I don't mean to be selfish here. I know this is the biggest discovery of my life; and, perhaps it will change everyone's perspective in general. It's just that I alone have to take this to the next step, without anyone else in harm's way. Let there be no misunderstanding; you are correct. I have completed the written proofs. The formulations and equations say it all. But, I have to be the guinea pig; no one else. I will let you read it all; and, if you agree, we go; I get the equipment. I don't know how to say it any plainer."

"Dr. Sheldon," Swanson sipped his champagne, "how soon can you give me the manuscript to study? The sooner I finish it, the sooner I can answer your proposal."

"Sir, with all respect," Jack seemed uneasy. "If anyone has to read my paper, I would prefer that only Matt here does it, if that's acceptable to you. After that, he can meet with you or we can meet together again. I would like to move as fast as possible, but with caution and security."

"That would be fine with me. I trust Dr. Bellos implicitly . . . done!" Swanson extended his hand to seal the deal. "At last; now tell me something, Jack, you have written in some journals about 'thought' and 'the process of thinking'. Tell me, in your opinion, exactly what is thought? Try and make it a simple answer for this old man, eh?"

"Well, I suppose the best short answer I can give is, 'Thought is the organization and expression of our senses'."

"Interesting take . . . I'm a bit of a scholarly type myself. I don't know if Mathew told you," Swanson chuckled. "Did you know that the word 'organization' has its root from the Greek word 'organon', as does our English derivative 'organ'?"

"No, I didn't."

"Do you believe our thoughts are really 'organs'?"

Jack paused a moment.

"Why, yes; I do."

"In that case, we should be able to transplant them, just like we do a kidney or liver, eh?"

Jack looked speechless, as Swanson continued, "Well, I suppose every time we speak, we transmit a thought to someone else, don't we, hah? I guess in that respect, we do transplant them; I mean; that is, if anyone remembers what we say, right?" Swanson winked. "By God, you are right, my boy; hah."

The evening went very well, and later, the three were outside the restaurant laughing and talking like old friends.

"Well, you two," said Swanson,"how long before one of you calls me?"

As they shook hands, Bellos said, "I'd like to read the manuscript right away."

"I'm certainly agreeable to giving it to Matt, tonight," said Jack.

"Really? Let's do it. You want me to follow you, or come with you, or what?"

Then, a white stretch limo pulled up to the curb. The driver got out and smiled at Swanson. "Hello, sir."

"Good evening, Mr. Mike. Mike, these are Drs. Jack Sheldon and Mathew Bellos. Gentlemen, this is my driver, Mr. Michael Warren. How long have you been with me now, Mike?"

"Sometimes it seems like forever, sir."

"Hmm, well, thanks for that, Mike, and thank you both. It was a most informative and enjoyable evening. The food wasn't too bad either, eh! I'll wait, with great anticipation to hear from you, Mathew."

Swanson saluted them as he got into the limo. Mike looked at Bellos and, with a wink, he got into the driver's seat. The limo made a U-turn and sped off. The two doctors stood, waiting for the valet.

"Matt, let's do this. I really need to start the ball rolling. We can go to my house. I'm sorry Rachel is gone for the night. She would love to see you. Anyway, I'll give you a copy of the manuscript."

"I'll follow you then."

The two got into their cars and drove to Jack's home, about 30 minutes away. Jack led Matt to his basement lab. Bellos sat down in one of the recliners, while Jack opened his desk, took out the book and handed it to Matt.

"You want me to start now, or go home?"

"If you want to read, I'll make some coffee and leave you alone. You may have some questions."

Jack smiled, went upstairs, and Bellos read the first 10 pages. Then he turned to the final pages, just as Jack returned with coffee and cake.

"Jack, can you give me a summary, before I get into your micro-tech lingo. You don't explain this Chemical Personality Transfer in the requisition. Just give me the substance. I'll read the proofs in private."

"Okay; fair enough . . . well, I've isolated what and where our personality/memory are located within the brain. I've defined it chemically. They are really one and the same, but manifest in different ways. You follow?"

"Not sure."

"You and I both know we learn everything through sensation and genetics, right? We become aware of whatever; then we think or behave accordingly. In any case, we remember it voluntarily or involuntarily. Matt, everything we know, everything we are, is eventually stored in one location."

"Am I supposed to differentiate between the brain and the mind, Jack?"

"Elementary, of course; the brain is the physical beast, and the mind is who we are . . . "

"Sorry," Bellos laughed, "it's just that I do remember some things about being a doctor."

"Anyway, if I may continue . . . personality/memory is a chemical cocktail. Our mind instructs all tasks required or chosen, and it eventually stores everything in a library of thought, in one location, for historical reference, a library of conscious and unconscious permanent records. You said summarize, right?"

"Go on . . . "

"Every action or thought triggers synaptic impulses within and between cells. I found the 'link' between those signals and the chemicals we produce. At the same time the signals fire, a record of that firing imprints in your library, as a chemical. Our library is our personality, you see. Matt, I have proven that we can withdraw the library. It coagulates after death. By extracting it and reintroducing it into the deceased, the patient will reanimate. So I called my proof C.P.T.–Chemical Personality Transfer."

Jack took a breath, "Well, that's most of it really . . . "

"Most of it; Jesus, come on Jack; what's the rest?"

" . . . Yes, well after reinjection, something unbelievable happens. The 'mixture' of the extraction and the catalyst bath redirects the patient's genetic makeup, issuing new instructions. The new chemical composition stimulates each cell to correct all flaws. The C.P.T. bath triggers anabolic growth within the genes. We grow more healthy cells than those that die off. I would not just live again; I would become healthier than I was before I expired. There has to be genetic compatibility, of course, which is why it has to be me. But the potential is staggering. Matt, eventually we could store people in small vials and reanimate them, when there is a genetic match."

Bellos' cheeks swelled and he let out a slow blow.

"Boy, Jack, I can only think of a thousand questions. You have proven this?"

"Yes."

"How?"

"Mathematics, physics, chemistry, microbiology; it is all in there."

"What about in a lab?"

"Come on; it's not like we can test rats, or animals, about personality."

"I know; but it seems to me that first you need a human host."

"Yes, and I need the equipment I've requisitioned, a controlled environment, and a genetic duplicate."

"And just how do we get your body?" Bellos chuckled. "It seems to be in use at the moment."

"It has to be me, Matt; my body. There is only one, unless you know something I don't," Jack smiled. "You are correct; so, I have to die; you have to extract the cocktail, re-inject me and bring me back." Jack hesitated.

"But here is a catch."

"Christ . . . I can't imagine 'a catch'."

"The window of completion begins after one hour of death and before 72-hours, I think. That is part of my new calculations. After that, the library is far too diluted; Death takes it."

"Listen to yourself, Jack. What are you saying? The brain dead isn't dead until 72 hours after the heart stops? Jack, what you are proposing is crazy . . . besides, why not invest in a cloning model? We have connections through affiliates."

"No, a male clone's DNA is incomplete. You know that. The brain would reject the serum in the first place. Ironic, isn't it? I mean 72 hours is exactly three days."

"What? Jack, when and from where, exactly, do you withdraw the serum? What are the guideposts directing the operation? Where is this 'library'?"

"Read the book! As the body begins to deteriorate, the mind protects itself. The memory cortex changes; and, in defense of dying, it coagulates the memory table, enabling a focused extraction; cool, huh? However, strange as it may seem, the extraction must take place after at least one hour of death."

"And this is explained and proven, here in your manuscript?"

"Yes"

"All this must happen pretty fast, Jack. Nobody knows when they are going to die, you know."

"Thanks for reminding me, but it's not when you die that this relates to, it's after death and before 72 hours are up."

"Hmm . . . "

"And one more thing; I am not prepared to share the formula for the catalyst bath, unless I am the guinea pig. If the extraction isn't embedded in the accurate catalytic compound, it will die within moments. The bath is what stimulates the C.P.T. to activate after reinjection."

"How long can the serum live—in the right catalyst?"

"I've calculated five days, so far."

"Okay . . . how, in God's name, are you going to know who is doing what when you are the one dead? Have you thought of that?"

"Yes, I have. I need a partner, whom I trust. Someone who keeps the catalyst, extracts the serum, measures the proper doses, revives me and stores the rest.

"In the catalyst bath?"

"Right, yes; placed with the right catalyst; there should be enough for six to seven injections. After the first extraction, each three-quarter-inch filled vial could be studied to try to extend the C.P.T. mix . . . Matt, if successful, we could not just re-animate me; but, maybe, we could change our view of death, completely."

"Jack, I'm still trying to figure out where this coagulation is precisely; and, for the record, I am not going to be a party to killing you."

"Well, there you have it. Details are in the pages. I need the equipment."

"It's all in here, right?"

"Yep. Will Swanson buy it?"

"There is only one way, my friend. I'll read this in detail, believe me; but, you have to let him read it, too. I know he is more than capable of understanding it. I trust him. Besides, you have no choice, as I see it."

Jack walked to the door, closed his eyes, sighed and turned. "Fine; I don't believe I'm saying this. Set it up. I have to know right away."

Bellos took the copy and put his hand on Jack's shoulder.

"I'll talk to you tomorrow."

Bellos left, and Jack fell asleep examining the original copy of his manuscript.

While he drove, Bellos took his Knofer out and put a headset on. He placed the manuscript over the Knofer and spoke, "Copy and transmit to Bellos GGM-TBN 010."

The Knofer input all information from the manuscript and transmitted it via headset, into Bellos' mind. He then pulled over to the side of the road, called Swanson, and sent the manuscript to him via Knofer. Swanson performed a similar procedure, and then he spoke to Bellos.

"Mathew, I don't see how we can help Jack right now. You know this is what I've been waiting for, but not this way. We cannot be a party to killing anyone, intentionally. Besides, it will take time for Ever-Life to digest and prove the details of the manuscript. You have to go back and tell your friend that I said 'no' regarding his proposal. Tell him we may be able to help in the near future, but we need to work with him, systematically, before committing. I am sorry, Mathew. I know how serious this is. But the potential abuse and chaos this could create are just as staggering as the potential medical advances it could bring. No one will be able to control this yet."

"I know, sir; but he wants to start now and get physical results within five months. Jack has been working on this for 35 years, and he can taste the end. I know how he feels . . . I, too, have many questions; but would you consider our being a blind financier, at least monitor him somehow?"

"We have very few options. Don't forget; he has to die, Mathew. I don't see how we can be involved in any way without drawing too much attention from the wrong people. Right now, this is a losing proposition. Patience is the key."

"I'll let him know in the morning."

CHAPTER 12

NEEDLES

AS THE DARK BLUE VAN SPED along the night desert road, Angie Esposito lay tied up and gagged in the back against the wall. Her muffled screams and kicking only annoyed the kidnappers. Finally, a cell phone ringing broke the maddening sound of the girl.

"Damn . . . give me that phone . . . hello."

"Marty, have you got the girl?"

"Yes, sir."

"And she is not harmed in any way?"

"No, sir, she's a bit uncomfortable. She's a fighter, that's for sure . . . now what?"

"You have to pull over and park the van; and please sedate her."

Marty tapped the driver, gestured to pull over, and the van stopped. Another kidnapper pulled a syringe out and stuck it in Angie's thigh, pushing fluid into her. They waited. A few seconds later, the voice on the phone said, "What's happening, Marty?"

"She's quiet and limp."

"Thank God. Now, please, gentlemen, the second syringe; and be careful; this is the big one."

Marty gave the phone to the man holding Angie. Then, he gently removed the hood from her head, undid her blouse and pulled the collar down from her neck. Marty followed his instructions and measured carefully. As he stuck the long needle slowly 1.25-inches into her neck, he shook his head and murmured, "It's times like these, I wish I never became a paramedic."

Very carefully, Marty pulled the syringe puck back, extracting liquid. "Jesus," he whispered, "it's not red."

He took the needle off and kept the filled vial from view. Then, he picked up the phone and heard, "Are you done?"

"Yes, sir, but. . . "

"Marty, put the vial in the case. Complete the task. Are you there?"

"Yes, sir. Are there any changes in instructions?"

"No, but be very careful. Make sure she is completely all right. Do you understand?"

"Yes . . . you don't need to worry."

Marty hung up the phone and laid Angie comfortably on a pillow in the back of the van. Then he climbed into the front passenger seat, and the van continued on its way.

CHAPTER 13

ANGIE AND RACHEL

RACHEL SHELDON LISTENED IN DISBELIEF to the call on her cell phone, while she sat in the downstairs lab of her house.

"What the hell are you saying, Brian? What are his vital signs? How can you be so sure?"

"Mom, listen, I hear footsteps. I have to go. I will call you as soon as I can. I don't know what else to say right now. Just wait; I'll get back to you."

The phone went dead and Rachel stood up in an adrenaline rush, pacing the room. Then, it hit her. "My God, Jack . . . "

She raced and grabbed his manuscript again and began to read it feverishly. She got a pencil and paper and started doing calculations in the book margins. The doorbell ringing interrupted her concentration. *Who is that?It's four o'clock in the morning.*

The bell rang again, and again. She put the book down, walked quickly upstairs and looked through the small door porthole, but she could see nothing, so she carefully opened the door. There, at her feet, lay the unconscious body of a girl. Rachel quickly knelt and turned her over. It was Angela Esposito. Rachel held her head up and felt her pulse. She seemed okay, but unconscious. She gently slapped her face and rubbed her hands. "Miss, Miss; hello . . . are you okay? Wake up, honey . . . "

Suddenly, Angie coughed and opened her eyes. "Oh, my . . . Where am I?"

"You are with me now, sweetheart. You'll be fine. Can you move?"

"Yes, I think so . . . " Angie looked closely. " . . . It's you."

"Me? Yes, I am. Can you get up? Let's get you inside."

" . . . Yes; no; I mean it is you, Mrs. Sheldon, Dr. Sheldon. You are Dr. Rachel Sheldon."

"Yes, I am." Rachel looked puzzled. "Come on, stand up. That's it; try to walk with me."

They limped slowly together into the living room.

"Mrs. Sheldon, I am . . . I am Angie, from Focus Ward at Andrews Hospital. I need to talk to you."

The two just made it to the couch, when Angie fainted again. Rachel gave her a cool, wet towel and a sip of water.

"There now; take it slow. Let's just be real careful here and relax, okay?"

Angie coughed and looked around. "Oh, my head; I can't believe I found you. How did I get here?"

"The doorbell rang. I answered. You lay at my feet." Rachel smiled, stroked her hair, and Angie forced herself to sit up.

"Please, Mrs. Sheldon. I have to talk to you."

"All right; you can call me Rachel."

"I am afraid something horrible is happening or at least something stranger than I have ever known."

"What is it?"

"Like I said, I am the nurse in charge of third floor Focus Ward at Andrews. Tonight your husband, Dr. Sheldon, was admitted as a victim of a car accident."

"I know, baby." Rachel's eyes flooded. "I was there. I just got home a while ago. He died."

"No, Mrs. Sheldon; that's just it." Angie grabbed Rachel's shoulder. "I saw him. I saw him alive."

Rachel jerked back, stood up and thought, Brian; his phone call . . . "I just talked to my son; he said something about the third floor and Jack being alive."

"Mrs. Sheldon, I'm not a fool or a weirdo. I have been working at Andrews for three years, always on Focus Ward. The surgical team operated on your husband for hours. They reattached his arm and leg, but his heart had stopped. He was clinically dead for the entire hour. I monitored him, there was no brain or heart activity. Then, I took a food tray into his room. He sat up. He just sat up." Angie took a deep breath. "I had to see you. Somehow, I thought you would believe me; please?"

Just then, she remembered; and, reaching into her pocket, she pulled out the two-inch long, blue test tube vial. "Look at this; I was supposed to inject it into his neck, but I freaked out and ran. I swear, Mrs. Sheldon, he was as alive as we are."

"What is that?"

"I remember; I got the original email around 10:30 p.m., from Dr. B. himself. It said I should inject Dr. Sheldon at precisely 2 a.m. with 'this' into his right carotid artery."

Angie handed the vial to Rachel. "After that, they took me away and locked me in Dr. Bellos' office. I found a book there. I read part of it, but I don't believe it. It said that Dr. Sheldon was alive, because of something called 'Ever-Life'."

Rachel's eyes swelled as she stared at the vial. "Oh, my God!" She took Angie's shoulders and squeezed. "Can you walk?"

"I think so."

"Come with me."

Rachel led her downstairs to the lab, grabbed Jack's manuscript and showed it to Angie.

"Did the book look like this?"

"Why, no; the book I saw was bigger. It had a kind of white leathery cover with gold lettering that simply said J.A.S. But inside, it described Jack Avuar Sheldon as being 'duplicated'. There were a lot of technical definitions and medical procedures regarding DNA. He was approved for something called transtosis. Yes, that's the word, I think."

"What does it mean? Angie, something is definitely going on . . . " Rachel sat down for a moment, " . . . That book; it couldn't have been written tonight . . . What is the last thing you remember, child? You didn't just appear at my door. Can you tell me?"

"Yes, I think so . . . " She recounted her evening to Rachel.

"Angie, we need to get back into the hospital. Can you get us into Focus Ward?"

"Yes, sure . . . "

"I know I'm asking a lot, but you are in this, honey; otherwise why kidnap you and then leave you at my door?"

"Yes, all right; besides, I have to find Ralphy. The last thing I remember, he was thrown onto the street curb by thugs . . . I know I am right about this, Mrs. Sheldon; I know it."

"We will go to Matt's office. You carry this book. We have to see the other one . . . wait, I have to see Jack first . . . The morgue, we will go there first. I know the department head. Come on; and Angie, whatever happens, don't lose this vial; and don't tell anybody you've got it, okay?"

"Okay; but, Mrs. Sheldon, Dr. Bellos wrote the email in the first place. He already must know I have it."

Rachel looked at her and paused with a confused look.

"You are right. Let's go."

CHAPTER 14

BELLOS AND JACK

DR. JACK SHELDON AWOKE NAKED in the corner of Room 309's bathroom shower. He slowly stood up, soaked, with no pain, and thought, *Okay, no bruises, no sores; Christ, I feel fine, good . . . now I have to get myself together. What the hell has happened to me?*

He put on the terrycloth robe behind the door, and walked back into the bedchamber. The room door lock clicked and the knob twisted. In walked Mathew Bellos.

"Matt, is that you?"

"Jack . . . " They smiled and embraced. "How are you feeling? God, it's good to see you up and about. Come, sit."

"Jesus, Matt, I had blood everywhere. I've been lying down, sitting; Christ, I fell in the shower and just woke up crouched in the corner. For God's sake, what the hell is going on?"

"I have a lot to tell you, but we don't have time right now. Here, I brought you some clothes. Get dressed. We have to leave. Your body is still reacting from everything. Obviously, you have no idea what happened to you; so, just trust me."

"Now what?" Jack started to dress, but almost fell from being lightheaded.

"Here, take a sip of this," Bellos handed him a glass.

"What is it, milky champagne? Not bad; guess I'm out of shape."

"Come on. You'll be fine; follow me. Try to be as quiet and quick as you can. There are people, who, if they are not here yet, they will be. They want you, and I don't mean in a good way."

The two walked out of Room 309 and down the hall into Angie's office. Bellos opened the closet door.

"Matt, did we miss our coats?"

Bellos turned with a sarcastic smile. Then he reached behind the hospital gowns, tapped a particular part of the molding and whispered strange words, "Yuopenzechduar GGM-TBN 010."

The wall slid to one side, revealing an elevator, much like the one in Bellos' office. They stepped in and Bellos continued speaking strange words, "Master secure, initiate directive-197."

The wall closed behind them, and both men felt a slight tug, down and to the right.

"What the hell was that? Is this some vampire castle with secret passages? And when did you learn Chinese—That Wong Tong, Wang Chang shit. What was that? Jeez!"

They both looked at each other and Bellos chuckled, "I'm glad you haven't lost your sense of humor."

"Thanks . . . that tells me nothing."

"The fact is, my friend, to quote your favorite science fiction—we are going where you have never gone before; or something to that effect."

"Like that's exactly what I was thinking . . . "

"Well," Bellos shrugged, "I have to get you far away and safe, fast. We are getting on a plane here at the Complex."

"Matt, I feel funny all of a sudden."

"Hold on, here we are."

The elevator door didn't open. It appeared to disappear—poof—to reveal a flight hanger and a small one-engine propeller plane, waiting for the two to board.

"So, are we back in the ancient 1960s? Where did you get the antique?"

"We're flying low and slow, to avoid detection . . . come on, up the stairs, watch your head. Just sit anywhere and put the belt on, will you?"

"I feel so sleepy."

"You need a shot. You might as well give into it for now. I have to see the pilot. I'll be back."

In a few minutes, even considering the noise, Jack drifted to sleep. It felt like only seconds, but it was 20 minutes in all, until the plane bounced on the landing strip and Jack woke up. To protect Jack, Bellos tried to give the impression that they were leaving the state; so, he filed the flight plan with the Complex, but actually had the plane take off from the Andrews Airfield, and then land at a small airstrip in a remote area on the campus.

"Jack, you up? We are here."

"How could I not be with that smooth landing? Where are we?"

"Let's go."

The two deplaned and the pilot immediately took off again.

"This still looks like desert, except of course for the huge concrete door over there. Oh, my head."

They walked toward a bright light shining at them on the door, about 100 yards away. A special ops guard in full combat regalia greeted Bellos with a smile and salute.

"Evening, sir. This way . . . "

"Well, this can't be Brazil," Jack joked. "I don't see any bikinis."

They stood before a large 20-foot square concrete door.

"Oh, great, something else ridiculous; it looks like some old 1950s bomb shelter?"

"Actually, it is, or was." Bellos gestured to the guard and the door slid open.

"Matt, I need to sit down, sorry. It's like I've had the crap beaten out of me."

Bellos held Jack's arm and guided him through the door into the first room on the right.

"Here, sit and drink."

"This is the same stuff you gave me before? What is it; where are we?"

"Just relax; you are going through some very radical changes."

"Really, ya think? I was in the hospital, you know."

"Just drink it. Look, Jack, I know you are upset. I said I would explain, and I will. But you have to be patient with yourself, the situation, and with me. This is life threatening. It's all very sensitive. The most important thing right now is that you take it slow, just for a while."

"Upset? I am way beyond upset. It's all so frustrating, and where the hell is Rachel? I have such a headache. Christ, I am a doctor and I can't even think. I feel like I have superpowers one second and the next; it's like I'm going to vomit my insides out from the pain."

"Side effects, Jack, side effects. They should pass; and, if they don't, this is the one place on Earth you want to be."

"And, where is this? I see four walls, a table and chair."

Bellos put his hand on Jack's shoulder, smiled and said, "Listen; you are having massive memory issues; and I don't want to repeat myself more than three times, okay? Do you feel up to eating something?"

"Yes, the only food I've seen is what that nurse dropped on the floor."

"Then you remember the nurse?"

"Not really, maybe; I don't know."

Bellos sighed, leaned into him and examined Jack's eyes.

"For now, I don't expect much. The only thing I am asking you for is patience. Are you feeling any better?"

"Yeah, as a matter of fact, I am. What's in that drink?"

"Good. Come on then, follow me; this way."

They walked out and down a hall, to another door. Bellos pulled out his Knofer; waved it over the icon, above the lock and the door clicked open. Jack walked into a very small room. "So Matt, you've brought me from one closet to another?"

There was one lounge chair and table in front of a small round stone fireplace. A video image of a world map displayed on the wall, and what looked like a silver refrigerator stood in the corner.

"Jack, please sit. We call this room a Unit. This one's young, I mean small. It's one of many here. If I had to describe the whole area, it's sort of like a beehive. You haven't seen this part of the Complex, yet. There is nothing to fear at all; but it is highly secure."

"Obviously, if you've kept it from me."

"The important thing is that you are safer here than if you stayed in the hospital; and you get much better service. We have a lot to cover in a very short time."

"Okay, what's next?"

"Actually, I need you to get comfortable. Here, drink more wine and maybe nap a bit."

"And how do I get food and the drink?"

"Well, that red button, just speak as you push. You can order anything. After you order, go around the corner and you will see a small 'lift door'. Open it. Whatever you ordered will be there. Use the remote on the table there. It will enable you to monitor hospital activities on the screen above the fireplace. You can catch up a little. We have no way for you to communicate with the outside though, sorry. As for the drink, more is in the refrigerator, over there, ready for you. Jack, this isolation is necessary for your health, just for a short time to guarantee your safety. Try to keep calm, will you? Just don't forget to drink the wine."

"In case you haven't noticed, I keep asking you, what is that stuff?"

"It's a very old and rare healing elixir. I couldn't really explain it if I wanted to, but it makes you feel a lot better, doesn't it? Drink all you want."

"You are just trying to get me drunk my first day back."

"Unfortunately, buddy, the drink's effects are only temporary; and it has no alcohol in it, sorry."

Jack swallowed every drop, sat back and felt the warmth spread throughout his body.

"You must listen. There are things at work here you never foresaw."

"I don't understand. Quit being so damn cryptic and just spit it out, will you?"

"Do you remember C.P.T.?"

Jack looked puzzled at first, but suddenly felt refreshed and alert.

"Yes, I think so, Chemical Personality Transfer."

"Right, what else? Come on."

"It's the transfer of our personality, our memory, from a dead person to a live host . . . yes, I remember."

"Where did it come from?"

Jack strained. "From me?"

"Yes, you, and what happened, Jack?"

"Jesus, what did happen? Did I screw up?"

Bellos smiled. "No, you did quite the opposite. You succeeded; you did it; you are the proof; well your serum is."

"What are you saying?"

"I'm saying that you took all the findings and research, you combined them into one fantastic hypothesis, your manuscript, and you proved it true. You found the formula, the chemical cocktail for yourself. Jack, you were dead, and now you are not."

"Dead?"

"You were in a car accident. It was very bad; yes, dead, but there are other things going on right now. I have to keep you going with the elixir you are drinking until we get the vial."

"Why?"

"Let's just say, you found the cocktail and how to extract and inject, but you weren't prepared for the corrective action required by your body. You were a wreck when we admitted you, bones broken, an arm and leg severed . . . "

"So, how did I survive?"

"Well, we gave you Fix-its to repair all body parts and functions."

"What the hell are you talking about?"

"You can't understand everything right now. Your mind is still fried. There is a lot more to hear. Right now, the drink needs time to work. Here, have another, doctor's orders, and I want you to put on this headset. Listen to the program; relax as much as you can. Drink all of the wine, little by little. Order some food."

"Fine, good speech, I remember something else, too. I had help."

"We knew something like this would happen. Please, eat and drink; it's critical. Listen to the headset. You will feel better."

"Who is 'we', Matt? Who knew this would happen, the hospital staff?"

"There are forces that want C.P.T. and all the vials. How much did you make? If they get it, they will try to duplicate it. Look, my point is that you may not even remember what we have said here, unless you do as I say."

"I remember five vials; I think. I'm well enough to talk. Tell me, where am I?"

"Why do you have to know everything, immediately? Right now, your wife and my daughter are in grave danger, and you have to get better ASAP to help me keep them safe."

"What? You mean Rachel. What do you mean, 'and your daughter?'"

"Yes, my daughter. She is in this up to her eyeballs, and she doesn't even know it, yet. Jack, she is the key to all this. We have to protect her. I can't explain it all right now. Listen; do you remember Marion Brock?"

"He was co-investor of Brock/Swanson."

"Right. Well, he invested in you and your experiment to prove out C.P.T. because Gordon Swanson . . . "

"Gordon Swanson? Yes, I remember that bastard. He turned me down."

"Yes, and for good reason; he didn't want to murder you."

"I was murdered?"

"Then, of course, there was your bad timing; your jackass impatience almost lost you your life. Now it's threatening us all. Getting Brock involved opened the door to profiteering and sabotage on a global scale."

"Wait a minute. Who is Swanson to judge and decide the future of C.P.T.? I don't believe that."

"Well, that's why we are here. Obviously, you don't believe anything bad about Brock. You don't realize the forces in play in all this. I can assure you, Gordon is one of the good guys." Bellos smiled. "And so are we. What you need to know is that we have to move fast. That means you have to heal fast. The drink will work, but it needs a little time, and you need to listen to this headset."

"Fine, I do need to eat. I am so tired again, all of a sudden."

Bellos patted Jack's shoulder. "It'll come and go for a while. Relax; I will be back to pick you up. Jack, you have discovered a miracle, but others have turned it into some cat and mouse game for the usual power and money. We are going to make it right."

Chapter 15

Why Me?

AS MARION BROCK DESCENDED with an armed guard in the Andrews hospital elevator, he reached inside his pants pocket and pressed the emergency button on his phone. It sent a signal to his Chief of Staff, Rash InVoy. InVoy was at his east European office in Istanbul, Turkey, when the signal came through.

"Archer . . . ARCHER! Get in here."

"Yes, sir."

"I want a team at Andrews Hospital, in Arden, New Mexico, within a half hour, ready to complete stage four; and we need to get Mr. Brock out."

"Yes, sir."

"Who have we got there?"

"We have four men, prepped at the Complex, in Mr. Brock's building. I can have them in the hospital within 20 minutes."

"Do it!"

Back in the Andrews elevator, Marion Brock looked like a man about to burst, thinking to himself and murmuring incessantly to the guard.

"Do you know what I've done for that son of a bitch, Jack? I should have fixed him six months ago. He is the one who came to *me*, after his precious friends deserted him . . . Christ! That irresistible letter started it all:

Dear Marion,

Thank you for your recent support with regard to our latest acquisition of the Dunn's programming software. It will allow us to control and read the viral stimuli variations within the quarantined floors.

Additionally, if you would consent, I would like to meet with you on a private personal matter. It is of great importance to me-to us, I believe.

Sincerely,
Jack Sheldon
Chief of Research and Development
Brock/Swanson Labs

"Jack was the first bastard employed at the Complex to see my home. Bet you didn't know that. For years, I kept faithful to my code. But smooth talking Jack, he was right about every issue he ever wrote about to me. I remember thinking, What could his letter mean? The big three; Shit! Visionaries of tomorrow . . . they sucked me dry, with researching the common cold, Alzheimer's, Down Syndrome, and now this . . . look at me, shit!"

Brock was raging red, staring at the guard.

"Within two years of knowing me, they were negotiating, on their own, with the Pentagon, Israel and China; funding new money, making new theories. They all needed me in the first place to finish this Complex. I was there for them, no one else. My help allowed them to become famous, and that son-of-a-bitch, Jack, he changed everything. How could I resist making that first farking phone call?"

Marion remembered every word . . .

"Hello, Jack?"

"Yes . . . Marion?"

"Yes, yes; how are you?"

"Fine, thanks for calling."

"Well, I know I'm somewhat of a recluse. It seems we only see each other when I'm awarding you monies at some conference. Jack, I got your note. Yes, I would love to meet. When would you like to come over?"

"Fantastic, great; I'd like to see you at your earliest convenience; if possible, today or tomorrow . . . ?"

"That's fine; as a matter of fact, I am home now. It's 4:30 p.m. If you would like to come over, I'd be glad to see you."

"I'm at home, too. I can be there at say 6 p.m.; how's that?"

"Good, I'll see you then."

So, at 6 p.m. sharp, Jack arrived and pushed the security buzzer to the penthouse entrance, outside the Fargo building. A guard answered. Jack gave his name and the door opened. Jack took the elevator to the penthouse, and his knock on Brock's door began it all.

"Hello, Jack," Marion said with a smile. "Come on in."

"Thank you for seeing me on such short notice." Jack shook his hand.

"It's fine. Can I get you a drink?"

"Sure, thanks."

"Something special, I think; champagne."

Brock opened one of his many bottles and filled two tall crystal glasses.

"Here. Now, sit. Tell me, what can I do for you?"

They had a sip; and then, Jack told Brock everything about C.P.T. and the meeting with Swanson.

"Jack, I am rarely at a loss, but this is beyond my understanding. As for me, I can offer my money and resources. What do you need?"

"I need this special equipment."

He handed Brock the proposal that he gave to Bellos.

"I also need a location to work and trusted assistance."

Marion sat and reviewed the 20-page proposal.

"You also need patent rights, copyrights, international protection, not to mention personal security, and transportation . . . things only money can buy. Jack, I'm yours; but, only on one condition."

"What's that?"

"Why, that we are partners in this, Jack . . . with my money and resources, along with your brains and medical know-how . . . why, it's a win, win, guaranteed. Here's my hand on it."

Jack took Brock at his word, and they shook hands with wide smiles.

That was months ago. Now, Brock stood in a silent rage, waiting for the guard and the elevator to take him to God knows where.

"Mr. Brock . . . Mr. Brock," the ops guard said, breaking Brock's concentration. "We're here, sir; please follow me."

The two men stepped off the elevator into the hallway on the sixth floor below the hospital. The guard led him to a small room and opened the door. It was quite pleasant, with a comfortable couch, chair and two tables.

"Please, sir, if you would be kind enough to wait in here, we can clear this up very soon, I'm sure."

"Well, all you had to do was ask, sonny. I'm at your beck and call, like I have a choice."

As the guard began closing the door, he heard, "You are fired, you know; you dipshit!"

Even though Brock heard the click of the lock, he grabbed the knob and tried to yank the door open.

"Shit, shit, shit!"

Then, he took his phone out and dialed InVoy; no reception.

"Damn it! Where the hell am I?"

CHAPTER 16

THE MORGUE

DR. RACHEL SHELDON and Nurse Angela Esposito arrived at the Andrews Hospital emergency room again, around 4:45 a.m. The reception staff had been too busy to notice them, so they both easily walked past the front desk and down the hallway.

"Angie, quick, into the elevator . . . " Rachel pushed two on the panel. " . . . I know Frank Bloom. If he stayed the night shift and Jack did die, maybe he will give us some concrete answers."

They both stood impatiently, and when the elevator door opened, the sign etched on the wall read:

ANDREWS HOSPITAL MORGUE ⟶

Rachel walked out and to the right. "Come on; hurry." Some 35 feet or so past a wide window that overlooked the hospital atrium, she pushed the glass double doors open, revealing the department's main area. In the middle of the room, there were four examining tables. Across from them, in the far corner, working on something, sat a man looking into a microscope.

"Excuse me, excuse me, Frank, is that you? Frank?"

The white haired elderly man looked up and turned around. He was obviously in quite good shape, while well into his seventies.

"Frank? No, Ma'am; Frank works in Research Lab 23, now; different building."

"Oh, really?"

Rachel seemed to wither a little.

"You look like I just kicked you in the belly. Perhaps I can help. I am Richard Bellos, The mortician here, extraordinaire. Okay, it is a bit late for that. What can I do for you two?"

Rachel looked at him with great surprise. "Bellos? Are you related to Matt?"

"Of course; I am his father. I know you."

"But, I always thought you passed away. I mean, I'm sorry; it's just a shock."

"I expect so; nevertheless, I am here in the flesh."

He held out his arms, and she instinctively hugged him. "Jesus, why would Matt let us think you were dead?" Rachel held on tight; her eyes began tearing. "It's just . . . Jack, you know?"

"I know. It'll be fine. Come; sit here." He walked them to a cushioned bench a few feet away.

"It's been just a horrible night. I'm at my wits end . . . Oh, excuse me, this is Angie, Angie Esposito."

"Yes, I know of Angie. Hi, we are all family here . . . "

Rachel sobbed and Angie took her hand. Dr. Richard stood before them and spoke reverently, "My deepest apologies and respects about your husband, my dear; I am so sorry for your horrible evening."

"Thank you. I am here to see his body. I need to see him."

"I understand; you have nothing to fear. Try to stay calm. Believe me; I will show you nothing to be afraid of . . . Please, come with me."

Richard helped her up, and then he turned, leading them through doors, which led into one of the main vault areas. "Now I assume that neither of you frequent this atmosphere much; so, first, you should know, things have changed radically throughout the industry in recent years. In particular, here at Andrews, I hope you noticed; there is no peculiar fragrance or nauseating odor."

The two women sniffed the air.

"For another, we lay our guests in bed-like comfort; they're not on a cold slab. It's to assure best in case potentia'.

"So what does that mean?" Angie asked.

"I mean, we address any question, about anything, at the bed. Let me show you."

He walked the two over to the wall, pulled the latch and a mahogany, twin bed-like casket drawer slid out.

"She was a small girl, who had been rushed here, having an immune reaction to asthma. She expired two days ago."

Rachel gasped. "Her color, she looks like she is asleep. She looks so alive. I had no idea. Do all the departed look like this, now?"

"Most, yes, unless it is a special circumstance."

"You mean, like Jack?"

"Yes, I am afraid so. I can show you something."

Rachel looked at Angie and the book she was holding. "Yes, please, I have to see."

"Well, follow me."

He walked into a smaller, dimly lit room that, somehow, radiated a pleasant warm feeling.

"I don't ever remember being in here," Rachel said.

"Well, I like to think that is because I redesigned it all. This way . . . over here."

The two women followed him to the far corner, about 35 feet away. There were four beautifully decorated 36 inch by 24 inch drawers on the wall.

"Mr. Bellos, all this looks more like a mausoleum than a morgue room."

"It is neither, really. Oh wait, I forgot."

Richard brought two cushioned chairs, and placed them facing one of the drawers.

"What is that?" Rachel said, pointing to the icon on the drawer.

"Very good, Mrs. Sheldon; you certainly can spot the unusual. It's an old glyph from a language long ago. Literally translated today, it means 'Money Comes from God'."

"Kind of odd, don't you think, especially on a coffin?" said Angie.

"Yes, but the point is, you see; it's not the meaning that is important, it is the shape."

Richard took out his Knofer and waved it across the symbol. The drawer clicked, and a larger than normal coffin slid out in front of the three. The casket was pearl white, almost perfectly oval and mildly glowing.

"I don't understand," said Rachel. "What is this?"

"Please. Don't be afraid. I've been waiting for you all evening. Now, we can begin." Richard smiled, turned and waved his Knofer over the same icon on the center of the casket top. The entire top half became transparent, and the girls shocked back at what they saw.

"Jack, oh, my God!" Rachel began to weep.

"Please, my dear." Richard held out his hand to her.

"Look a little closer; come."

Both Rachel and Angie stepped forward. The light inside the casket was perfect, enabling them to see every detail. There lay Jack Sheldon, wearing nothing but a faint smile.

"This can't be," Angie said. "That's not him. He is on Focus Ward, in 309, broken and bloody. This man is perfect. He has no marks, no stitches."

"Actually, he was not broken or bloody at all, my dear."

"What are you saying?" Rachel snapped, as she studied the body. "What are we looking at, Dr. Bellos?"

"Oh, this is your husband all right, every cell. You can believe me. Please, will you two sit, just a moment? I have to tell you something."

The chairs were comfortable; but the women sat rigid, still staring at the coffin.

"Angie, Rachel, there is much more going on that I want you to know, because, well . . . because we are more than just hospital family."

The women looked at each other. "What?"

"Angie, my dear . . . " Richard knelt, in front of her, with his hands on the chair arms. " . . . I know what a night this has been for you, and it's far from over. But, I tell you the truth when I say . . . You are my granddaughter."

Angie looked wide-eyed, as he smiled and extended his arms to her. "But, I don't understand." She put her hands to her mouth, and then, instinctively, leaned into Richard.

"I know, my dear, but it is true."

He started to cry, too, and then gathered himself together.

"Angie, both of you, listen; pay close attention. First things first, and then your questions . . . Angie, your father is going to be here soon; and, as this day begins, it's going to be a new life for you, him, me, Rachel and Jack."

"My father? Who is my father?" Angie gasped. "You mean Dr. B?"

"It is quite a story, but for another time. We are in a horrible rush. I realize this isn't easy, but I have to expedite here."

"What about my husband, Jack?"

"As I said, that is Jack all right. Angie, do you have the vial that Dr. Bellos told you to inject?"

The two women looked at each other,and Rachel nodded to Angie.

"Yes, I have it here." Angie reached into her pocket, withdrew it and handed it to Dr. Richard.

"Thank you." He waved his Knofer over the icon on the casket again. Rachel stood up and watched as the coffin slid around and lowered. Richard took a syringe out of his pocket and filled it with the liquid in the vial. He turned to Rachel and spoke softly, "You know, my dear, it was your calculations, over the early years, that were the motivation and the stepping stone to Jack's putting it all together. Without you, this would not be possible. Remember that."

Richard leaned over Jack's head, with his back to the two women and injected the vial. "Now we wait,"

Then Richard reached over and pushed a small button on the wall to the left of the coffin. A 10-inch by10-inch door opened, revealing a filled wine glass, which he took out.

Rachel stared at Jack's body in disbelief. She thought she saw his right hand quiver. "Jesus, his eye twitched; he is blinking." She caressed his face and leaned into him.

The first thing he saw was her smile. "Rach?"

She held his hand and kissed him, "Hi."

With tears of happiness flowing, she began gently caressing him. "Thank heaven, Jack, my darling."

"Please, you two . . . " Richard patted Rachel lightly. "I hate to interrupt; but Jack, you have to drink this."

He handed Rachel the wine glass and nodded. She took it, lifted Jack's head and fed him.

"You two have very little time," Richard whispered, "and you may want to pull that blanket over your husband. Now, Angie, will you come with me for just a minute? We need to talk. Then, all of us need to move out of here."

"What is going on?" Jack asked, as he tried to sit up, shaking. "Who are you?"

Rachel put her finger to his lips. "You've done enough for one day, honey. We are going to do whatever the doctor says. Now, be quiet, and drink."

"Thank you," said Richard.

Just as he was about to begin, there was a bang; then two, three, coming from the outer rooms of the morgue. Richard ran to the door; but, by that time, it was too late. He had just enough time to turn and yell back at Angie, "Get to the closet, Angie, hurry! Get in there, now!"

Richard felt the first bullet hit his leg. Angie screamed and instinctively made it into the closet, the door slamming behind her. Jack heard the shots and jumped up and out of the casket, naked. It all happened so quickly. Rachel saw the next two bullets explode through Richard's torso and into the walls. She screamed as Jack reached to help Richard. But, he too stepped into an array of gunfire. He turned to Rachel, just as the men entered the room. There were loud sparks everywhere.

"Rachel!" Jack yelled, as he fell.

The gunmen had no mercy, pulling the triggers repeatedly, spitting bullets into Richard and Jack. Then, they turned to Rachel. One black-hooded man yelled, "Fuck you! Fuck him! Fuck all you assholes!"

Rachel stood in terror. The last thing she heard were the shots of the automatic machine-guns, as she felt the bullets go through her chest. She fell, face down, hitting the floor, her eyes in a glassy glaze, and her mouth spitting blood as she reached for Jack. Smoke and silence filled the morgue. Three bodies lay limp, with pools of blood spilling all over the floor. The gunmen looked and saw both the vial under the casket and the manuscript that Angie dropped. One of them picked them up; and then, they all left, out the Atrium window onto ropes that took them up into the morning sky.

Barb Sawyer heard the commotion and hurried down the hall into the room where she saw Rachel, Jack and Richard soaked in blood. She screamed and ran back out, bumping into Dr. Mathew Bellos.

"Barb, what is all the noise?"

She was hysterical, shaking. "My God!" She pointed. "There, in there; they are all dead!"

Bellos let her go and walked into the bloody scene. He stood, stunned at the horror. "Dad, no! My God, Rachel?"

All three were riddled with bullets. Bellos went to his father first and turned him over.

"BARB!" he yelled. "BARB, COME HERE!"

In seconds, Sawyer appeared again with a crash cart.

"Help me! Take his feet. We have to get him in the casket over there. Hurry!"

Within a minute, they managed to lift Richard up and into the coffin bed. Bellos took his Knofer, waved it over the casket lid, and the bed slid back into the wall. Then, he looked down at Rachel, up at Barb and spoke quickly and succinctly into his Knofer, "Team red to floor two of the Andrews morgue, immediately! Set up Unit-4 for gunshot victims. Notify Dr. Lu, two for transtosis."

Barb watched astonished and transfixed. Within seconds, Bellos' emergency team arrived and moved with lightning speed. They put Rachel on a gurney and wheeled her out into a private elevator. Bellos, gently but firmly, took Barb by the shoulders, looked her straight in the eyes and said, "Barb, look at me. Go to the nurses' station and call emergency and the police. Get them here right away. Then call Frank Bloom in Research Lab 23. I need him here to autopsy Jack, and get me those results stat. Have you got that?"

"Yes, sir."

"Okay, good, this was a pro job. We need to move quickly. Also, call Dave Marshall, Chief of Security. Have him come to my office, ASAP . . . and Barb; I don't need to tell you, do I? You didn't see anything. You weren't even in here. Only one person was shot . . . period!"

Barb closed her eyes and nodded yes.

"Now go!" Bellos turned around again to survey the room and he heard a faint noise coming from the closet. He walked slowly to the door and listened to crying inside. He swung the door open and Angie exploded out into his arms.

"Dr. B . . . Dad!"

"Thank God; you are all right, child."For a moment, nothing else existed. Bellos spoke with quiet surprise, "Angie, you know?"

"Yes, Dr. Richard told me. He said he was my grandfather. What happened?"

"A lot . . . come with me. You will be safe."

He turned her around and they walked back into the closet.

"But where are we going?"

Bellos tapped the wall and spoke strange words that meant, "Master secure, GGM-TBN-010."

The wall slid open and the two stepped into a lighted elevator.

"Angie, put your left hand palm on the panel and say after me, 'Master's daughter, Angie Bellos.' Can you do that?"

"Yes."

She repeated the phrase phonetically. The door closed and the elevator moved upward. When the door opened again, they were back on the tenth floor, in Bellos' office foyer.

"Angie, are you okay enough to reach on top of that bookcase, there?"

"Sure"

Andrew Sarkady

"Get the shiny white book with J.A.S. on it. Bring it to my office down the hall, over there."

Bellos walked ahead to his desk and used his Knofer to call Gordon Swanson. Angie felt her body start going into shock. She concentrated and thought, *This is not going to happen*. In a most determined way, she took a high-back chair from the dining room and stepped up to reach the book; the same one she had read earlier. Holding it to her chest, she walked into the computer room; but she stopped at the door, shocked once again at what she saw. Dr. B. was talking to a two-foot tall hologram of a white-haired man. The image seemed to grow out of a small rectangular object on the desk. For Angie, everything that night had a dreamlike quality; but, now, the weak, dizzy feeling started to overwhelm her, as she listened.

"I'm afraid they have assassinated DP-1, sir, and Dr. Richard and Rachel Sheldon both need procedures."

"What about Angie?"

"She is safe, here with me." Bellos turned and smiled at his daughter.

"Thank God. What about the vial and Jack's manuscript?"

"Gone, unfortunately; the police are en route. Marshall will be here in a few minutes."

"What about Mr. Brock?"

"He is in a Unit, down on six."

"Good, I will notify 'Ever-Life'. You confirm all DNA. We have to get the vials, Mathew. Did you find out how many there are?"

"Jack said five, but we really can't be sure."

Angie stood watching and listening, in disbelief.

"Angie is the most important thing right now; so, keep her safe. Then we must meet. Have you seen young Mr. Sheldon, yet?"

"Marshall and I will do that."

"I think it best to bring the lad with you, Mathew. Take a Carrier to Jerusalem. I have a meeting on the surface in Geneva regarding 'Time Trust'. After that, I will meet you, in the reception tunnel beneath Judah villa. We know they have to stop and trade the merchandise, in the Holy City, before going on to Turkey."

"Why?"

"Too many ears, Mathew . . . "

Bellos glanced to the side, at Angie again. "Yes, sir, be safe."

"You, too."

CHAPTER 17

MEETING THE MAN

MARION BROCK'S CHIEF OF STAFF, Rash InVoy, sat in his office, in a meeting with Greek Orthodox Pappas Kristos Alieri, who was first assistant to the local Ecumenical Patriarch. The diocese headquartered in the modest Church of Saint George, within the Phanar district of Istanbul, Turkey. Father Kristos was liaison to the Christian Orthodox Hierarchy, most heavily populated in Russia now.

"Rash, you know I appreciate you keeping me updated on all this. Everyone is so excited that completion is in sight. This is a Godsend to help us understand our Lord's resurrection."

"You're welcome. Just to be clear, Father, your brothers and leaders have agreed to everything, correct?"

"Yes, I have assurances; this is our greatest opportunity to unite the faiths and merge science with religion. We have agreed to work in harmony, as long as no one is hurt and no major conflict results."

"Nothing worthwhile is easy, Father."

"Has something happened? Our briefing was to include Mr. Brock."

"We have just heard from Mr. Brock. He has been delayed; he will call as soon as he can."

"Were you able to confirm securing the formulas?"

"Yes, the good news is we have the manuscript, and a vial is on its way to us, right now."

Kristos took a breath of relief. "How long before we know?"

"A few hours; we have a lab set up, where the trade will be made. Are you prepared for the exchange?"

"Yes, my son. As you know, after I met with Mr. Brock, I approached the local synagogue and mosque leaders. We all have been very persuasive in record time throughout our individual hierarchies. I have commitments totaling $16 billion in U.S. currency. We are all ready to transfer shares, upon receipt and confirmation."

"Good . . . pardon me for asking, Father; but, this has to be the biggest transaction so far that you've negotiated between Russia, Israel and Iran, no?"

"Yes, it is, by far; it is the greatest treaty in the history of the combined faiths. We will bring peace between the Christians, Jews and the Muslims, finally, all in the name of our Lord."

CHAPTER 18

BRIAN

THE FAINT LIGHT OF THE MORNING SUN began to change
the horizon as Brian Sheldon arrived at Marion Brock's Fargo
building.

The entrance guard was ready and admitted him without
question to Brock's penthouse on the top floor. Brian waited
over a half hour, pacing and looking out the living room's great
bay window. For a moment, the beauty of the sunrise hitting the
desert flowers erased the jarring emotion of all that happened
that night. As he studied it all, he noticed four men, dressed in
SWAT team garb, running toward the building from the
direction of the hospital. They were carrying what looked like
automatic weapons. Brian pushed his face up against the
window, to try to see exactly where they entered. His nerves
kicked into gear, again. Suddenly, Brock's multi-line phone
monitor rang. It was built into the glass tabletop covering the
couch's side table. Just one light blinked and beeped. He stared
at the light and thought for a split second about what to do.
Then, he touched the light and a speaker turned on. He heard
two men talking.

"Yes, sir, we have part of an empty vial and the manuscript,
but we couldn't find Mr. Brock."

"Stay where you are. We will bring him to you."

The line went dead. Brian pushed the dot again, sat down on the couch and thought. Then, he raced downstairs to the security guard.

"Excuse me, sir, I saw men run into the building. They looked like military. It looked like they were wearing SWAT clothes."

The guard snickered, "I assure you, if anyone came in, I would have seen them. This is the only entrance. No one gets by me."

"You know," said Brian, "I think I'm going back to the hospital and meet Mr. Brock there. Don't worry; I've got all the codes, and I locked upstairs."

Before the guard could react, the lad skipped out the door and ran, as fast as he could, along the long paved path back to Andrews. After almost 10 minutes, he staggered, out of breath, into the first floor ER-1. There were police all over, so he stopped one of the plainclothes men.

"Excuse me, officer, what's happened?"

"I'm sorry; I can't say."

Brian showed his Brock Intern I.D. to the officer.

"Young man, that doesn't do anything for me. If you have a question, you can ask for a detective on the second floor, if they let you in up there."

Brian rode up to floor two and cornered the first cop he saw, "Hello, sir? Sir, I am Brian Sheldon. I work for Marion Brock, out of Washington, D.C. He owns this place. Can you tell me what happened here?"

"Sheldon, eh, good for you; I am Detective Inspector Burns, of the Arden City Police, homicide. You must be here to answer questions because this is a murder scene, and I need answers."

"Murder? Who was murdered?"

"What's your name again, Sonny?"

"Sheldon, Brian Sheldon . . ."

"Come with me, over here." Burns led Brian to a bench in the hallway outside the morgue.

"You are Brian Sheldon, eh?"

"Yes . . . "

"Do you have relatives here at the hospital?"

"My father was in a car accident last night. I'm here to see him."

"What about your mother?"

"She's home. I talked to her, a little more than an hour ago."

"Ah well . . . I am sorry, son. But your dad was shot tonight, in this morgue."

"What? That's impossible! It can't be true!"

"Yes, well, it is. Someone shot him at least four times. I am sorry, son. Is there anyone else you know here?"

Brian coughed and looked like he was about to throw up. He began to sway and hyperventilate . . . *Dad? Impossible, we monitored him; he was on the third floor* . . . "I want to see him! Let me see my dad!"

"I can't do that, right now, son. Try to settle down . . . you go with this officer; she will take you somewhere safe. I'll meet with you later; I'm sorry . . . go."

The uniformed policewoman took Brian by the arm and escorted him back down to a secure room in ER-1.

"You just wait in here, Mr. Sheldon. I'll be right outside if you need anything."

Brian sat down on the hospital bed, shaking, disoriented and angry.

I have to get out of here.

Back on the second floor, Detective Burns yelled out, flippantly, "Sergeant Wells, did we get anything on the wife yet?"

"Two detectives went to her house, Jake. Nothing; no answer; but, downstairs in the ER, one of the receptionists thought she saw Mrs. Sheldon in the hospital, about an hour or so ago."

Jake Burns rolled his eyes in disgust. "Christ, I need a vacation."

CHAPTER 19

BREATHLESS

NURSE ANGIE STOOD AT THE DOORWAY of Dr. Bellos' computer room inside his tenth floor suite at Andrews Hospital. She watched, mesmerized, as her father completed his call to GGM Gordon Swanson.

"Angie, come take a seat, here. Are you okay?"

Angie sat on the chair beside his desk, laid the Ever-Life book on top and spoke. "I just can't believe all this is happening. This is the night from hell."

"In some ways, yes, but right now, the important thing is that you feel okay. You have been through so much, and I'm afraid your body may go into shock."

"I know; I just started feeling a bit shaky, lightheaded and weak; but I need to know why." Angie's eyes filled with tears.

"I know." Bellos reached for her. "I'm sorry, Angie. I've been a fool. Forgive me?"

"But why did it happen? I don't understand."

"Some very bad people have wanted to get a serum—a formula—for a long time; and they finally stole it tonight."

"Why? Tell me. I've seen a man rise from the dead; I was almost murdered, and I can't believe three people were just killed not 10 feet from me. I think I can hear whatever you have to say."

Bellos sat back and began, "Angie, I've wanted to tell you about us, and other things, for a long time; but, I couldn't, for many reasons. Partly, I guess, because there's a bit of a coward in me about you. Believe me, though, it's more than that. I thought I was protecting you. I thought I was doing the right thing, for years, not telling you I was your father. I didn't want others to find out and use you. I've been torn between telling you, and worrying if I did, your life would change so radically, you might lose yourself, blame me; and I'd lose you. Lately . . . well, time and events do strange things to people. The truth is, I guess I put some things out of my mind to protect my sanity too. So, I hope you can be patient with me. I will fill in gaps, as best I can, I promise."

"It sounds confusing."

"Yes, I guess . . . it all started when your mother died." Bellos reached and took his Knofer out. "Do you think about your mom a lot?"

"Of course, Carla Esposito, we lived a strange life in those days . . . and I remember you were there."

"I know, I never told you this, but, when she died—it seems like only yesterday sometimes—we were married at the time, but we couldn't tell anyone. If you remember, natural born citizens were not allowed to marry emigrants. She had to keep her maiden name. Your mother made me promise not to cause a stink about the whole issue. She thought it would ruin my status in Washington if it came out. Later, I filed papers, through my contacts, which made you my legal protégé. After your mom passed away, several extremist bastards tried to deport you; the papers stopped that. You never knew. We settled into a routine of academia and life. You were so smart. Eventually, your interest in nursing assured you a future, freedom and independence. The country needed anyone in medicine, and I was well-known enough that they stopped harassing us. By that time, my books, patents and lectures gave us the financial security we needed to move on. When I got this position at the Complex, I didn't tell you anything for your own safety. I know it's no excuse; but here in New Mexico, you were safe and seemed happy. I concentrated on my work; and I vowed to bring Mom back."

"Bring Mom back?"

"My position here allowed me to research her death; and, at the same time, I could keep an eye on you." Bellos stroked her hair and shoulder. "Focus Ward was the perfect place to keep you safe with me."

"But why did I have to be safe? Something is missing."

"Some aspects of what I am involved with right now are very dangerous; and there is more you have to hear and see."

Bellos spoke into his Knofer in the strange Ever-Life language. Three small holograms—a sphere, a square and a triangle—appeared above his Knofer. He grabbed the triangle, tossed it on the floor and spoke to the Knofer. "Please set Carla Bellos program, authorization: Bellos GGM-TBN 010 . . . "

Angie stared, focusing in disbelief, as Bellos talked to her, "Angie, I am not just head of this hospital. For years, I have been a leader in training of a very old, secret organization, an underground society, really. That is a good part of why I didn't tell you everything. It would have put you in danger, sooner. Now, you have to know."

Angie stood up, shaking uncontrollably. Bellos reacted quickly, "Angie; your body is going into shock; try to calm down."

He went to a cabinet, pulled out a sealed foil-wrapped glass and handed it to Angie. "Drink this; it should settle you. Sit down; concentrate on the hologram."

Bellos then turned to the triangle and said, "Activate."

It began spinning on one tip and projected a light beam to the ceiling. Then, a skeleton began to grow up. First two feet, and then leg bones appeared like plants growing in fast forward. The complete skeleton grew within a minute. When the bones were finished, there was a beep.

Angie sat in awe, staring in wonder

"Yeah, they don't teach you this in nursing school."

Bellos had a faint smile as he reached for the next sphere and tossed it into the skeleton. A spinal cord and nerves began to grow from the base of the backbone out to the head, hands, and feet. Angie watched a brain flower inside the skull. Nerves sprouted out, like beautiful ivy growing on a castle's walls in quick time-lapse photography. Angie stared in wonder, and she stopped shaking. When the nerves were complete, Dr. B. tossed the square into the beam and said, "Features—Carla Bellos."

Then, he turned to Angie and watched her expression. Within seconds, muscles and skin covered the body. A light tan beautiful skin color with detailed feminine features appeared. Finally, body hair and facial hair finished the image. As it rotated, Angie involuntarily placed her hands over her mouth and reached out, "It's Mom! How is this possible?"

Bellos gently grabbed his daughter's hands before they could touch the hologram.

"Listen to me. I need to tell you a lot . . . I am part of a secret society that can do many wondrous things, like this. I show you this, because I – we – have no time. I need you to trust that everything I tell you is true. The form here, what you see, is Mom."

Bellos helped Angie up and they stood together, staring at Carla.

"Now, you need to be strong and open minded."

Angie took a breath. "Why? What now?"

Dr. B. went to the closet and took a bathrobe out, which he always kept for his wife. He turned, looked at Angie and they both watched Carla, as he spoke one word into the Knofer, "Employ." Her hologram changed and became fleshy. The triangle and beam of light disappeared and the body slowly lowered onto the carpet. Carla Bellos stood before them. At first, she moved ever so slightly, and then she blinked and looked at Dr. B.

"Hello, darling," Carla leaned in and embraced Bellos.

"Hi, babe. Here, put this on. I brought someone to see you. Look."

Carla turned and saw Angie. After several blinks, she recognized her daughter. She held out her arms in surprise, "Oh, my heavens . . . Angela?"

"Mom?"

"Oh, my baby! How wonderful! My goodness, how you've grown."

They hugged tightly. "Oh, Mom . . . it is you."

Then, Angie turned to Bellos. "Dad, how did you do this?"

Angie started to shake again.

"It's all right," Carla said. "I am here, just in a different way. I am still Mom. I can't be exactly like you and Dad anymore . . . Mathew, please."

"Angie, Mom is real, but in a different way. It's similar to the principles regarding clones. From our research, we are able to create solid holograms. Each is similar to a clone, but synthetic, sort of. In your mom's case, I programmed most of the memories into the holographic data; but I have been limited. She can function in every respect, up to the degree we have programmed. The important thing right now is that you two can be together; but Mom can only do so many things. We can talk about this and a lot more, later. Right now, you two should enjoy the moment. I have to go to a short important meeting. You stay here with Mom, and I'll be back in about 10 minutes."

Bellos kissed Carla and left the room. The two women went to the couch on the far side of the room.

"Mom, I'm a nurse, so I understand medical technology, up to a point, but it's hard to accept this."

"I know. Your dad tried to explain everything to me some time ago. I never understood."

"You feel real, just like me, like anyone else; and you sound like Mom. It's so good to see you."

"Tell me all about you . . . what you've been doing?"

Meantime, Bellos left and refocused on the morgue murders. Work demanded it. He walked to the front door and opened it. Chief of Security Dave Marshall stood before him.

"Dave, come in; sit down."

"Sir, we caught the men who did it."

"Good. Were they Brock's?"

"Yes, their communications are primitive. We traced contacts to Rash InVoy, Brock's Chief of Staff, and Archer Smythe, InVoy's hatchet man. Smythe made the 'go' call from Istanbul, Turkey. Here's the phone he used. We took it off one of the murderers. The whole thing went down within 15 minutes. If we had more time we may have found out why . . . "

"Dave, that's not the point and you know it."

"We are examining the room now. The Carrier-Unit malfunctioned from the bullets. We think it died."

"What?"

"I know; I thought they only died from sunlight, right?"

Bellos squinted, "Or apparently something else . . . "

"Ever-Life is searching all databanks and testing a four-foot square wall section struck by bullets. At this point, we don't have answers."

"All right; keep me posted. Make sure Ever-Life gets all necessary DNA data for processing Dr. Richard and Rachel?"

"Yes, sir. One other thing— young Sheldon is in ER-1."

"Hmm, good; deliver him to Carrier Unit-17. We will all be leaving from there. Thanks, Dave."

"I am sorry about this."

"I know. Tell the police I will be available to interview tomorrow . . . oh, and Dave, tell Barb Sawyer to go home. She and I won't meet until I get back."

They shook hands. Marshall left and then Bellos went back to his office to see Angie and Carla.

"Hi, you two; I'm sorry, I had to leave."

"That's okay, luv. We had a wonderful time; didn't we, sweetie?"

"All this is wonderful; I just need a little time," Angie said.

Bellos kidded, "Your Mother and I understand. After tonight, I'm surprised you haven't gone mad by now. But you have stopped shaking . . . listen, I do hate to break this up, truly, but Angie, you and I have several things we have to do. We have to go."

"No," Carla reacted, "not yet; please Mathew, it's too soon."

"I'm sorry, honey, it is necessary, only for a short time, I promise."

After a few seconds, Carla looked at her daughter and said, "Yes, right, we will be together soon. I love you. Remember, it is just a little different, that's all. Give us a hug, baby."

Angie leapt into her mother's arms and held on tightly. Carla gently pushed her daughter back and whispered, "Bye for now." Then she stood straight, with tears in her eyes, and said, "End program."

Her image pulsated, blinked, and suddenly, she was gone. Bellos took Angie in his arms. "I know this is difficult. I know this morning has been too much for anyone. But, Angie, you are not just anyone. I believe you can handle all this. There are changes coming fast, and I promise, you are a big part of them. You will be with your mom again."

"I hope so." Then, with a smile, she stepped back again. "Okay, what's next, Pop?"

"Have you got the book you brought in?"

"Right there, on the desk . . . "

"Grab it and come on then; we go."

Angie followed Bellos out of the room and back into the elevator by the front door. Bellos spoke with conviction, "Down-red 6, STAT . . . " The elevator pressurized and fell fast, down below the hospital some 1300 feet. Within 10 seconds, the door opened and they walked out into a lighted, rock wall corridor. Once again, Angie stared at everything.

"Dad, where are we? Wonderland?"

Bellos chuckled, "Interesting you say that; I thought so the first time I came here. This way; follow me."

They walked through the hallway, passing five numbered doors. Bellos opened the sixth, which had the number 17 on it. They stepped into an empty white room.

"Angie, this is the inside of a Carrier-Unit. Remember repeating those words in the elevator, before?"

"Yes."

"Well, now your voice print is part of a very special database, and consequently, in rooms like this, you have authority to request most anything you want. So, don't be bashful or afraid to ask for it, within reason of course."

"I don't understand."

Bellos waved his arm out, "I mean, like a chair."

146

He said it and, immediately, a high back cushioned chair appeared.

"Table with hors d'oeuvres."

A dining table with a large plate of various appetizers appeared out of nowhere.

"Standard programming is Victorian style furniture. You will learn as you go. You try."

Angie said, "Lobster dinner with asparagus, baked potato, and champagne."

A filled plate and glass appeared on the table.

"Try not to get caught up in it too much, though, all right?"

"What do you mean?"

Bellos turned, as if he were speaking to the walls.

"Please provide a couch, fireplace, tables, lamps and 60-inch wall monitor. Decorate walls in style of Bellos house-1017."

Angie watched the room's lighting pulse, and then, like magic, everything Bellos requested appeared out of nowhere, neatly positioned around the room.

"That's impossible!

"Yeah, rather nifty; isn't it?"

"Nifty . . . please?"

"Yes, nifty . . . obviously, I am sort of stuck on Victorian Santa chairs, fireplaces and ancient clichés. You practice . . . decide what you like. Just remember, if you abuse the Unit, it will cease to function. Honey, I have to go for just a little while. Try to relax. How is your body shock?"

"I feel better."

"Good." He turned to walk out and heard, "Dad, wait, you can't leave without telling me; what is a Carrier-Unit?"

Bellos stopped and did a double take. He turned around and took a breath himself. "You're right." He scratched his head and looked at her, lovingly. "Do youremember in the nurses' lounge, how I acted?"

"Yes, I was hurt, shocked really."

"I am sorry for that. I didn't think you were going to be so upset at what you saw. After all, you are a nurse."

"What did I see?"

"You saw something wonderful; but yes, scary, especially if you are not prepared."

"I feel safe now. Tell me."

Bellos leaned back in the chair. "As I started to tell you before, some years ago I was recruited by a medical research organization. The organization is a subterranean culture of people, who base their lives on healthcare research and well-being. They have lived deep beneath the Earth's surface for centuries, much longer really; but, the point is, they—we have made unbelievable medical discoveries, discoveries that far surpass anything mankind has done up on the surface."

"Like what."

"Like how to bring a person to life."

"You mean, Dr. Sheldon, don't you?"

"Yes; and very soon, your mom, I hope. Dr. Sheldon discovered a serum, a formula. It's a bit complicated."

Angie sat up straight and attentive. "So, Frankenstein?"

"Far from it; however, we have not been able to duplicate the formula, completely. We are working on it as we speak. Anyway, his serum can only survive and will only react properly, in a special catalyst bath. That catalyst exists in its raw state, within a single primary source, a person, who contains a very special DNA mix."

"Okay, so the combination of serum and catalyst bath can bring dead people back to life. I get it."

"Well, it's not just that. Follow me on this one point, please. I am referring only to the catalyst bath."

"Fine, go on."

"So far, within all the known gene banks, our family, Bellos/Esposito, has the only DNA structural combination to make the bath. It's one of the reasons they recruited me, my DNA . . . and it has been passed on to certain relatives . . . "

"Your genes?"

"More specifically, in this case, regarding the catalyst bath, you—your genes."

"What?"

"Angie, you alone, you are the only person who has the genetic carrier proteins in the raw state; in the right sequence combinations. You carry the bath that will insure Dr. Sheldon's serum will live long enough to re-inject into a patient."

Angie sat still, staring blankly, for a moment. She furrowed her brow, rolled her eyes a bit and looked around the room. "So, what are you saying, exactly?"

Bellos pulled his chair close to her and took her hands. Just as he was about to speak again, Angie blurted out, "Dad, did you know I was kidnapped tonight?"

"No . . . when?"

"Earlier, after Ralph and I got caught in the elevator."

"Jesus, I was the one who authorized the Elevator-Unit to take you out. I thought you would be safer."

"We made it to a road, and then a van came. There were men with black hoods. They took me, drugged me and left me on Mrs. Sheldon's doorstep. She and I talked, and we took Dr. Jack's manuscript to the morgue. Dad, Dr. Richard injected Dr. Sheldon with the vial you gave me, and he woke up."

"I expected that, but that particular Dr. Sheldon was a duplicate body, developed with a process called transtosis . . . it takes more explanation. We don't have time right now. That book you have describes everything, including how we do it. We can reanimate cells, grow organs, and even grow complete bodies. Unfortunately, however, the memory/personality of the patient is temporary. We keep the duplicates comfortable and normal with periodic non-invasive procedures."

"That must be the wine Dr. Richard gave him, right?"

"Yes; I'm sorry about all this, kiddo, dumping it on you like this."

"It's okay; I'm a nurse, remember? Take a look at this, on my neck. Is it a needle mark?"

Bellos studied the tiny dot. Then, he rolled his eyes, stood up and paced. "They kidnapped you to try and get the catalyst bath. They are making more vials. The shelf life of the serum is too short to study."

"So, am I in danger?"

"Not until they realize your neck is the wrong extraction point."

"What do you mean?"

Bellos stopped pacing and looked at her. He snapped his fingers, as if a light bulb turned on.

"Jesus, we have a traitor in our midst. They know you are the bath, and that means they know this, Ever-Life, us . . . we have to get the serum vials back before they mix the wrong catalyst, unless, of course, they redid the chemistry already? Angie, I know all this is shocking—the morgue, Focus Ward. I will make this up to you. I'm going to bring you into my world, unless you are too exhausted."

"Dad, I think I'm already in your world."

"I'll trust you with everything. Are you hungry?"

"Yes."

"Let's get you refreshed, and eat. You can't afford to go into shock again."

Bellos grabbed his Knofer, "Authorization Bellos GGM-TBN-010 . . . transfer this Knofer to Angie Bellos . . . here, look into the red dot."

Angie did and then she gave it back to Bellos.

"Activate defensive posture 001 to protect Angie Bellos."

Here, now it's yours. If you get lost and can't find anyone, it will show you the way."

"I don't think I'm going to wander off. Anyway, I am tired and hungry."

"Eat your lobster. Around the corner, over there, is a bath area. I have to go now, just for a short time. I will be back very soon. Meanwhile, you can freshen up and enjoy whatever you like. After that, I'm going to send you on a learning effort. You are going on a tour, and will witness exactly how we do what's in that book."

"Where are you going?"

"I'm going to save what we have started and begin beating the bad guys. I'll be back by the time you are ready."

CHAPTER 20

UNIT 17

ANGELA BELLOS SAT IN UNIT 17, which was on lower level six far below Andrews Hospital. She had finished her meal, refreshed herself and sat comfortably watching the monitors, waiting for her father to return. There was a knock on the door and a guard walked in.

"Hello, Ms. Angie, are you all right?"

"Yes, fine; just waiting."

"I see. The doctor asked me to bring you company. I hope you don't mind."

"Well, I can't imagine any more surprises. Sure; that's fine."

The guard turned, motioned, and in walked a young man, with his face down. Angie studied him for a few seconds, and then he looked at her.

"Ms. Angie, this is Brian. Brian, be nice. Ms. Angie has had an evening to match yours . . . Ms., the doctor said he will be here shortly."

"Thank you."

Angie stood studying the young man and then said, "Brian, Brian Sheldon? Is that you?"

Brian looked perplexed, until he took a moment to examine her face. "My God, you're Angie Esposito, what the heck! I haven't seen you since . . . "

"The party week; at college . . . "

"Was that it? Jesus, that was years ago."

They both held out their hands to each other. Brian smiled and said, "You are the last person I thought of seeing today."

"Why are you here?"

"I really don't know, to tell you the truth. The cops were in the hospital, when I got there. They ended up interrogating me. Then, they locked me in a room in the ER. They said my dad was killed. Maybe they think I'm involved, a suspect or something. For God's sake, I just wanted to find my boss; and, all of a sudden, I murdered one of my parents."

Angie paced, went to the couch a few feet away and sat down for a minute.

"Brian, I am so sorry. I wish I had better news. This has been the strangest night of my life. I am the one, who was monitoring your dad on Focus Ward."

"Focus Ward, I was there, just tonight. No one mentioned your name. I was there with my boss, Marion Brock. We met Barb Sawyer. Do you know her?"

"Sure, my dad said that she relieved me."

"Your dad? I thought you lived alone, after your mom died."

"I did, for a while; Dr. Bellos did so much for me. I never understood it all, until tonight. He is my father."

Brian sat speechless, beside her, as the door opened again . . . in walked Dr. Bellos.

"Hi, sweetie . . . " They hugged. "You look refreshed."

"I took a shower, and had the food."

"Good . . . "

Then, Bellos turned to Brian and extended his hand.

"Hello, young man. It's been a while."

"Yes; hi, Doc . . . Please, tell me what's going on. They told me Dad is dead."

"I know, Brian; but that is just not true. Everything is going to be fine."

Brian looked confused, while Bellos turned to Angie again. "Remember, honey, I told you before to be strong? Now is the time."

Bellos walked to the door, opened it and Dr. Jack Sheldon stepped into the room. Angie gasped. Jack looked immediately at Brian.

"Son, thank God."

Brian jumped from his chair into Jack's arms. Bellos closed the door and locked eyes with Angie. He pursed his lips, gesturing with a finger for her to be silent. They both watched Jack and Brian.

"Dad, what's happening? They told me you were shot. Where is Mom?"

"The truth is, I don't know." Jack glanced at Bellos. "But, we will work this out. I promise. That's why I'm here."

They embraced, and after the shock wore off, Jack fixed on Angie.

"Matt, Angie is your daughter?" He stepped over to her and took her hand. " . . . Wonderful; apparently, your father has several secrets."

"Yes, I'm learning. Apparently, he knows how to keep one."

"Matt, where exactly are we? Did the young ones take a plane ride, too?"

"No, sorry, and once again, we have to move on, buddy. Time is of the essence. Look, you three have legitimate questions. I'll start by telling you, Brian; your boss, Marion Brock, has taken something very precious from your dad. Without it, he may not live. We have to get it back. That means we need to work together. You understand?"

"Not really; my boss, Marion? I was with him on Focus Ward. We were just trying to see Dad."

"Brian, think a minute for me," said Bellos. "Do you know anything about a big deal; some negotiation Brock has been involved with?"

"Why, yes, I think so. He and his whole team are about to close a big deal, to make peace for the first time between religions, or something."

Jack and Bellos looked at each other.

"Brian, son, do you have any idea where the deal is taking place?"

Brian paced, thought and said, "I think it's with some Greek Orthodox priest, in Jerusalem or Turkey, or somewhere like that. I remember Rash InVoy saying they are supposed to meet at some church."

Bellos took a breath and then walked over, opened the door and said, "Dr. LuAnne, please come in . . . this is my daughter, Angie; and this is Dr. Jack Sheldon and his son, Brian."

"Hello, everyone . . . " She focused on Angie. "I understand you are going to tour with me for a while."

"Yes, I think so."

They both looked at Bellos, and he nodded.

"Well, then, I guess we are off," LuAnne said with a smile.

"Fine, that's a good idea." Bellos embraced Angie and whispered, "Good luck; everything will be fine. I should be back to see you early this afternoon. You are in good hands with Dr. LuAnne."

"I'll be okay." She pulled his head down, kissed his cheek, and then looked at Brian. "See you later I hope, Brian."

They both walked out, Dr. LuAnne shut the door behind them, and Bellos turned to Brian and Jack. "Okay, you two; take a seat, please. Listen carefully. We are all going on a trip in a very special vehicle. It's called a Carrier. When you get in, just relax. I should tell you both, this Carrier is very fast; but, neither of you should feel any sense of moving or speed. Our objective is to retrieve up to five small vials, which were made from and for you, Jack."

"Jesus, Matt, you're talking about C.P.T."

"Vials?" Brian asked. "Do you know where they are?"

"We think so. Our security team has tracked and located the courier carrying them. He is negotiating with us as we speak. We plan to intercept him, in Jerusalem."

"Uh, Jerusalem, as in Israel?" Jack asked.

"Yes, and if all goes well, we make a trade. They end up with fake serum, we get the real thing; and then, you, Jack, get C.P.T. We should return here to Andrews, sometime after noon, U.S. Mountain Time."

"Shortly after noon? This Carrier vehicle must be very fast . . . and who are the 'they', Matt? And what are we trading?"

"I will get to that. Like I said, you two shouldn't feel any sense of speed in the vehicle. However, you both should be aware of the jet lag factor, because, while it is now 8:14 a.m. here; in real time, we will arrive in Jerusalem in a little over one hour from departure. That part of the world is some nine hours ahead of our Mountain Time."

All three looked at one another, as Jack commented, "Jesus, Matt, if I do the math, that's spaceship speed. You said we were going where no one has gone; but, should we be taking the kid?"

"No, we shouldn't. He will stay in the Carrier at a villa, outside Jerusalem. You and I will go the final distance. I need you to be okay and focused, Jack; can you do this?"

Brian stood up and blurted, "I know I won't! I'm better trained and stronger than either one of you two. God knows what shape Dad is in right now. You are only doctors, for Christ's sake, not astronauts. I am not leaving Dad again."

"Brock taught you something, eh?" said Bellos.

"I'm good, Matt," Jack replied. "I'm fine, really; one thing though . . ."

"What?"

"Can I have another drink of that elixir?"

"Yes, sure."

Bellos walked across the room, over to the curved wall, opened a small door and took a wine glass out.

"Here . . . "

"What is that?" Brian asked.

Jack smiled and toasted his son. "Food for the Gods, son, food for the Gods . . . "

He drank the whole thing in one gulp. Bellos held the door open and gestured to both.

"Okay, you two, let's go."

CHAPTER 21

HOLMES

DETECTIVE JAKE BURNS STOOD staring at Jack Sheldon's naked body on a slab inside Andrews Hospital Morgue. "Who are you, Mr. Sheldon, besides a bloody mess? Sergeant, Sergeant Wells . . . "

"Yes, sir?"

"Where is Dave Marshall, Security Chief?"

"I am right behind you, officer."

Burns turned around to look up at a 6'2" handsome 45-year-old man in a tan shirt and dark brown pants. There was nothing on his person except a small device, which was holstered at his waist.

"That's *Detective*, Mr. Marshall. Exactly, where have you been?"

"Tending to duty on the 7th floor. What can I do for you?"

"And, what is on floor seven?"

"Psychotic and bi-polar patients . . . "

Burns raised his eyebrows and shook his head. "Great, more suspects . . . I'll tell you what, Mr. Marshall, first, you can give me an idea of why this man was shot. What were these pros after? They were pros. But this was no hit. The line of shots indicates more than one automatic weapon, and look at these bloody footprints. They have the same shoe tread. Tell me, Mr.

Marshall, where was your security squad while all this was happening?"

"Okay; so, they were pros. How did they get in? They left, breaking the hall windows. Where would they go? We searched the campus and found nothing. But, I'm sure your men will do better. It is only a 600-acre campus. Listen; I have no idea what they were after. We try to save lives here, not take them. None of my staff carries weapons; only special ops have guns. You can interview everyone. Look, this is 2nd floor Cancer Treatment, Mortuary and Maternity. These are not major areas of concern for murder. I have one person who monitors this floor every hour. That's it."

"What about your Chief of Staff, Billows?"

"Dr. Bellos is not here. He is out of country."

Burns looked him square in the eyes. "Well, you better call and get him back. I want to see him."

"I already did."

Burns turned to the investigating team. "Sergeant Wells; get me that nurse, Barb Sawyer. Thank you, Mr. Marshall; if we need more, we will call you."

"Detective Burns" Sergeant Wells said, "I've been informed Barb Sawyer has gone home."

"What? Well, find out where she lives and get over there."

"Excuse me, Mr. Burns," Marshall interrupted, "Barb Sawyer didn't see anything. I interviewed her. She has been on the verge of a breakdown; she needs sleep. If you insist, I'll bring her to your office and you can interrogate us both after she has a break; just give her a breather for a few hours."

"Oh, I see. Well, in that case. . . Sergeant, forget it. Mr. Marshall says don't bother . . . he has interviewed her . . . I guess he is in charge . . . after all; it's just a homicide investigation. Tell her to take the week off and go to Florida, on me . . . Jesus, how did these people get on the Complex in the first place, with such fantastic tight ass security protection? I hold you responsible, Mr. Security Chief." Jake took several deep breaths, before continuing. "Now, Mr. Marshall, may I call you Dave? . . . Dave, why do you think this man, lying there, was in that position? I mean, his son says he was in a car accident earlier tonight and recovering on floor three . . . why would he show up on the morgue floor, naked, with his face shot off? So far, we know he ran toward the gunshots, not away from them. Why? He is naked, why would a living man be in the morgue and run naked toward machine guns?"

"I think you asked me the same question twice . . . Yes, he does look naked. Well, I am sure it wasn't the heat in here. We keep the whole building at 65 degrees."

"And why are there two other pools of blood; one there, and one way over there in that corner; no bodies, right, just lots of blood? There is no trail from either of the pools to over there; and, there is nothing on any of the walls except nice green paint and bullet holes . . . Boy, this one is going to be fun, eh Dave? It's a real security puzzler . . . any thoughts?"

"Yes, do you need me here anymore, Detective?

"No, please; no thank you."

"Jake, I found something else," said Dr. Watzin.

"Well, spit it out, Doc. That's why you forensic guys are here."

"Look at this."

"Yes, well, I'm sure it's significant. It looks like a broken half of a test tube . . . no odor . . . remnants of blue liquid . . . "

"Yeah, it was in the corner over there."

"Get it to the lab; and get me anything. I want to know what was in it; what it is made of; are there any fingerprints; and get all this blood, bullets and clothing tested yesterday, damn it! And, Sergeant, where is that kid?"

"He is gone, Jake."

"What did you say?"

"I just got the call from the uniform cop outside the room in ER-1. He is gone. She doesn't know how or when, but he is not in the room."

"Oh, for Christ's sake; find me his boss, that Marion Brock. He should know something. Didn't the kid say he was here in the hospital? Turn this place inside out, but get me Brock; or at least someone I can yell at."

Burns turned and started walking out to the main hallway when he saw someone.

"Hey! You there, stop!" Jake cornered a young man at the atrium window. "Where are you going? How did you get in here? Who are you?"

"I am Ralph Walker, a second floor nurse."

"Oh yeah, where were you when the shit hit the fan?"

"I have been out of the building . . . "

"Doing what?"

Burns' angry tone did not sit well with Ralph.

" . . . Witnessing my girlfriend get kidnapped. Who the hell are you?"

"Homicide . . . " Burns flashed his badge. "When did you get here?"

"I got back about 10 minutes ago and was coming up to tell my supervisor about the whole incident when I walked into you."

Burns pointed to the bench against the wall. "Over here; come sit down . . . I don't believe this; just when I thought I could leave . . . .I am Detective Burns, Arden Police; tell me everything, boy."

"Fine; I work third shift and break at 3 a.m., I met my girlfriend, Angie Esposito, for lunch and a walk. We ended up on the highway, not realizing where we were, romance, you know? And the next thing I know, this blue van stops. Three men whisked her away to God knows where."

" . . . And then what?"

"What do you mean, *then what*? Then, I was alone on the road. I didn't do anything wrong. Why are you interrogating me?" Ralph was more angry than nervous. "Angie is gone. I don't need this shit; I'm out of here!"

"Hold on a minute, Mr. Rush-Rush; I have a murder/homicide here, and hemorrhoids. You just admitted to being involved in a kidnapping. So fess up, partner; or we are going to lock up, right now. Got it?"

"Fine, whatever . . . " Ralph rolled his eyes and continued, "The oddest thing was after they drove off, I heard a cell phone ringing. I found it on the side of the road and answered it."

"Yeah . . . and?"

"And a voice said, 'If I were you, I would get my ass back to the hospital. You don't want to miss any of this'."

"What?" Burns sat down next to Ralph.

"Yeah, I know. So I ran, but in the wrong direction. Finally, here I am; that's it."

"So, why didn't you use the phone to call 911?"

"It was dead."

"Where is the phone now?"

"Here, in my pocket."

Ralph handed it to Burns.

"Sergeant Wells . . . take our man here down to the station and get his statement. Give this phone to the engineers. Tell them I need everything on it. Sonny, I'll need a picture of your girlfriend and work details about her."

"Mr. Marshall or Dr. Bellos will have to tell you about her work. Angie and I do not discuss our jobs much, if you know what I mean."

Ralph stood up and accompanied the sergeant out of the building.

"Oh, Sergeant, call me, after the guy signs his statement."

Burns walked the other way, over to the nurse's station and interrupted the group gossip. "Hey, one of you, will you page Mr. Marshall. Tell him I want Barb Sawyer in my office tomorrow, the earlier the better. Here is my number. Have him call me if he has any questions."

Then he turned around and walked toward the elevator, talking to himself, "Jesus Christ! Murder, kidnapping, missing mother, pros in ops boots; what am I, Sherlock Holmes? I never should have left New fucking York."

CHAPTER 22

THE CARRIER

BELLOS, JACK AND BRIAN WALKED down the long hallway from Unit-17, toward an Ever-Life Carrier substation.

"Matt, how far is it to this vehicle, or whatever it is?" asked Jack.

"Just down those stairs, over there; are you okay?"

"I think so. Strange feelings come and go."

"Dad, is there anything I can do?"

Jack smiled. "You're with me. That's plenty."

"Here we are," Bellos gestured, "just down that stairwell and beyond."

Jack walked, holding on to Brian; and, halfway down the stairs, they saw the Carrier and stopped in awe.

They were staring at a smooth oval structure some 100 feet long, shaped like a combination of a football and a fish, lying on its side. Jack was hesitant about letting Brian board.

"Christ, Matt, is this thing alive? Is it safe?"

"Everything is fine. Yes, it is safe."

It had four thick-sectioned tentacles extending from one end, each moving independently of one another. The most striking feature was its body color variations. Some sections radiated florescent green, while others blinked in bright yellow or translucent orange.

The three men stepped closer, slowly, staring, and a door appeared behind one of what looked like a large round fish eye. Brian stopped.

"Dad, this is not my idea of a subway. It looks like an ancient blinking disco light?"

He turned to his left and noticed two other men entering a second door, some 75 feet away, closer to the tentacles.

"Dad, look! That is my boss, Mr. Brock. Why is he in handcuffs?"

"Son, go on; get on board."

"What is going on, anyway?"

"I'm sure Dr. Bellos will explain."

They all walked into a hollow, pearl white, wet looking, large oval room; but, actually, it was dry and pristine, with clean circulating air.

"Dad, how do they light this place?"

"Yeah, Matt; are the lights behind the walls?"

Bellos stood behind the two, and announced to the room, "Authorization GGM-TBN-010 . . . Please furnish standard furniture, wall monitors, and a bath center. Please supply refreshments for all."

Before their eyes, everything appeared out of nowhere. Jack flinched and looked at Brian. "Don't be afraid . . . sit down, Son."

They watched Bellos walk to the far sidewall. He took out his Knofer, pushed it into a slot and spoke to the wall, "Master secured . . . Security Directive GGM-001 and GGM-010 . . . destination group number two, Post 4-A . . . we await instructions."

The deep, articulate voice of the Carrier, itself, spoke for all to hear, "Acknowledged."

Then, silence . . . after 15 seconds, or so, the voice spoke again. All Carrier-Units were capable of communicating, in any language the human mind could understand; and each spoke as representative of their hive mind.

"GGM-1-000 is in danger. There has been a security breach in Andrews Hospital-level-three. The courier you seek in Jerusalem Section Post 4-A is Muslim. He is holding a hostage and primary C.P.T. formula for Ever-Life. Dispatch of three Carriers is available from Jerusalem location. Please acknowledge communication."

"Communication acknowledged," Bellos said. "Recommendation?"

Bellos heard a two-second *ding*, and a small door appeared at the far end of the room. He walked over and opened it. There was a single small two-inch vial filled with a blue liquid. He took it out.

"I don't understand," Bellos said. "Please acknowledge?"

"Please, sit down, Doctor."

Everyone could hear an air blowing sound, as the cabin pressurized. The Carrier began to move and accelerate. The three sat in silence.

"Dr. Bellos; Dad, what just happened?"

The Carrier's voice spoke again, but this time, so only Bellos could hear.

"Listen carefully, GGM-TBN. You have precisely 1.75 time hours to complete the trade for the hostage. It is essential to our continuing cooperation with your species."

Bellos replied quickly, "Who is the hostage?"

There was no answer.

"Please, reply," said Bellos again. "What about our passenger to trade?"

Silence filled the cabin. They all waited; but nothing happened. Then Bellos took his Knofer from the slot and called Swanson. His image appeared life-size in the Carrier.

"Mathew, I take it you heard? We have received the same instruction here."

"What do we do with Brock, sir?"

"I will detail after you arrive. We know InVoy wants the serum and Brock, but what else, I wish I could say."

"I thought they had vials."

"Yes, and someone we need . . . damn! Why Brock thinks he can do this is beyond me. I will meet you at the dock. We will drive to the checkpoint. Security is fine, but we have no idea where we go from there. See you soon."

"Sir, there is something else."

"Yes?"

"It appears we have a mole in the Complex."

"Perhaps . . . "

Communication ceased.

ᔑ·ᔫᔦᘓᔢ·ᔥ

General Facts Regarding Carriers:

1] Each time a Carrier travels, it burrows through rock, lava or anything in front of it. It can shroud itself within a bubble-like protective shell, and, as it burrows, it displaces anything from in front to behind it, leaving no evidence that it was there. Alternatively, without the bubble shroud, Carriers move through rock like fish swim in water, but their bodies spin, as they reach speeds close to that of a rocket in space. Also, without the shroud bubble, they leave a tunnel behind, rather than displace the rock or lava.

2] Carriers have lived within the Earth for millions of years, and those that reach adulthood have grown large enough to burrow tunnels a half mile in diameter. However, there are no records indicating how big they have grown.

3] Carriers and humans share a synergistic relationship. When a Carrier travels with a human passenger, it absorbs an indefinable sustenance, which humans alone contain. After an adult Carrier has accumulated enough human sustenance, it may be stimulated to reproduce, by secreting a gooey jelly from its skin. In that case, they leave tunnels with their offspring glued to the walls. The gel sticks indefinitely, and, those few that grow large find their way to the Earth's core, where they prosper as adults in a hive environment by withdrawing magnetic power from the Earth's core The greater the sustenance they derive from humans, the more gel they secrete. The goo contains trillions upon trillions of microscopic offspring, organisms that may or may not grow into larger Carriers. Carriers mature into many sizes. Rule of thumb is the older, the bigger.

4] Very few tunnels exist without gel, but those that do, remain lifeless and function as vents, allowing magma to reach the surface.

5] Ever-Life negotiates annual treaties with the Carrier hierarchy, which governs all Carrier behavior with humans, including:

A] To communicate with the Ever-Life GGM as he requests via direct mind interface or Knofer. Based on Treaty 91776, called the Michael Plan, Carrier hierarchy agreed to provide instant information to the standing GGM, regarding whereabouts, pertinent events and hive activity. In fact, it is all done in trust. Certain questions have arisen in treaty council meetings, which do remain unanswered, including what the Earth's core is really made of; why the great beasts don't go into it; and why sunlight is supposed to kill Carriers? Fundamentally, it is an accepted fact throughout Ever-Life that the large Carriers are at the top of the food chain, below Earth's surface. New short-term agreements can be negotiated as needed, with a Carrier ambassador—a Tyree Master, if emergencies dictate; however, these are usually done within the deepest hottest known Carrier habitat, the Core Post.

B] To take passengers from any one point within the colonies, to any other, like public transportation on the surface. In return, each Carrier derives sustenance from that passenger and shares it with the hive mindset of their species.

6] Smaller sized Carriers not only engineer and construct their own hive communities, but they also build all the new habitats in the Ever-Life colonies. They are capable of completing tasks which might take the surface years to construct in only a few hours.

7] Carrier offspring supply utility and insulate the colonies from the intense heat and magnetic radiation output of Earth's core. The waste-excrement, of the microscopic Carrier gel is what lights, sanitizes, supplies oxygen and a mean temperature of 65 degrees for all life within the colonies. For well over 10,000 years, Ever-Life has endured, prevailed and prospered within the environment provided by Carriers.

8] There are very few Grand Carriers, which are enablers of time travel.

9] All Carriers have a collective, hive mindset. No one, in the public, knows to what extent the beasts understand humans.

10] The biggest mystery regarding all Carriers is that no colony anywhere has been able to study one. There are no factual estimates of how many offspring exist or why certain ones mature to function in one way while others grow to enormous sizes and function in other ways.

11] The vast majority of Carriers live and reproduce at the microscopic level. The big ones reside below 500 miles, deep within the bowels of Earth.

12] It is an acceptable miracle to all citizens of Ever-Life, that each Transport Carrier can provide anything that a human traveler requests, instantaneously.

13] Ever-Life's Post Staff Hierarchy are the only ones who are privy to updated maps of hive locations, and even those are constantly outdated.

14] Except for scheduled transports, no one knows where or how often any Carrier moves within the planet.

CHAPTER 23

EVER-LIFE

DR. LUANNE AND ANGIE BELLOS walked through Ever-Life's meticulous tunnel system below Andrews Hospital. Eventually, they stepped onto a people mover, which took them toward Lab 202. Angie held the railing and studied all the people and sights. One area in particular caught her eye. Across the walkway, through a large 30-foot by 20-foot pink tinted window, men and women, dressed in monk-like garb, appeared to be writing, sitting at desks with their backs facing her.

"What are they doing over there? It looks like an adult school class of some sort."

"Not exactly; that's book finishing. It's where the manuscripts like the one you're holding are handwritten, proofed and bound. Only the greatest of our successes are prepared in those books. Then, each is shipped to an Ever-Life Post Commander, where they are stored for medical reference."

"Everyone seems so focused."

"Yes, they are dedicated and so patient. Honestly, I could never do that. I'd get too bored . . . each one of them is trained, committed, and every book is a priceless work of art. What has always amazed me is, if you tried to compare the handwriting between them, even an expert couldn't find any difference. Of course, they don't have much fun, as I see it. What you see them doing is what they do all the time. It is truly a calling."

"Why not just photocopy the books? Don't you have printers down here; or reproduce them electronically, an e-book thing?"

"Yes, we have similar processes; however, over eons, these scribes have accepted the task to guarantee every single character in each manuscript is perfect. Not only does each book contain a case study and specific directions for reanimating life, but also each one is a masterpiece, a treasure of historical reference for future generations . . . by the way, have you read that book you're holding?"

"No, not completely, but I hope to make time."

"I think you'll find it very interesting; come on, we're here; watch your step."

Dr. LuAnne escorted Angie into the lab. The bodies of Richard Bellos and Rachel Sheldon arrived earlier.

"I've never seen anything like this."

"Not if you have never been here." Dr. Lu smiled. "Do you feel well enough to do this right now?"

"I've got my second wind, I think. Besides, I have no idea what time it is."

"This way then . . . "

They moved from the main outer room to one of four attached smaller work chambers. Chamber 2 was sterile, well lit, warm with two gurneys and an operating table, which looked like glass; but, when Angie touched it, she flinched, "Whoa, it feels warm and cushy, almost lifelike."

"Actually, it is alive. Most everything here is alive; a subject for another time, but nothing to be afraid of."

Angie noticed a few unfamiliar instruments lying on a table, and the curved walls displayed video and audio information. Dr. Lu touched an image, and the screen image became 3-D. There were no wires or plugs anywhere. Dr. Richard and Rachel each lay, side by side, on two separate stretchers with nothing hooked up to them. There was only a quarter-size coin, a control device, stuck to their left underarms, which maintained their body temperatures at 34.5 degrees Fahrenheit.

"Angie, take Mrs. Sheldon there, to the next room, through that door."

"Mrs. Sheldon? Please, no. I don't think I can; it's too soon."

"I'm sorry; it's okay; I'll do it."

A moment later, LuAnne returned.

"Doctor, I apologize," Angie said. "I am a nurse; it's just that after what just happened . . . "

"Not a problem; no explanation needed."

"Who are you working on first?"

"Dr. Richard, maybe he can help."

LuAnne brought Richard's genetic records up on monitors.

"What do you mean?"

"He has been a part of Ever-Life for quite a while, you know."

"No, I didn't. I thought he was the mortician at the hospital."

"He was; he is; but he has also been a colony citizen for a long time, as was his grandfather. Dr. Richard had been researching our duplication and transtosis programs for years. Recently he conducted experiments of his own, even while acting as your mortician. I hate to think he has to go through this procedure again . . . yes; we will do him first. Maybe he can give us insight to something we may miss otherwise. His knowledge is invaluable."

Angie looked perplexed, but she listened intently. "Since I'm not familiar with anything here, can I ask, what exactly is Ever-Life?"

"It's both the name of our network of colonies, and it's a healthcare program which we began long ago to improve quality of life. As it evolved, the goal has become everlasting quality of life. We don't seek to conquer death, really. Our goal is to keep postponing death's inevitability by controlling life's processes better through genetic manipulation, rather than death controlling life's limits. In many ways, it's not much different from your modern medical goals on the surface; but we have been at it much longer. We make discoveries and share them with 'up there'. It has never been vice versa. I hope that makes sense."

"A bit much to take in . . . "

"Yes. Anyway, you will find some things familiar and others not so much. We have two procedures, which we are going to address, today. One is duplication and the other is transtosis. It is important for you to understand the difference."

"Okay . . . ?"

"In order to be duplicated one has to have a particular genetic code."

Dr. LuAnne slowly pulled the gurney's sheet back, revealing Richard's body.

"I can't believe I just met my grandfather, and now, he is here, like this." Angie took a breath. "What do you do first?"

"I know this is hard for anyone, even a nurse. First, with Richard, we are not duplicating; we are reviving him . . . transtosis. You may know it as reanimating, or cellular activation. Also, it includes thought reproduction."

"Transtosis, hmm; why not duplicate? I mean, look at the bullet holes . . . "

"Because; although our technology may be futuristic, by your standards, unfortunately, one can only be duplicated once; and Richard has undergone the process once before."

Angie giggled sarcastically, " . . . another thing they didn't teach us in nursing school."

"Sorry?"

"It's not important. Okay; so transtosis, how do you activate cellular growth?"

"Well, principally, you understand the concept of jolting a heart, when electric shock is administered to defibrillate?"

"Yes, fibrillation—electrical signals gone wild, the heart does not pump, it flutters out of rhythm. It may stop beating altogether."

"Exactly, so we administer electric shock to defibrillate and stop the fluttering, zap it back into normal rhythm. Or, if it is altogether stopped, the hope is to start it beating again."

"Basic nursing to us, too. I understand."

"Additionally, at the same time, we rejuvenate individual body cells, not just the heart. If a cell dies, we can shock and nourish it back to health, too."

"Really? So, can you stop the aging process?"

"You are way ahead of me. Let's stick to this patient."

"Sorry, go on."

"We are going to send cell doctors in, to make a house call on every cell in his body. They are sort of machines, but not. I believe your ancient researchers on the surface coined the names, Nanites or Nanoprobes."

"What do you call them?"

"We call them Fix-its, but Nanites is fine. Anyway, we grow them, we don't build them. And they are not part of any semiconductor chip technology. We construct each one based on a patient's DNA. We program them, inject, and then they do their thing, and each cell's synaptic profile is defibrillated and reactivated. Then, they nourish each cell back to health."

"That is what you are going to do, here?"

"Yes, partly; listen, Angie, I am sorry you had to witness the shooting in the morgue. But here, you will see the wonder of Ever-Life . . . you ready?"

"Wonder of Ever-Life, huh? Yes, ready."

LuAnne went to the glass refrigeration cabinet behind her. She withdrew a five-inch by seven-inch mirrored box. In it, were four, small, clear cylindrical syringes, covered at one end.

"I hate needles," Angie said.

"We gave them up long ago,"

Angie picked up and studied a cylinder. "We had courses on Nanite technology, but ours are microchip-based, not organic. I never got close to the real thing before, much less, witness anything like this."

"Each Nanite is about a hundredth of the size of an average cell. We have organic computers that construct and program each one, based on many variables: cause, time of death, medical history and most important of all, each contains the information of the patient's DNA."

"Organic computers?"

"Yes, for all practical purposes down here, they are as alive as we are, and quite fascinating to work with. I am sure you will learn as you go."

Angie smiled respectfully. "I hope so. I could spend a lifetime studying this alone. What is the next step?" Angie handed the cylinder to the doctor.

"As they are injected into the blood, the Nanites self-circulate, while they multiply to the same number of synaptic connections in every system of the body. Then, they position and synchronize to deploy-activate, as close to the same time as possible. Just to give you an idea of the magnitude here, we calculate between 500-750 trillion synaptic connections in the average human body. So, the Nanites have to multiply very quickly."

"Whoa, the wonder of medicine."

"Yes, it is unbelievable to me at times, too. After the successful defibrillation, they feed and nurse the individual cells. Once the cells are functioning normally, the Nanites dissolve. They expel as waste, through normal body secretions and digestion, leaving no trace. If activation does not happen with the first charge, they will try again. If no success after three cycles, we inject again."

"So, they can multiply that fast and attach to every single nerve's contact?"

"Yep, every one, bone, muscle, fat; any organ, the brain, blood . . . I am sure I left something out, but the point is, all of them will defibrillate in unison."

Angie watched, as LuAnne sprayed her hands with a peculiar pink colored aerosol, which dried on contact. "This is a combination of a sterilizing wash and surgical gloves."

Then, Dr. Lu picked up a cylinder and took the small cap off the top. Each cylinder was a one-inch in diameter by five-inches long, clear material, but not plastic or glass. Carefully, she touched it against Dr. Richard's chest just below his breastbone. Angie saw her squeeze the cylinder gently and heard a poof. The doctor repeated a second injection into his right inner thigh. Angie stared at the body. "When will we know?"

"Watch the wall monitor."

Dr.Lu touched the image, and a full size hologram of Richard's body appeared at her eye level. The two watched the Nanites spread.

"They look like a swarm of bees," Angie said.

Within 10 seconds, the entire hologram filled with Nanites, and Dr. Lu looked at her Knofer. "They are synchronizing now. Angie, please go to the refrigerator over there. Yes, there. Open the small door and bring me the wine glass inside."

"I remember this. In the morgue, Dr. Richard had Mr. Sheldon drink from one, just like this."

"Yes? It stimulates the part of the brain that processes memories. Without getting too long-winded, and considering our different definitions of structures, let me just say, the drink enables the patient to remember certain life necessities and experiences."

"Excuse me?"

"Your heart is not the only thing that beats in rhythm. Besides, as you know, it has its own electrical system. My point is that every system in the body has a rhythm. Every atom in a cell has a tone or vibration. Duplicate a particular tone and you duplicate the energy, which affects the mass. In this case, it means kick-starting the function. The body has to remember how to live. Each cell has to remember its involuntary behaviors —to breathe, to sense, to function. The Nanites jumpstart everything by duplicating the energy; and then they hand it off to the original player—the particular mass—the cell. But, the entire effort is short term. The patient must drink this elixir. The chemistry in this feeds the body and triggers functional memories, which each cell stores within its nucleus. We consider a cell's functional memories a shadow of a thought. Obviously, the brain also remembers all functions. You've heard it said, 'how big is an idea,' right?"

"So, where is this shadow of thought?"

"It is within every individual cell, at the point of origin. However, in cases of duplication this may or may not be the case. The elixir helps overall cellular recall, but we are not sure how much."

"And you are not sure how long the drink's effects last?"

"True, that is a big question. We must continue timely drinks until we can replant the entire adult memory, permanently. We do that via our headset process. That is why Mr. Sheldon's C.P.T. is so revolutionary to us. It allows for total cellular recall and complete personality trait transfer."

"Wow, good thing you know so much about Mr. Sheldon's discovery. And there is an alternative to using his C.P.T.?"

Dr. LuAnne took a headset out of the cabinet and showed it to Angie.

"This is what we use, in addition to the drink. It enables transplant of thought, but it does not insure all personality traits, like C.P.T. does. The truth is, the math and physics say C.P.T. is full proof. I've done the calculations, and I have the instructions to perform it; but, I don't have the catalyst bath needed to hold the serum extraction. That is critical for success. So for now, it is the drink and headset."

"Dr. B. says I am the bath. I would be glad to help any way I can."

"I don't understand. He told you that you are the catalyst bath?"

"Yes; he said my DNA, genetic code, is the serum donor bath."

Then, LuAnn's Knofer ticked; and they both turned to Richard.

"Look," Angie said, "he is moving."

"Yes . . . lift his head . . . give him a sip."

The glow in the hologram stopped. Dr. LuAnne touched the wall and the 3-D image disappeared. Angie gently lifted Richard's head and touched the rim of the glass to his lips. Dr. Richard blinked and sucked in a quick deep breath. Then, he took a sip of the drink and opened his eyes.

"Thank God," Angie whispered. "Dr. Richard . . . Grandpa?"

The first thing he saw was Angie's face. "Hello, my dear . . . " Then he turned and saw Dr. LuAnne. "Well, Dr. Lu, hello. I did not expect you. Angie, may I have a little more of that?"

"Yes, of course."

Richard drank again. Slowly, he moved his arms and legs and looked at his chest. "Did a freight train hit me?"

"You will feel better with time," LuAnne said. "You know the drill, Doctor. Keep drinking . . . Angie, watch him. I will be back in a minute."

Luanne went to her private office, through the doors on the other side of the room. She put a headset on, took out her Knofer and made a call.

"Sir, we have revived Richard. Angie says her DNA has the correct genetic code to duplicate the catalyst bath."

"Do you have both manuscripts there?"

"Yes, Dave Marshall recovered the other one, and gave it to me."

"Can you use her?"

"I don't know. I'll see."

"Can Richard help?"

"I will talk to him, when he is up to it."

"Time is running out, Doctor."

"Yes, sir."

"Contact me as soon as you know anything."

CHAPTER 24

THE POLICE STATION

RALPH WALKER SAT ALONE, tired and hungry in the Arden police station waiting for a copy of his statement about the kidnapping of Angie Esposito.

"Mr. Walker, thank you for your time," Sergeant Wells said. "Please sign this and you can be on your way."

Ralph scribbled his name and, at the same time, noticed a woman walk by the office door.

"Oh my, that's Barb Sawyer . . . It's 8 a.m. I'll bet she is not a happy camper. She was on night shift with me."

He shook hands with Wells, walked over to Barb and tapped her on her shoulder. "Barb, good morning. I don't believe you are here."

"Morning, Ralph . . . No, I'm not, really. They had a car come and get me . . . you?"

"Me? Hah. I was on my way to see you when they stopped me and brought me here. Angie was kidnapped."

"What?"

"Yeah; I just signed the police statement. Have you met this guy, Burns, yet?"

"No; what about Angie?"

"I wish I knew."

"Well, you wouldn't believe what happened at the hospital while you were gone, either."

Just then, Jake Burns walked into the station, sipping his coffee. He noticed the couple right away and snickered, "Good morning, you two . . . long night? You must be Barb Sawyer."

"Yes, I am."

"Ms. Sawyer, please follow me. Mr. Walker, right? You can go. Don't get lost again. We will need you."

"What about Angie, for God's sake?"

"Believe it or not, sonny, we don't just interrogate people . . . we put a team on it five minutes after you told me. They went to the site you described, and, right now, they are following what they think are van tracks. If we get anything from the phone you found, we will let you know."

Burns left Ralph, standing there, escorted Barb Sawyer into his office and shut the door. "Please, sit down, Ms. Sawyer. I understand you were the first to see the bodies in the morgue last night, right?"

"Yes."

"Tell me, how many were there?"

"I didn't go in the room all the way. I just saw the one bloody naked man. I ran out and called 911."

"Hmm, you heard the gunfire?"

"Yes."

"How many shots?"

"They sounded like pops . . . machine guns, I guess. I really don't know."

"Ms. Sawyer, who do you work for?"

"Dr. Bellos, Chief of the Hospital."

"And, when was the last time you saw him?"

"I saw him just before he left to go out of town before the shooting."

"Ms. Sawyer—Barb—may I call you Barb? Barb, we found a lot of bloody footprints in the morgue room. Most had the same tread, or so the blood tells us. We believe they were professional killers."

"Oh, my . . . "

"But, there were also two sets of footprints, which didn't match the others, and one set was obviously a woman's. The prints seem to indicate, two people were carrying something, together. Do you have any idea what they could have been carrying?"

"No."

"Barb, what size shoes do you wear?"

"Why? Size eight. Why?"

"I want you to know that, as we speak, there is a team of forensic specialists at your house, checking your clothes, the garbage, your shoes, your toothbrush; everything. Ms. Sawyer, I think you saw more than you're telling, and I think you helped move something—maybe a body with the help of someone else. I think you are lying . . . I think you ran into Dr. Bellos, just as one of the orderlies suggested, and the two of you moved one or more of the bodies. What do you say to that?"

Barb broke down and cried, "My God! All I did was hear shots and run to the room. Before I walked in, I saw a naked man . . . there was so much blood . . . I ran back to my station and called 911."

"Where is Dr. Bellos' office?"

"On the 10th floor," Barb couldn't stop sobbing.

"I want you to take me there, right now. Do you have a problem with that?"

"No, but, he's not there. He is out of town."

"Where did he go?"

"I'm not privy to his itinerary."

"Who is? Does he have a secretary?"

"Not that I know of; I think he books his own trips."

"All right, let's go."

The two left Burns' office and walked toward the front door.

"Sergeant Wells, call Dave Marshall at Andrews. Tell him to meet us at Dr. Bellos' office on the 10th floor in 20 minutes."

"Yes, sir."

" . . . and get any info to me that was on that phone from the Walker kid. Call me with an update on our team in the desert as soon as you can. Come on, everyone, let's go! Chop, chop . . . the day is moving . . . we have a girl to find."

CHAPTER 25

SET UP 1

HALFWAY AROUND THE WORLD from Andrews Hospital, GGM-Gordon Swanson watched five computer monitors in his private Ever-Life office below Jerusalem. He had his Knofer on in case Bellos called. He was monitoring various Brock enterprises and particular theological communications, which he suspected might be terrorist related. A call came in from New Mexico and he put it on hologram.

"Dave? Dave Marshall, is that you? How are you?"

"Yes, fine, sir, good to see you."

"Dave, what is the status there?"

"We disposed of the Brock people, who shot the Carrier-Unit, and we are processing the three doctors; but, the police have a particularly inquisitive detective."

Swanson giggled. "Yes, that's Jake Burns. He was very good in New York, years ago. He even found a serial killer who dismembered one of our people. He does not know about us, but he is trustworthy. I met him twice, both times in D.C. at conventions for new weaponry. Have you talked to him?"

"Not really; but, he knows I am hiding something. I am supposed to meet with him in Dr. Bellos' office shortly."

"Have you secured the floor?"

"Yes."

"Well, I do like him. I'll tell you what. Set it up to bring him down to Red Level 6. We will all meet there when we get back. He loves a good mystery. We will give him one he won't forget."

"Yes, sir. How goes it there?"

"Mathew's Carrier is due shortly. We are set up to trade. We don't know who he has, but we will. The courier is scared of the Brock team. He wanted a strategic advantage, so he took a hostage. Dave, handle things there, will you? I expect we will be back this afternoon, your time."

"Yes, sir, of course. Be safe."

"You too . . . "

The Knofer cut the image, and Swanson took one last look at the monitors in front of him, reading the tapes from Iran, Russia and Istanbul. Then, a lone, single message spelled out across his Knofer, "I am ready . . . but, you must come quickly. They are watching. I can feel the guns."

Swanson replied, "Our people are there . . . fear not."

CHAPTER 26

SET UP 2

PAPPAS KRISTOS ALIERI SAT in a waiting room, outside Rash InVoy's second floor office, in East Jerusalem. He made the hurried appointment to see Brock's chief of staff, because of the serious phone call received from the Muslim consulate, in Istanbul, Turkey. After 10 minutes, the door finally opened and InVoy walked out.

"Kristos, it's good to see you. Come in."

"Thank you . . . I am most disturbed. I received calls from our Russian Church and the Muslim council in Turkey. Then, on my way here, I received one from our local consulate. Is it true, there has been a kidnapping by a courier? Is he the same one who has our vial?"

"Please, sit, my friend. All will be fine. The courier is below the Church of the Holy Sepulchre, here in town, as we speak. He is just trying to insure his own safety. It is a bit of a surprise, but we have arranged a meeting and the trade. I assume the money is safe and ready, correct?"

"The money is in place, but we cannot afford to let one man destroy this effort."

"Father, be assured. This is too big for one man to ruin anything. The courier will make the trade."

"Who is the poor soul he has captured?"

"That is his secret; but we will know soon. We have agreed to guarantee him and his family's safety; and, we have increased his price . . . don't worry; we are paying the difference. We will deliver his share within three hours. He will give us the vial. I will give it to you. You give us the $16 billion."

Kristos took a deep breath. "These methods . . . they are not God's will."

"Stop it, Father. This is what you wanted and planned for months. You cannot expect everything to go smoothly. Nothing ever does; especially when this kind of deal or so much money is involved. Our people have him in sight. It is all going to be over within hours. Talk to your people; tell them to be patient. You can either wait here or, if you like, I will call you at your parish, when I get word."

ॐ⬥꒰�০ꜱ⬥

In the center of Jerusalem, 50 feet below the Church of the Holy Sepulchre, a dark 5'5" Muslim man, Ahmed, sat in shallow cave, facing his bruised and battered prisoner.

"I am sorry you have to be here; I am not a bad man. I will not harm you. But, I have a family, and these people are very bad. They will kill me and my family if I do not do this."

The black-hooded prisoner squirmed and moaned; but, the duct tape and ropes were too tight; no one heard.

ॐ⬥꒰�০ꜱ⬥

Meanwhile, within Bellos' Carrier-Unit, rushing toward Jerusalem, Bellos, Jack, and Brian talked.

"How much longer?" asked Brian.

Bellos looked at his Knofer. "About 20 minutes or so."

"Frankly, Matt, it really doesn't feel like we have been moving at all," said Jack.

"If I told you how fast we were traveling, you wouldn't believe me."

"I could figure it out, if you give me some statistics," said Brian smartly.

"No thanks, son . . . what I'm curious about is, are we in a tunnel or under water, or what?"

"You want the truth?"

"No, lie to me."

"All right . . . we are traveling up to five times the speed of sound inside a 6000-year-old, organic life form that is synergistic with our subterranean culture, Ever-Life. And it has the capability of burrowing through solid rock as well as molten lava. It glides like a spacecraft going to the moon."

Jack and Brian nodded their heads at one another.

"Yes, well, that's great," Brian said rolling his eyes. "How are you feeling, Dad?"

"I'm fine, a little weak and confused, but pretty good, really."

"Yes, well, I need to get this over with, and you back to the hospital, Jack. Brian, I have to talk to your boss. He is in the next cabin. Do me a favor? Keep an eye on your dad for me? If he turns green or any other color, yell out, okay?"

Bellos walked to the far wall of the Carrier. "Open, please."

A door appeared and slid to the side. Bellos walked through. Marion Brock was sitting with handcuffs on, and he calmly, nonchalantly looked up. "Hello, Mathew, I didn't expect to see you. Will you tell me what is going on?"

"Yes, I will." Bellos slowly paced in front of Brock. "It seems you have been very busy . . . you blackmailed Jack Sheldon into trusting you and giving you the secrets of C.P.T. Your people cloned him, knowing the procedure wasn't full proof. Then, you stole the formula to sell it to religious groups for $16 billion.

You had the clones killed and you arranged for Jack to have a fatal car accident. You had mercenaries break into Andrews Hospital, kill two doctors, steal Jack's original manuscript and take a vial of the original C.P.T. serum so you could duplicate it, and sell it for power. Have I left anything out?"

Brock chuckled. "Yes, you kidnapped me. That's illegal in this country. You can't prove anything. I've been here, tied up . . . . you have no idea what you are getting into. You are going to let me go. I guarantee it. Whatever you think you know, you don't have a clue. Whatever you think you have, you are wrong. Now, go back to where you came from, and come to me when you're ready to let me go . . . Mr. GGM gofer."

Bellos raised an eyebrow cynically. Shaking his head, he turned and walked back into the other cabin.

Chapter 27

Team Burns

IT ONLY TOOK 15 MINUTES for Jake Burns to drive Barb Sawyer back to Andrews Hospital. He pulled into a handicapped spot, just 20 feet from the front door.

"Well, I completely understand why we parked here," said Barb, irritated.

"Yeah, well, I have a bad elbow."

"You can't be serious. You would break the law just for convenience. You cops are all alike."

"Really? Just look around. No one parks in any of these handicapped spots. Count them. There are at least 50 spaces, and not one car, besides mine . . . and, I'll tell you why . . . because you ticket violators $400.00 each . . .

. . . let's see . . . that's $20,000 revenue for your great hospital administration, for absolutely no reason but greed. Get off my back, lady! We will park right here. Let's go!"

Within minutes, they stepped out of the 10th floor elevator to greet three forensic doctors, two uniformed police and Dave Marshall.

"Good morning again, Jake Burns," Marshall said.

"You may call me Detective or Inspector, Security Chief. Now, if you don't mind, please unlock Dr. Billow's office."

"That's Bellos . . . yes, sir." Marshall opened the door.

"Let's go, people." Burns waved the team through the foyer.

"Quite a spread, Jake," said Watzin.

"People, listen up. I want everything examined with the finest detail. We do this by the book—my book. I want swabs—bag anything that you can pick up; get photos—use everything in those suitcases and get me something. Don't forget to put on shoe covers because this man, Mr. Marshall, is using ultraviolet on the floors. Got it? Any questions? Good. Well, then . . . go on, get to it . . . all right, Mr. Chief Marshall, show me around."

Marshall led Burns and Sawyer into the oval room. "All this is Dr. Bellos' hospital living quarters, as well as his office suite. He has every medical reference book you can imagine in there—many from other countries, in different languages."

"How many languages does this guy speak?"

"Several, I think. Over there are chairs, and original paintings are on the walls, and that's a window, as you can see."

"Very funny, Chief. Where's the office?"

"Through that hallway, follow me."

"Mr. Burns," Barb Sawyer asked, "Why am I here?"

Burns stopped, and turned toward her. "Because you are in this up to your thigh highs, missy, and I know you are going to break. So tag along until you do."

"Through here, Lieutenant," Marshall said sarcastically.

"You've got a real sense of humor, don't you, Boy Scout." Burns looked around the computer room. "Hmm, nice laptops, and those screens have to be 60-inch monitors. Impressive."

"Yes, the doctors can conference on strategic orphan diseases from anywhere in the world without getting a headache . . . anything unusual you would like me to clarify?"

"Yes, as a matter of fact." Burns walked around the room and studied. "How long has Dr. Bellos been Chief of Hospital?"

"I've been here one year, two months, four days, 20 hours, six minutes, and 42-43 seconds, now. None of us speaks for Dr. Bellos."

"I don't like wise-asses, Mr. Marshall."

"I don't like men who pick on innocent women . . . look, Detective, I was told you are good . . . real good. Do you know Gordon Swanson?"

Burns did a double take and grinned. "Yeah, I know him a little. That's not going to buy you a dime."

"Well, maybe not. But, I'd like to cut the crap. We do want to help. You know neither Bellos nor Barb is the shooter. Gordon Swanson's name is on the marquee here; I did talk to him. Actually, he asked me if you would consider talking to him in person."

"Really, I'm flattered. Is he going to tell me what happened?"

"I think he is going to have Dr. Bellos with him, if that tweaks your interest."

Burns turned his back to Marshall, as Watzin came in. "Jake, I found something . . . "

Burns followed Watzin back to the foyer.

"Look; this door, it's not a closet. None of us can get it open."

Burns turned to Marshall again. "Well, Chief, what's this?"

"It's a sealed elevator shaft from two years ago, when we renovated the 10th floor."

"Break it open."

"Wait, look down here." Watzin was kneeling in front of the door. He pressed a weak spot in the wall and pushed his fist through, creating a five-inch hole.

Burns watched and then turned to a uniformed officer. "You there, give me your flashlight." He bent down and shined the light into the hole. "Concrete? Shit! Watzin, are your people getting anything else?"

"This may take a couple of hours, Jake."

Burns walked down the steps and looked at Marshall. "Okay, Chief, you win. Where's Swanson?"

"Follow me . . . "

"Watzin . . . God, why did your parents name you that? Have the office call me when you are done. By the way, any feedback on Walker's phone yet?"

"Yes, as a matter of fact. There were two calls made; one from Turkey, and one looks like it came from the van."

"Turkey . . . like gobble, gobble . . . "

"No, Jake . . . like, from across the other side of the world Turkey."

"Fine . . . shit . . . wish I was in Turkey."

CHAPTER 28

THE EXCHANGE

THE TIME WAS 5:30 P.M. when Bellos' Carrier arrived at the post platform in Jerusalem. Gordon Swanson and a three-man guard team stood waiting to greet them.

"Mathew, it's good to see you in the flesh, bad circumstance."

"Yes, sir. You remember Jack Sheldon?"

"Of course. Jack, how do you feel?"

"A bit rocky, at times, but Matt says he's going to fix that."

"That is the plan."

"This is my son, Brian."

"Brian, you have quite a dad, here."

"GGM, we are ready," a guard interrupted.

"Good. Let's walk, everyone. Where is our guest?"

"Still in the Carrier . . . he called me GGM-TBN."

"Well, that confirms the mole, eh?"

"Sir, we have 30 minutes," the guard said.

"Alright, I'll brief you all in the car . . . Brian, my boy, I know this has to be the strangest day of your life; but, I have to ask you a favor . . ."

"What is it?"

"Would you mind riding with my guards here in the second car? Now, before you react, there is a good reason I ask. Your dad needs a fresh dose of medicine. We have no choice but to go on ahead to be at the trade point on time. Otherwise, this all fails. I'm asking you to go and get the medicine; then, the car will bring you to us immediately. None of my people has clearance to carry what your dad needs. You do by virtue of your genetic link to your dad. It is only a short trip to the villa and back. Will you do that for us, for your dad?"

Brian looked at Jack. "Dad, no!"

Jack insisted, "Brian, please . . . we all have to do our part."

"Fine . . . " Brian said, frustrated. He hugged his dad and walked away with the guards.

"Where are they taking him?"

"To safety, Jack, let's go."

Bellos gestured and they all walked quickly up to Swanson's car. But it wasn't a white stretch limo; it was a tattered looking 1960 four-door Lincoln Continental that had a bulletproof body and tires, a special engine, and sprayed graffiti all over it. It also had four transparent swivel guns mounted above the front and rear lights. Each one looked like a tiny airplane jet. The four men got in the car and drove off into the heart of Jerusalem.

Swanson began briefing them, "Now, gentlemen, we are going to meet our courier, Ahmed. He approached a contact that we have had in the Brock camp since Jack started their partnership. He is Muslim, and, over the last five months, has been running money between here and Turkey for Rash InVoy."

"Then, we must know everything . . . " Bellos said.

"No, he swings whatever way profits his family. But I know he hasn't said anything about this. They would have killed him, already."

"Why the kidnapping?" asked Jack.

"To guarantee we would insure his life and his family's safe future. He wants out of Brock's hold permanently. You see, we are not trading anything. We are taking him two hours before he is supposed to give the vial to InVoy. We get the vial, the hostage; and, in return, he and his family go to an unknown location to live out their lives safely."

"It sounds a little James Bondy, sir," Bellos said, "if you don't mind my saying."

Swanson smiled. "Yes, it'll be fun. I haven't even told you the Hollywood stuff."

"Oh no . . . "

"What?" Jack asked.

"I just love Hollywood," Swanson said. "Diced Hard . . . Bruised Wullus . . . remember that classic . . . when the gun was taped to his back? Exciting!"

"Sir," Bellos rolled his eyes, "not many of us remember that. It was a long, long time ago; and his name was . . . "

" . . . Yes, right; I digress." Swanson lifted a satchel onto his lap, opened it and started handing things out.

Jack looked at Bellos and commented. "Matt, this is about C.P.T. and medical research, right; not war games?"

Bellos just shook his head.

Mr. Mike turned the car lights off and pulled into a dark concrete lot, just two blocks south of the Church of the Holy Sepulchre.

"Are we close?" Bellos asked.

"Somewhat . . . " Swanson chatted, as he handed things to the two doctors. "This entire area is nothing but church buildings. We have to walk quickly and silently. Here, you two, take these vests and put them on under your shirts."

Then, he took out what looked like two pistols.

"Guns?" Jack said, "I'm having trouble remembering how to piss."

"Just take these. They won't hurt you, and they won't kill anyone. They don't shoot bullets. They are set for wide, so, you just point and pull the trigger . . . "

"Wide? What's *wide*? If they won't kill anyone, what good are they?"

" . . . And put these glasses on, too."

"Holy crap," Jack said. He did so and looked out the car window. "It's like daylight; what the hell?"

"Okay, Jack; take a minute; focus and drink this." Swanson handed him a canteen.

"Boy, whatever this stuff is, it's better than water."

"Hmm, don't you just love history, men? Did you two know that this church commemorates the death and resurrection of Jesus of Nazareth? Just like the one in India . . . "

"Sir . . . " Bellos whispered.

"Yes, sorry, well, that's another story. The important thing to remember is the sensitive nature of these people. Watch out for yourselves! Be alert! For over 6000 years, those we now know as Orthodox Christians, Jews and Muslims have claimed ownership of these buildings. Factions fight constantly, over everything, from its validity and when to worship, to where to place a chair. Brock's camp negotiated with all three theological leaderships to get your serum, Jack. And they will pay handsomely for it. Somehow, they are convinced that the serum will prove resurrection is possible, thereby uniting the faiths. Therefore, there will be some very tight security, all around here. Stay with me. We are following Mr. Mike, here. He's not just a pretty face."

"I don't understand. Why do I have to be here?" asked Jack.

"You don't. It is Brian we wanted. Other than monitoring your health; and, of course, we know you do want to make all this right again, now; don't you, Jack?"

"What?"

"You went to Brock, remember, Jack? He's had Brian for 18 months, right? We are going to check your son out, completely, to make sure he has no illness, and no implants. Don't worry; he has no idea. He was Brock's insurance that you would convince Matt to do what he wants. You wanted us involved from the start. Remember the café and wanting my help. Well, now you have it. We all need each other, now."

Jack sat stunned.

"Okay, Mr. Mike, let's go."

They opened the car doors and got out. The three had the weapons under their coats; they looked like lost tourists. Mike led them to the end of the parking lot, through narrow winding streets for about a quarter mile. Then, he stopped, above a five-foot wide rock stairwell.

"The church is about five blocks from here, over there, sir. Look, up on the roofs, to the right and left."

"Yes, I see. Look there, you two, be careful." Swanson pointed, and then he spoke softly to Mike, "They are Brock's men. Are we good to go under?"

"Two Carriers are about a mile away."

"Hmm, let's go, fast and quiet."

Mike led them down the winding stairwell to a door at the bottom. It opened into a small room, which had an eating table, two windows and a closet.

"Through there, sir." The closet was an entryway to an old tunnel system, put in place by the Palestinians, during the Seven-Day War in the ancient 1960s.

"I can't get over these glasses," Jack said. "Flashlights are obsolete . . . "

"Heads up and watch your step. Follow me."

They walked single file into the tunnel about 100 feet, and then they stopped. Mr. Mike pointed his Knofer toward the walls and read it. "This is it, sir; best reception point."

"Yes, good." Swanson took his own Knofer out and tapped it several times. Then, he put it on the dirt floor.

"Activate catacomb details."

Floor Plan of the Church of the Holy Sepulchre

The Knofer displayed a five-foot tall hologram of the church, mapping all its rooms.

"Now comes the hard part, men," Swanson spoke again, "GGM-001 . . . Statistics on all life forms within 50 meters, spherical of church."

The Knofer placed glowing dots, representing people, throughout the hologram.

"Zoom 10 times . . . look there, Mike, below the Edicule. It looks like they are in one of the Kokhims."

Swanson touched the hologram, and it magnified the image with even more detail.

"Yes, sir, that's them . . . look; that one is clearly lying down unable to move."

"Excuse me," Jack said, "Kokhim, Edicule?"

"Edicule is the church location of the tomb of Jesus." Swanson pointed and explained further, "That Kokhim is one of the small short tunnels throughout the underground, where the Jews buried rock like containers—ossuaries, holding the bones of their dead . . . Mike, can we get a Carrier to collapse the flooring below them?"

"No, sir, too dangerous, the whole church could come down."

"How far is the closest Carrier from that spot?"

"On the other side of the church, sir, one has tunneled maybe a quarter mile . . . "

"All right, give me your Knofer." Swanson transferred all detail information about the church. "Mike, go back; have the Knofer pinpoint every Brock operative in the outer perimeter . . ."

"Can you do that?" Jack asked.

"Take them all out. Meet us at the Crusader Facade entrance to the church; bring guards. We will give you 15 minutes. By then, we will be at the Facade."

"See you soon then, sir." Mike left.

"Have a seat, you two."

"What now?" Bellos asked.

"Just this . . . " Swanson put his Knofer on the floor, again. With one touch, he pulled up a close holographic view of Ahmed and the prisoner in the tunnel. "Now we are going to say hello."

Swanson did something Bellos didn't realize was possible. He projected an image of himself into the tunnel, in front of Ahmed. Right before his eyes, in the pitch black, there was a flickering light the size of a candle. Ahmed froze in terror. Out of the light, a laser dot began tracing the image of Gordon Swanson from the shoulders up. Ahmed reached for it, trying to slap it. He threw dust at it, but it continued to draw the three dimensional image. Ahmed recoiled in fear, and within a minute, it began to speak, "Hello, Mr. Ahmed. Do not be afraid. I will not harm you. I have come to take you to safety."

Ahmed shook fearing the worst. "Praise be to Allah," he stuttered. "I am not your enemy. Please do not kill me."

"Ahmed, calm yourself. I will be with you soon. Your family is safe; but why do you hold this hostage?"

"I am afraid . . . "

"If I can do this miracle and you see me now, surely you know I am not lying to you. Look and see your family."

With those words, a different hologram replaced Swanson's head, showing Ahmed his wife and two children boarding a plane with two GGM guards.

"At some point, Ahmed, you have to believe. This would be a good time to start."

"I do, I do! I am frightened, but thankful."

"Good, my friend. Now, there is no reason to keep your prisoner blindfolded. You are not the only one who is afraid."

"When will you free us?"

"We are leaving now. Target 6:13 p.m. You have the clothes to wear?"

"Yes, my lord."

"Please, make your guest comfortable. If they suspect, it is over. Do you have the vial?"

"Yes, my lord; and I have something better."

Suddenly, the Knofer cut the image.

"Alright, you two, let's hurry," Swanson said.

From directly above the underground Carrier station, one-quarter mile from the main Facade entrance, Mr. Mike instructed five special ops guards . . .

"Okay men, set your weapons. Be quiet and quick. You all have precisely seven minutes, starting now . . . go!"

The Ever-Life guards ran silently into the night.

৯৽৪୦⅃Ƈঌ৵ও

No moon was shining that night. As Swanson, Bellos and Jack left the tunnel and entered the streets, the GGM-glasses enabled them to see as if they were in sunlight.

"This way, Jack. Try to keep up!"

Swanson led the three through the dark, narrow streets, winding to the church. Suddenly, there was a ping next to Jack. He never heard a real bullet ricochet. He had no idea where it came from; but, his reactions were quick and surprisingly accurate. In one motion, he turned to the left, looked up toward a building rooftop, pulled his weapon out, pointed it and pulled the trigger. The noise sounded like the pop of an air rifle. A Brock mercenary fell behind the three, splat, onto the street.

"Holy shit, Jack," Bellos said. "Where did you learn that?"

"Hell if I know."

"Watch it! They have silencers . . . "

"Silencers?" Jack yelled in a whisper. "I can't see a fucking thing."

"Come on! No time to chat! Good job, Jack. Our men should be in position by now."

They began to run fast, crouching, weaving in and out, back and forth, listening to the pings hit the walls beside them. After 50 yards or so, the gunfire had them bogged down at the edge of an alley.

"Christ! This is insane," Jack said.

Then, they heard three, four airbursts fired from the right and left rooftops above. All went quiet.

"Those are our men." Swanson stepped quietly to see around the alley's corner. "Over there, there is the church . . . and there is Mike at the Facade entrance.

Mike was waiving and yelling in a whisper, "Sir! Come on! This way!"

The three ran across to the Facade entrance and huddled together with Mike.

"Well, that was exciting, eh?" Swanson said out of breath. "Are we ready, Mike?"

"There are three of Brock's men inside the church, two on the way to the Edicule, and one at its entrance."

"Where are our men?"

"In position and ready, sir."

Just then, the unexpected happened. They all saw a man and woman walking quickly directly toward Swanson from the tomb. The man had a long dirty brown shawl with a tan straw fedora pulled over his ears. The woman was wearing a babushka, pulled low over her face, and dirty white pants. They had their heads down. Behind them, there was a loud commotion and then gunfire. The couple started running toward Swanson, and Mike listened to his Knofer.

"Command-1, command-1; Brock man down at the Edicule . . . Do you see the couple?"

"Yes, we see them. Take all Brock men out, in the church, now! Repeat; take all Brock men out now!"

With another three airbursts, it was over. Brock's special-ops fell silent, no blood spilled.

Mike stepped between Swanson and the couple. Everyone's eyes fixed on the couple, as the man reached into his pocket.

"Sir, my lord, it's me, Ahmed. I saw you in the tunnel. Please do not shoot. Here, here is the vial."

Swanson extended his hand and received the small tube. Behind Ahmed, the hostage stepped forward and lifted her head.

Bellos was stunned. "Angie, Angie?"

She leaped into his arms.

"Get to the cars, Mike." Swanson said.

"Yes, sir, this way."

They all turned and walked quickly out the doors, across the courtyard to two waiting cars. Swanson stopped in front of one and spoke to the couple.

"Ahmed, you and your family are safe now. We have arranged for safe passage to the destination your wife gave us. You go with this man and all will be right."

"Thank you, my lord," he bowed and kissed Swanson's right hand. Mike led the man to a small, inconspicuous car, a few yards away. Ahmed got in the back seat and looked one more time at Swanson. As he rolled the window up, the car drove away.

Angie, on the other hand, was shaking and held tightly onto Bellos. Once in the limo, she broke down, crying again, "Oh, my God, oh, my God."

Bellos tried to console her, "Angie, it's all right, now. Believe me; it's okay. Can you tell us, what is the last thing you remember?"

"I was in a van. Then I woke up with tape over my eyes and mouth . . . oh, my God, oh, my God!"

Swanson took out two hand-held medical extractors from the glove compartment. He stuck one into the vial that Ahmed gave him, extracting a small amount of liquid; and then, he turned to Bellos.

"Mathew, please hold her steady, for just a second."

"No, please, she's been through enough."

"Doctor, come to your senses. Look at her. If she is Angie, who is at Ever-Life? We have to know now; then we pick up Brian and go back. Mathew, she's not the one who knows everything."

Angie looked up at Dr. B. terrified.

"Do we have to do this right now?" Bellos pleaded.

"Yes, we do."

Dr. B. gently lifted her chin. "Angie, trust me, this one last time. I will explain everything. Believe me; you are safe now, child. I promise."

Angie nodded, shaking, with tears in her eyes. Bellos held her head to his chest firmly. Swanson pressed the round edge of the other small tool to her neck and touched the button. There was no pain, just a short slurping sound. The syringe swelled and filled with liquid. Swanson leaned forward and handed the tool to Mike.

"Transmit all data. Let me know immediately."

The car drove through the narrow streets to the Carrier station. The four men and Angie got out quickly, and went down to the tunnel platform.

"Mike, where is young Mr. Sheldon?"

"They are bringing him down now, sir. There he is; over there, very interesting; one implant removed; lots of information, and we told him what it was. He is quite the sport."

"Everyone is here then. Let's move."

They all walked into the Carrier. Swanson stepped across to the sidewall away from the others. He seemed to disappear as the wall extended out and wrapped around him. Once alone, he turned on his Knofer and called Ever-Life.

Dr. LuAnne appeared and spoke quickly, "We tested bath samples from both females; the one that you just sent and one obtained here. I am sending analysis now. I estimate her age at two weeks. She could start breaking down within two to three months, sooner is my guess, given the butchery of those lunatics. Bottom line is; we have only one dose."

Swanson took a deep breath and replied, "Thank you, as always, Doctor. I hate these people. How is Dr. Richard?"

"He is slow . . . transtosis was successful."

"Hmm, you have my approval; go ahead and use the vial there; inject him with the C.P.T."

As Bellos held Angie, they watched Swanson reappear again from containment.

"May I have your attention? Jack, we have the catalyst bath needed for you; we will proceed with your C.P.T. as soon as we get back. But, we also have a big challenge. Brian, I hope you have clarified your loyalties."

"I've always been loyal to my family first. I had no idea what Mr. Brock was doing."

"I believe you, son. Will you help us now?"

Brian looked at his dad, "Yes, of course, but what can I do?"

Swanson whispered to Mike, "Please escort Jack to Dr. LuAnne upon arrival." He then turned to the group. "Mathew, Angie, Brian, please come with me. Unfortunately, we still have work to do."

Bellos hugged Angie and then released her, "Come on; it will be all right."

The four stepped to the opposite side of the room. Swanson studied his Knofer for a few seconds, and then he faced the wall and spoke in the strange Ever-Life language, "Swanson GGM-001 . . . Open."

The wall became a thin, and a transparent door slid to one side. Marion Brock looked up and smiled, as they entered one by one.

"Well, Dr. Bellos, I knew you would be back. I didn't expect you would have such esteemed company, though. Hello, Gordon; Brian . . . "

Swanson had a slight smirk. "Hello, Marion. Please, everyone, sit."

Immediately, four comfortable high back Victorian chairs appeared.

"Impressive," Brock said, a bit surprised. "Glad you know how to do something, Gordon. You should take your magic show on the road."

"Yes, well, we are on the road, Marion. It is time to finish this long stupid farce."

"I agree," Brock said, yanking, trying to free himself. "Let me go!"

"Marion, I can't believe you thought you could do this and walk away with everything."

"I will, you idiots! You don't have a clue!"

"It's over, Marion. I wonder why people like you think money is God. You really thought all you had to do was sit in that luxury condominium, with bank accounts all over the world, think up silly schemes to make more money and dictate to your gofers. You thought your silly plan was too complex for us to figure out. Even now, you really think C.P.T. is yours and you will live forever . . . my God, Marion."

"You are the one who is mistaken, you pompous ass!"

"I'm afraid he's not, not at all."

For the first time, Brock heard the Carrier's voice; and with those words, the walls began to thin, and the cabin separated, splitting into two parts like a bubble. The one section containing Jack and Mike continued on, back to Ever-Life, without any sense of change in speed or direction. The new section stopped, and everyone felt it. Part of the wall became a viewing monitor.

"You silly, pointless man," Swanson said. "My real concern has been the children. You don't have any, do you, Marion?"

"This has gone far enough, you control freak!" Brock yanked at his cuffs. "Release me, or you will never see the vials."

"Your mistake was stealing them yourself." Swanson spoke, like a prosecutor giving closing remarks to a jury. "You thought a kidnap within a kidnap would fool us all. Ahmed was in the van, and he is safe now, as is Angie. You see, Marion, somehow your people did get the right bath from Angie; and poor Ahmed did as instructed. He put Angie at Mrs. Sheldon's front door. Your henchman had everything in place with the theology's three fathers. All you had to do was get the vials."

At that moment, a video appeared on the wall showing Brock opening security station box 1120, after his meeting on Focus Ward with Barb Sawyer. Swanson walked over and touched the screen. The image became a frozen life-size hologram of Brock with his hand holding the vials. Everyone watched as the image slowly rotated.

"That was your big mistake, Marion. It wasn't enough to have billions and play with adults. You had to spite these children for your own profit."

"Look," Bellos said. "There, on the table, next to the box, that note. Enlarge that."

The screen zoomed in on the note.

"I'm sorry, Mathew," Swanson said.

The note clearly read, "Dr. B.'s email says the vials are in box 1120. The combination is 2fy947t."

"The error here was Angie not erasing your email, Mathew. We knew Brock was planning something. It was your suggestion; we have been monitoring him ever since he started the effort with Jack. After Angie left the ward in terror, her clone, sitting here, walked up to the guard, and he let her right in. He has been dealt with; but, Marion, you did not trust her to take the vials, because she is a clone. She just got the combination for you . . . pride and arrogance . . . you had to do it yourself."

"Clone?" said Bellos. He turned to Angie.

"Unfortunately, Mathew, she has a very fundamental mindset, the one Brock gave her to take his simple directions, and, that is all. I am so sorry. You see, Brock had no idea his van dropped the real Angie off at the Sheldon's house because, one, he was in Focus Ward, and two, he is here with us now." Swanson chuckled cynically. "Ahmed took the clone hostage."

Angie sat in a chair, whimpering, while Brock wailed, "I'll destroy the vials. Let me go! You bastards!"

Swanson smiled, took his Knofer out and said, "GGM-001 authorization: I release this man to Carrier 2211. This is the operative who authorized the shooting of Carrier 2210, in the morgue." Then, Swanson put his Knofer away and spoke kindly to Brock, "You, Marion, have always had the vials, safely in your pocket; and, you thought you would be able to negotiate, even now, at the last of it . . . "

The wall hologram disappeared and a green glow appeared around Marion Brock. He could not move.

" . . . Brian, please reach into Mr. Brock's right coat pocket."

Brian walked over, reached in, pulled out two blue vials and gave them to Swanson. At the same time, Bellos withdrew the single vial, which he retrieved from the Carrier, when it spoke during the first part of the trip.

"Sir, I completely forgot about this one."

Then, the Carrier's voice spoke again, for all to hear, "You have done well, and we thank you GGM-001. That vial is our gift to you . . . so many years together; this is the first time we clash. Take the vials and go. I take these two with me."

The cabin went silent; and the room began to split once again. Bellos, Swanson and Brian watched Brock, through the transparent membrane, as he became completely rigid. A green glow intensified around him. His face and eyes swelled and he began to scream wildly. Clone Angie fell unconscious in the chair beside him. Then, the membrane wall became opaque and the section containing Brock and Angie detached. They were gone. Bellos covered his tearful face and cried.

Swanson gently squeezed his shoulder. "Gather yourself, now. This is hard, I know; but it is your job. We have a lot to do; and, you have a daughter waiting at Ever-Life."

CHAPTER 29

InVoy's Office

PAPPAS KRISTOS ALIERI had been sitting in the reception area outside Rash InVoy's office for over an hour waiting for word on the trade.

"May I get you anything, Father?" the secretary asked, "A coffee or bread of some kind?"

"Thank you, perhaps a coffee, if you'd be so kind."

"I'll see what I can do."

಄ఠౙఴ಄

Meanwhile, inside InVoy's office . . . "What do you mean, they are all down? The trade isn't scheduled for another 45 minutes. What the hell are you saying? That is bullshit! You know what? You're fired!"

Kristos could hear the yelling.

"Archer . . . Archer! Get your ass in here."

Before Archer could appear, three GGM SWAT-guards swung into the second floor open window, in front of InVoy. They pointed their weapons, and the commander took off his dark hood.

"Hello, Mr. InVoy," he said quietly, but quickly. "Please, do not move! Now, step away from the computer."

InVoy reached for the keyboard, so they shot him, two airbursts, barely audible. InVoy fell backward behind the desk. Archer came in a private entrance, across the room.

"Shut the door, Mr. Archer. Sit down, right there! I am going to make this easy for you or easy for us. You can contact the banks, correct?"

"I have no account privileges."

"Too bad . . . good bye . . . "

All three pointed weapons at Archer.

"No . . . wait!"

"Mr. Archer, what I'm looking for here is cooperation, not money. You decide, but do it now."

"Fine, cooperation."

"Smart thinking . . . " The commander smiled and they lowered their weapons. "I need you to do three things. First, log out of the computer . . . next, in one half hour, I want you to call Father Kristos and tell him that the trade failed."

"What?"

"Tell him it went sour, and Brock is gone."

"I can't do that."

"Yes, you can, and it's true. InVoy will anyway, when he wakes up; but, if you don't do it, he'll wonder why, since he won't be conscious for an hour or so. Now listen closely, the final thing is the most important. If you don't do exactly as I say, we will be back for you. If you do this, you will never see or hear from us again, understand?"

"What is it?"

"Give this to Father Kristos. Don't let anyone see it."

The commander handed Archer a sealed envelope.

Archer took it and raised his eyebrows. "Yes, okay. All right, I will."

The commander went to the dead computer and typed something on the keyboard. The monitor blinked, then it went blank and he stood up. "We're done here." He looked Archer in the eye for just a second, and then the three leapt onto ropes out the window and disappeared up.

As Archer walked out of the office, the secretary walked back in from the hallway and handed him a cup. "Father, here is your coffee."

"Thank you, my dear."

"Father," Archer said, "may I see you for just a minute please?" Archer escorted the father out to the hallway. "I have this for you." Archer handed the envelope to Kristos. "I'm afraid Mr. InVoy is tied up with everything at the moment, you understand . . . he asked if you might be patient just a bit longer and wait at your parish. He will contact you. It shouldn't be long."

Kristos rolled his eyes, looking disgusted. He turned around to walk back down the stairs, and, as he did, he opened and read the note:

> *My Dearest Friend,*
> *Things are not what they seem for you at this moment. Please trust me. It is urgent that you join me for supper, tomorrow at 3 p.m. . . . at the Jerusalem villa. I request this because my health is failing, and I would like to give you something before my passing."*
> *S*

Kristos looked up, with a lump in his throat, and quickly left InVoy's office building. He made several calls while driving and arranged to fly on the next available plane to Jerusalem.

CHAPTER 30

THE MOLE

EVEN CONSIDERING THE TIME DIFFERENCE between Arden and Jerusalem, the Carrier holding Jack Sheldon and Mr. Mike arrived at the Andrews underground platform at 1:05 p.m., U.S.A. Mountain Time.

Jake Burns and Dave Marshall had paused, so Jake could take a call from the Arden Police Station about Angie's kidnapping.

"I appreciate that, Sergeant, but that doesn't tell us what happened to the girl. If they traced it to Sheldon's house, have the team keep doing the tire treads and follow the van. That's it! I have too much to do here right now."

Burns slapped his cell phone shut and turned to Marshall. "I'm sorry about that, Chief . . . long conversation. I just can't figure out why they wanted a young nurse from this place. You know her, right?"

"Where in heaven did you get that old phone?"

"I collect them. It's a hobby."

"Angela Esposito; yes, I know of her, but not well. She is a good nurse."

"Hmm, well, we should get to it; enough time wasted, eh? You are taking me to meet Mr. Swanson and Dr. Bellos, right?"

"This way, Detective, follow me."

Marshall continued to lead Burns down the stairwell to the main floor of the hospital, then through the back hallway to a narrow private elevator.

"Interesting, Chief, this looks just like the door in Dr. Bellos' office."

"Just like it, except this one works . . . " Marshall pushed the hall button and the door slid open. "After you, Detective . . . " Marshall followed him in and spoke aloud, "Security Chief-060 . . . Red-6 . . . stat."

"Some kind of code, eh?" Burns asked.

"Yeah, hospital code."

When the doors opened, Marshall walked out first; and, Jake stayed inside, apprehensively looking at the rough rock walls.

"Looks like a cave, Chief . . . all sparkly; are we still in the hospital?"

There were shiny ornately decorated glowing characters etched into the rock wall, designs of all kinds that were completely unfamiliar to him. He stepped out onto the platform, looked at Marshall and called upstairs, but there was no reception.

"Okay, Chief, we are going back upstairs; come on, get in."

Marshall stood grinning, while Burns pushed buttons on the bezel.

"What's going on, Chief?"

"Nothing is going on. If you'd care to follow me, you have nothing to be afraid of here."

Burns looked out and around again. "Afraid? I'm not afraid. Lead on, let's go . . . I'll follow."

Marshall looked at him, snickered and began walking, slowly, past several doors including Unit 17. Then, they both walked into a wider tunnel and stepped onto a moving tram that carried them downward and to the left. Burns watched as people passed them, going in every direction, living their lives no differently than on the surface.

"It looks like the bloody airport," Burns said.

The people mover took them to the main vertical chasm. They approached and walked off the tram toward the railing. Marshall gestured Burns to look over, into the sheer drop. Burns grabbed the railing with both hands and surveyed the unbelievable cavern and architecture.

"Not quite the airport, is it?"

"No, I confess I've never seen anything like this. It's almost like a fantasy movie set."

"Yes, I know. The first time I saw it was over two years ago. There are underground cities like this, everywhere, miles below Earth's surface. It is all still quite new to me. The people here have never been up to the surface; and, if you ask anyone, they would insist they'd never want to be anywhere else."

"Unbelievable. And where does all the light come from? At first glance, it looks wet, damp and chilly. I mean, given the rock walls, but it isn't, is it? It's quite beyond pleasant."

"I hope you understand if I plead ignorant. They have told me 'it's technical'. After all, I am in the security business, not lighting. But, as I understand it, the light comes from microscopic algae, or something like the glowing jellyfish in the deep oceans. That's probably where they originated, anyway. Everyone takes them for granted once they have been here a while. Look, Detective, Mr. Swanson and Dr. Bellos will be here shortly. I'm supposed to show you as much as I can, but, honestly, there is not enough time for much. I'd like to take you to one place that may answer all your questions."

"That would be a nice change. Fine . . . lead on. I'd prefer not to get lost down here."

The two men walked along the outside path of the main vertical chasm. Burns said nothing. Rather, he filled his senses with the awesome sights and people. Finally, Marshall opened a glass door and the two walked into Ever-Life Lab 202.

"Well, Chief, you have my undivided attention. You can start talking anytime."

Marshall had a faint smile. "Welcome to Ever-Life, Detective. Andrews and the entire Brock/Swanson Complex above rests on the cave catacomb structure we walk within now. This is all part of a self-sustaining, subterranean environment, far below Earth's surface and between planetary continents."

"You mean we are in some Jules Verne novel?"

"No one has ever written about this, I guarantee it."

"So Ever-Life, what is that?"

"It's where the bodies are, Detective."

"Bodies?" Burns stopped dead and turned to face Marshall. "We only found one body. I think it's time you explain yourself, Mr. Security Chief."

"Yes, well, that's why you are here. Come this way."

The two walked over 300 feet. Burns saw many medical tables with Knofer's on them, holograms, naked body parts floating, and even some full bodies suspended in midair. In another area, there were transparent rooms, one after the other, with doctors operating.

"Is this your hospital's Frankenstein parlor, Chief?"

"Not exactly. Here we are . . . "

They walked into chamber two of Lab 202 where Dr. LuAnne stood waiting for them.

"Good morning, Dr. Lu."

"Good morning, luv," she patted Marshall's face. "And who might this be?"

"This is Detective Jake Burns of the Arden City Police Department."

The doctor looked him over from head to toe.

"Hmm, good stock, you must be Scottish?"

"Scots, Irish, English and Hungarian, actually . . . but, I am a New Yorker by profession. I moved to Arden 10 years ago."

LuAnne giggled. "Whoa, some temper, I bet . . . interesting genetic package, too."

"He is investigating the shooting at Andrews."

"Ah, well you've come to the right place."

"Really, why's that? Who are you people?"

Dr. LuAnne grinned. "Over here, Jake, I think you'll find this most entertaining."

She turned and they followed her through the double doors of the lab's operating room.

"Hello, Dave," a voice said.

"Dr. Bellos? My God!" Marshall grinned and embraced the 74-year old man. "I'm so glad you're back."

"Thanks! I can tell! Me, too."

"Excuse me," Burns chimed. "You are Dr. Bellos?"

Dr. Richard turned to Jake. "One of them. And you are?"

"Oh, Dr. Richard, this is Detective Burns from the police. He's investigating the shooting at the hospital."

"Ah . . . " Richard looked at Marshall. "He's been cleared by GGM?"

"What?" said Burns. "You know, I'm only going to take just so much of this crap. One of you better start talking to me."

Richard replied kindly, "Well, I guess that would be me, Officer. My name is Dr. Richard Bellos. I am the mortician at Andrews Hospital. Early this morning, I was with several people in the morgue lab. Some very nasty military types broke in and shot up the place. I remember being shot several times, falling, and then, nothing. Beyond that, I can't tell you anymore."

"So you were shot?"

"Yes, rigorously . . . " Richard opened his lab coat with both hands to reveal his chest. " . . . Here, here and here, as you can see . . . oh, and here, my leg."

Burns looked and walked closer to study and feel the bullet scars. He turned to Dr. LuAnne with a look of amazement. "How is this possible?"

Just then, Mr. Mike and Jack Sheldon walked through the lab's doors.

"Good afternoon, everyone," said Mike, as he looked at LuAnne. "Are we ready for Jack?"

"Yes, I hope so. Will you excuse us, Jake? You may watch; but, preferably from over there," she pointed.

Burns and Marshall stepped backward to the side to give the others room.

"Who's that?" asked Burns.

"Mike Warren, Mr. Swanson's driver, and that is Jack Sheldon?"

"Sheldon? There was a Sheldon shot in the morgue, right?"

"Yes, as a matter of fact, there were two Sheldons shot. He is the one you found on the floor quite dead, at the time. The other was his wife. She is here, too, shot by the same men. She will be next, I think."

"Next?"

"You will want to pay special attention. You see, we found and already eliminated the special ops boys who did the deed, as well as their boss and the conspirators. All that remains is to bring everyone back to life."

Burns pulled Marshall's arm and yanked him back out, through the room's double doors.

"What do you mean you've eliminated the special ops boys and all that remains is to bring everyone back to life? I think it's time we all go back to my police station."

Out of nowhere, two GGM guards appeared beside Marshall.

"Sir, is there a problem?"

At that moment, a familiar voice interrupted.

"No problem, men, you may go. Mr. Marshall is quite correct, Detective. Hello, Jake."

Burns turned and released Marshall's arm.

"Gordon Swanson . . . as I live and breathe . . . "

Swanson extended his hand. "Good to see you again, Jake. To my left here is the mysterious Dr. Mathew Bellos, whom you've been looking for."

Jake shook hands and quipped, "Well, Swanson, I trust you are here to solve this puzzle?"

"Yes, my friend, I wouldn't have it any other way. Now, please follow us. We don't like good people to stay dead, do we?"

Swanson led the five, including Brian, back into the Lab Unit.

"Hello, Doctors. How are our patients?"

"Fine, so far . . . " LuAnne said.

"How are you, Dr. Richard?"

"I'm fine, sir. It's quite something. LuAnne gave me C.P.T. I feel so, hmmm, so complete. Yes, complete is the word."

"Well then, wonderful." Swanson handed Bellos two blue vials. "Don't you think it's time you do this, Mathew?"

Bellos looked at Swanson and then at Jack. "Yes, sir, I do."

"Dad?" Brian said.

"Sonny, everything is okay. This is what we have been waiting for. I'll be just fine."

Dr. LuAnne went to the refrigeration cabinet, pulled out the box and gave it to Bellos. He turned and smiled at his longtime friend. "Have a lay down, Jack. Up you go, right here."

At the same time, Burns turned to Swanson. "May we have a word?"

"Of course, this way . . . "

Swanson led Burns into Dr. LuAnne's office and leaned back on the desk, while Jake paced.

"I know you have a job to do, Jake."

"Yep . . . " Burns cleared his throat. "But, my question is, why have you allowed me to see all this? I'm not a stupid flatfoot. I have to take you all in. You know that."

Swanson put one hand in his pocket, turned around facing the wall monitor and touched the screen. It immediately turned into a full size hologram of Jack, and Bellos performing C.P.T.

Jake stared at the hologram. "My God, man, what is all this?"

Then, the two heard a young woman's voice and watched Angie Bellos come through the door. "Some place utterly wonderful . . . excuse me, my dad told me I could come in and that Mr. Swanson was here."

Swanson smiled and extended his arms.

"Yes, I am."

He embraced her.

"So good to see you, Angela, you've got quite a dad, you know."

"Yes, I know. Thank you."

"Angela, this is Mr. Jake Burns. He is a policeman, trying to solve the shootings in the morgue."

The two shook hands. "How do you do . . . That was the scariest 30 seconds of my life, except for seeing Dr. Sheldon on Focus Ward, that is, and being kidnapped, of course. I almost didn't make it to the closet."

"You were there?"

"Oh, yes. I saw those men shoot Mr. and Mrs. Sheldon and Dr. Richard."

"Jesus!" Burns sat down, looked at the two and the hologram and took a long deep breath. "I guess it's time for me to retire."

"Not at all, my friend . . . " Swanson patted Jake on the shoulder. "It's just time for you to change careers. Come on, both of you."

Swanson led them back into the Lab Room, just as Bellos finished injecting Jack and gave him a glass of wine. "Here, buddy, this should be the last drink of this you need. Then, you're good to go."

Swanson stepped behind one of the gurneys, looked at everyone and announced, "Please, all of you. I need your full attention."

Everyone stopped talking and paid attention: Jack, Bellos, Marshall, Burns, Richard, LuAnne, Angie, Brian and Mr. Mike.

"I have two things to do, and the first is in this room. I have thought a great deal about this. As some of you know, our laws require that we relate properly down here—with each other and the Carriers. No one is perfect, but we cannot tolerate extreme felonious behavior. We must deal with it in a timely manner. Usually, we would do so within the confines of our own culture. However, in this particular case, this behavior has affected the lives and deaths of several people here and from the surface. This is Detective Jake Burns."

"Jake, I invited you here to arrest the person who allowed all this to happen."

Swanson walked around and forward to the left of Mathew Bellos. As he did so, two armed guards walked into the Lab.

"Mr. Marshall, I am so much more than disappointed. You see, everyone, Mr. Marshall has been our Chief of Security for over a year. He is the only person who could have authorized Angie's clone to get into Focus Ward. No guard would just let her in. Either she had the door combination, which she did not, or you, Dave, called the guard and told him to open the door for her . . . and that wasn't enough. Then, you notified the Brock camp, when Angie was in the hospital morgue. You are responsible for stealing Jack Sheldon's manuscript and the shooting of three people." Swanson looked Marshall squarely in the eyes. "Do you have anything to say, Dave?"

Jake Burns looked on with a blank stare, watching as Marshall stood at attention.

"Sir, I thought I was helping the surface get a piece of life they deserved . . . Mr. Brock was very convincing to me, sir. After all, his name is on the marquee with yours. I didn't think so many would be hurt."

Everyone looked in shock. The guards tied Marshall's hands behind him, as Swanson continued, "That's usually the way it is with people like you. The problem, Dave, is that you knowingly disregarded your part in this horrendous conspiracy. You know how we work . . . how I work. You have obviously been involved with the Brock camp for months. There is no jury system here . . . these are your choices. You are going with Detective Burns. Whatever happens within his legal system, well, you are lucky. We would put you in a dry Unit and let you rot. If they do not punish you to the full extent of their law, I will personally see you again. If you say anything about us up there, I will personally see you again. If anyone you know ever mentions me or anything about us, I will personally see you again . . . I trust you understand me?"

"Yes, I do."

"Guards . . . take Mr. Marshall to Carrier-Unit 4. He should be comfortable there until Mr. Burns is ready to leave."

As the guards left the room, Jake turned his palms to the ceiling. "What just happened?"

Angie turned to Jack and helped him off the stretcher. "Hello, Mr. Sheldon, do you remember me?"

"Yes, I do, young lady. How are you now?"

Swanson asked Burns to rejoin him in LuAnne's office.

"Jake, I have to tell you, we are all thankful you got into this so fast. However, you know better than anyone does what the practical aspects of a murder case are. Take Angie's kidnapping, for example; who can say how long it would have taken you to trace that van? And, you would never find out there were two of Angie, one a clone."

Burns' eyes bulged.

"Jake, I have a proposition for you . . . I'd like you to consider something, seriously."

" . . . and what would that be?"

"I'd like you to become our new Chief of Security. We need you. I trust you. You would work for Mathew. This Ever-Life station would be your home base. However, you would report directly to me. I say it that way because this is not just a position to be located here in Arden. It's a worldwide career." Swanson grinned. "You can hire your own team and coordinate everything from here . . . I'll tell you what—think about it. Mathew out there will take you around, show you our home here, in some detail, and answer all your questions. You two have to get to know one another, anyway. Then, you arrest and take Mr. Marshall back. Take this and call me."

"I have a cell phone, thanks."

"Not one like this, my friend. Do me a favor, Jake; wait here for just a few minutes. I'll be right back."

"Yeah, fine."

Jake shook his head, surrendering with a grin.

CHAPTER 31

C . P . T .

GORDON SWANSON WALKED OUT THE DOOR of Dr. LuAnne's office, back into the Ever-Life Lab. He leaned in and spoke softly to his driver, "Mike, please prepare Carrier-2400 for departure, destination is Post 4."

Then Swanson turned to Bellos. "Mathew, may I have a word?" The two left Lab-2 and stood in the main module area. "Mathew, we have four hours. Will you take Mr. Burns on a tour, and then meet me at Platform 6."

"Are we keeping the cop?"

"I hope so. I have a sixth sense about both of you."

Meanwhile, Brian Sheldon helped his father get his bearings, "Dad, are you okay now?"

"Yes, son, better than I've been in a while . . . "

Dr. Richard squeezed Brian's shoulder. "I believe your father's going to be just fine."

Jack smiled, but his entire face and demeanor changed suddenly. "Doctors, where is Rachel? Where is my wife?"

Richard turned to LuAnne. "Where is she, Doc?"

"Through there," she pointed.

"Do you have a vial, Lu?"

"Yes, GGM gave me another one . . . here," She handed it to Richard.

"Not this time . . . this one goes to Jack."

Dr. LuAnne smiled and put the vial in Jack's hand. Jack stared at the small tube. Then, he looked at Brian and said, "Yes, I can do this . . . Dr. LuAnne, show me where."

She, Richard, Jack and Brian walked into Lab Chamber 3. LuAnne tugged on Jack's sleeve, "There under that sheet . . . that is your wife."

"Brian, stay here."

Jack walked over to the gurney and carefully pulled the sheet back, revealing only her head and shoulders.

"Oh, Rach, look at you."

"Dr. Sheldon?" Dr. LuAnne said, "We gave her two injections of our Fixits within the last hour, sadly there has been no reaction."

"Fix-its?"

Richard tapped Jack's shoulder and handed him a syringe, "Nanites to you, it doesn't matter anyway. Here we don't use these, but this is your show now. Spray this on your hands; it's better than those old gloves we use up there."

Jack looked at everyone and then he took the syringe, filled it with the contents of the blue vial and attached a needle. "Okay, honey, here we go . . . Brian, get on the other side of Mom. Help me roll her toward you . . . good, now hold her there."

Jack took the half-filled syringe and stuck the needle just above her C-1 vertebrae, just under the base of her skull. Slowly, he pushed up into the bottom center of her brain, exactly 2.25 inches, at a 35-degree angle.

"Okay, this is it."

He looked at Brian with a tear and then he pulled the plunger back. A distinct coagulation appeared in the syringe. Jack continued, until only a thread of the gel like quality was left. "That's it." He sighed anxiously, slowly extracting the needle, and then he studied the liquid. There was a jelly-like bubble floating in the blue bath. It began to move by itself. Suddenly, it popped. The coagulation completely defused in a microsecond. The liquid in the syringe now looked like blue bubbly champagne.

"My God! All right, son, let her down onto her back."

"Dad?" Brian began to cry.

"It will be all right. Be patient."

Jack changed the needle and focused on Rachel. He leaned over and kissed her cold forehead. "Okay, babe . . . come back to us."

He gently moved Rachel's head to the side and carefully stuck the longer needle into her right carotid artery, pushing the contents of the syringe in completely. Then, he pulled the needle out, ever so slowly, gave it to Dr. LuAnne and sat on the edge of the gurney caressing his wife. "Rachel, honey, can you hear me? It's Jack . . . come on, babe; you can do this."

Jack waited; nothing . . . he turned away and covered his face with his hands. "Oh, my God, Rach . . . "

"Dad," Brian said, "Dad, look at her hand."

Jack wiped his eyes and lifted her right hand. A finger twitched.

"Rach, Rachel Ann Sheldon, you wake up right now . . . it's me! Honey, please!"

"Look, Dad, her eyes!"

As they all watched, she blinked and saw Jack's tears.

"Hi," she said, smiling.

Jack cupped her face and kissed her tenderly. She reached around his neck and they embraced.

"My God, Rach," Jack whispered in her ear, "Thank heaven it works . . . I love you so."

He pulled back a bit, looked at her nose to nose, but he really couldn't see through the happy tears.

"Where have you been?" she said.

"Welcome back, my only." Jack smiled. "Look, I have someone here to see you."

Jack sat up and she saw her son.

"Oh, my heavens, Brian . . . "

The three embraced and cried.

Richard and LuAnne watched, standing arm in arm. "I guess this would be a good time to leave them alone," Dr. LuAnne said, weeping.

"Yes, I guess," Richard replied, as he put his arm around her. "Come on, I'll buy you a drink of water."

CHAPTER 32

CARLA

ANGIE BELLOS AND JAKE BURNS WAITED inside Ever-Life's Lab 2, while Rachel Sheldon underwent C.P.T.

"Young lady, may I call you Angie?"

"Yes, certainly . . . "

"You have had quite a day, so far, eh?"

"All of us have, I think." Angie smiled and crossed her fingers. "I can only hope it's over."

"Well, I do have one final gift for you," said her father, as he walked back in. "Hello, Mr. Burns, if I may call you that?"

"Why don't you just call me Jake? After all this, I think we are on a first name basis now."

"I appreciate that." Then Bellos turned to Angie. "Honey, will you come with me, and you, too, Jake. I think you may find this especially interesting."

They all walked out of the lab, down the hallway into one of the Ever-Life private modules. The room was a transparent oval glass-looking structure, which contained several items of distinction: several wall monitors, a floating transparent full size mattress, three chairs, each also transparent, with plastic looking cushions, but they were warm to the touch. In addition, a wizard-like, black wand hung from the ceiling above the bed on an attached short cord. Bellos walked in, pushed a button on the door molding, and the entire room changed from transparent to an opaque white, giving them privacy.

"Jake, please sit there if you would . . . Angie, I need you to go into the bathroom there, undress and put on the gown hanging behind the door. When you come out, hop up on the mattress."

Angie did, while Bellos put on a lab coat and washed his hands thoroughly.

"You know, Angie, the wonders you have witnessed today have happened, to a great extent, because of you. Remember in my office, I was trying to explain things?"

"Yes . . ."

"Remember I said you will see Mom, again?"

Angie's eyes widened, as she stepped through the door tying her gown. She walked over, sat on the corner of the bed and looked at Dr. B.; her heart began to race. "Yes, of course."

Bellos approached her. "In order to make that happen, I have to take a sample of a very important part of you. I have to get a specific link, which is in your DNA chain."

"But, how do you do that, in a direct procedure?"

"I use a special instrument. It won't take long; however, it may be painful. I have to go around one of your ovaries; and, I cannot give you any anesthetic, because it would contaminate the protein mix. Look, sweetie, you are a great nurse, but you are also my daughter. You know medical risks. There are no release forms to sign here. If you don't want me to do this, I won't. We will just find another way."

Angie thought of her mom's hologram. "No, if you think this will work, I've always trusted you; it's fine . . . do it." She scooted up onto the mattress, lay back down and discovered nothing was cold plastic. "Yep, definitely, let's do this . . . Jesus; this bed is heated . . . what is this material?"

"Feels good, doesn't it? There is a constant sterilization process going on. That's what you feel. The material is organic. We can discuss it over champagne, if this works."

Bellos turned to Burns. "Jake, you may witness, but I need you to be silent and keep still, okay?"

Burns swallowed nervously. "I won't say anything."

Bellos focused his full attention on the procedure. He took out a small one-eye/one-ear wireless headset from the bedside table and positioned it over the left side of his head. Then, he sprayed his hands with the pink sterilizer, which when dry became surgical gloves. "I wish we could use this stuff at the hospital."

He leaned over the bed and opened Angie's gown, revealing her lower abdomen. Then, he looked up at the hanging wand and spoke in the Ever-Life strange language, "GGM-TBN 010 . . . Application Bellos, procedure Unit Med 111172; initiate."

The wand detached from the cord and floated down into Bellos' right hand. He gripped and squeezed it gently, and a bright light shined from its tip. It seemed to pull his hand gently over her skin until it found the right spot.

"Okay, Dad, interesting gadget."

"First, this is sterilizing the area . . . I won't let anything happen to you, honey. Try to relax. You've seen something like this many times, but here we call it a transfer micro-laparoscope. I'll try to finish, as quickly as I can."

"That's fine; I'm just a little nervous."

"I know."

Behind Bellos in the center of the room, there was a round, metal pedestal, which stepped up ten inches from the floor. He began to speak to his Knofer. "Master control GGM-TBN-010 . . . Issue full spectrum program Carla Bellos, immediately."

Within 30 seconds, the Knofer constructed her solid hologram on the pedestal.

"Employ", he said.

"Hello, Mrs. Bellos," Dr. B. said with a loving smile.

Carla moved her body slowly, shook her head slightly and looked around the room. "Hi, you two; and who is this?"

"This is our friend, Jake Burns. Jake, this is my wife, Angie's mother."

"Hi," Jake said without thinking.

"Mathew, what are you doing, for heaven's sake?"

"It's a surprise. We are performing a serious medical procedure, and I need you to behave professionally, please. I've been working on this for a very long time. Finally, we think we found the answer."

"Answer?"

"Yes, babe, here . . . hold this, will you?" Bellos handed her a small, three-inch tall, sterile drinking glass. "Now, please, honey, just stand there, quietly. Don't move, just for a few minutes."

With that done, Bellos turned around and pointed the wand against Angie's abdomen again, just to the right of her navel. At the same time, he tapped the wall monitor above Angie's head, and a hologram of her reproductive system appeared six inches in front of his eyes, parallel to the bed.

"Angie, if you need to, close your eyes; it's okay."

"No, I wouldn't miss this."

"Try not to wince. You are going to feel a sting and discomfort . . . now."

"Ooh, yes, Oh my."

"Try not to move. I'm just about there."

Angie was torn between the pain and the wonder. The hologram of her abdomen automatically enlarged, as the wand's micro-wire extended and maneuvered from its tip inside her body. Bellos studied the hologram, watching the magnified wire poke through the mesentery, outside Angie's intestines. It weaved over, around, and toward the right side of her uterus. Then it stopped, and he studied her reproductive anatomy, closely. The hologram's 3-D imagery magnified again, adjusting to Dr. B.'s vision, so he could focus on every detail.

Angie stared at everything. The image of her abdomen rotated. The headset enabled Bellos to instruct the hologram to focus and position, as he thought-willed. Within a moment, the tip of the thread seemed to search on its own. When it reached her right ovary, it appeared to peck around it, like a chicken feeds. Fortunately, there was no sign of bleeding, and Angie had no sensation of the micro-wire's tip at all. Her only discomfort was at the point of entry.

Jake Burns had never imagined such a moment. He sat mesmerized in silence, watching the images and Bellos operate the wand. However, Carla reacted as a concerned mother would.

"Mathew, darling, what are you doing to our child?"

"Shush, please, saving us all, I hope. Ah, there it is . . . got it."

Focusing on the hologram before him, he squeezed a small point on the wand with his index finger. As light from the micro-wire's tip shot against Angie's ovary, Bellos twisted the wand. It sucked the contents up, into the reservoir in the handle; and then the micro-wire recoiled back out, into the tip of the wand. Dr B. carefully withdrew his hand and held the wand up to study the thumb-size syrup in the reservoir. He took off the headset and covered his daughter with her gown. She had no entry mark or wound, of any kind.

"There, have a look, Angie. This is it."

"What, exactly, is it?"

Bellos kissed her forehead. "You have been the bravest patient ever. No one could have gone through what you have in the last 12 hours, and then this. I'm so proud of you."

"Thanks, Dad; now what? What is that?"

"Hopefully, it's the answer to my research and getting your mom back . . . " Holding the wand, Dr. B. turned to face Carla. "Unfortunately, it has to be ingested raw, within five minutes of extraction. It's too new to synthesize, hon." Bellos squeezed the wand handle, ejecting the syrup into the small glass, which Carla held. "Now, you have to drink it . . . "

"Not on your deathbed, darling."

"Go ahead, down the hatch; Doctor's orders, ma'am."

Carla looked at Bellos, made a horrible face and held the glass straight away from herself.

Bellos sighed in frustration. "Honey, this is the culmination of all my research over decades. It's a viral syrup for you and you alone. Besides, you can't taste anything anyway. Sorry, babe, now just drink it!"

Carla lifted the cup, and, in one foul gulp, she swallowed the contents.

"There, satisfied?"

Angie sat up in pain, but it was worth it. Bellos put the wand down and slowly backed up. Jake Burns stood up and stared at Carla. As the syrup fell to her stomach, it seemed to change into a round glowing glob. Carla's holographic body also changed to a beautiful transparent peach-like color. The three watched, stunned, as the pasty glob rotated and glowed brighter. Once in her stomach, it dissolved, liquefied and then spread throughout her body, like tiny shooting stars.

"Look at it, Angie. I never imagined this. So many years of medical school; I've seen so many unexplainable things, but this; it's magnificent . . . " Bellos' eyes filled with tears. "I finally found my own C.P.T. Jack's manuscript gave me the clue to solve my own viral hypothesis. I found the solution to reanimate your mother within you, Angie. Quite by accident for me, really, it appeared within Jack's catalyst bath formula. That's what led me to the gene mix in your ovary. You have the only natural DNA for the bath; so, logically, I started with you. I found a shadow of memory, in a protein mix, within one c-chain of one gene; one c-chain mix, in one singular gene; quite remarkable."

Carla was changing before their eyes. The liquid quickly traveled to her heart and seemed to engulf it. Her heart began to move slightly, and then it began beating in a normal sinus rhythm. Bellos sat down on the bed with his arm around Angie, and they watched in disbelief. Jake stood by his chair, frozen.

"My God, Dad, you are going to have to explain all this."

"Yes, I know; just not now."

"What's happening to me, Mathew?" As Carla spoke, Bellos' Knofer monitored her vital signs. Carla was a hologram, changing into a real person. Within minutes, they could see red blood moving. Organs, nerves, muscles, skin and hair appeared. Then, she was done. There, before them stood a beautiful, warm, flesh and blood woman. Bellos stood up and approached his wife. He held out his arms and grinned.

"Hello, Mrs. Bellos."

Carla looked at her husband without expression, as if she were choking. Finally, she took a deep gasp, sucking in her first gulp of air. As she did so, she fainted and fell off the pedestal into her husband's chest.

"Yes!" Bellos said, holding her tightly, "Yes!"

He kissed his wife repeatedly. Carla felt the sensations of life spread throughout her body. She held onto Bellos and wept.

"Oh, Matt, you feel so good."

He helped her up and she looked over at Angie. With one arm around her husband's neck, she reached for her daughter and the three embraced.

"I think maybe you all should be alone," Burns said. "I'll just wait outside here and give you privacy."

Carla looked at Jake and up at Bellos with a smile. "I don't suppose one of you could get me a coat or robe; it's a little chilly in here for skinny dipping."

Bellos turned to Burns. "Please, the closet, grab a robe; will you Jake?"

Burns took one of the standard folded white robes from the shelf and gave it to Carla.

"Thank you, Jake," Carla said. "Believe me; it pleases me just to be able to feel embarrassed. Don't go. This is my birthday, and you are welcome."

"Honey," Bellos said, "Are you hungry?"

"My God, Matt, can I eat?"

"Yes, you can do whatever any gal can do. We have to run some tests, of course, and do a couple of additional procedures, regarding memory; so, you'll be here for a time; but then we can go home."

"Home . . . oh my . . . "

Angie would not let go of her mother. They spent the next few minutes hugging and laughing. But Bellos had to bring them all back to reality. "Carla, honey, the hardest part for me is, Mr. Burns and I have to leave, just for a while. I'm sorry, I have to go, but it is necessary. I will be back." Bellos stoked her hair and kissed her tenderly. "Until then, at least we don't have to 'end the program' . . . Angie, you stay with your mom. You both will be taken to a Unit. So, make sure you are both comfortable, okay?"

"I will; she'll love it!"

"Mathew, I just got here . . . "

Bellos put his fingers to her lips. "I know; I have to finish something. It's another life and death situation. We will all have our time now; I promise."

Bellos kissed and hugged them both; then, he turned to Burns. "Time to go, Jake . . . " He walked over to the door and pushed the button that turned the walls from opaque back to transparent. Bellos opened the door for Burns and winked as Jake walked by. "I hope this Ever-Life experience has lived up to your expectations, Mr. Burns."

As the door swung closed, Jake smiled and quipped, "Mathew, I have no words to speak except this could be the beginning of a very interesting friendship."

CHAPTER 33

THE END OF THE BEGINNING

THE JUDAH VILLA WAS JUST TWO MILES outside of old Jerusalem. It was an oasis within an exploding urban setting. Two new ranch structures jutted out from the back of the original stone tower, which was 20 feet by 20 feet by 100 feet tall. At least part of the original tower was over 6,000 years old. Palm trees and olive orchards bound the entire estate. After the terrorist wars, the entire villa had been converted into a hospital/hospice, for several terminally ill patients. There were 10 master suites. Each had sliding doors to a center garden, where patients could at least enjoy clean air and the fragrance of flowers, if they felt well enough to venture out.

Today was a special day for patient S in Suite 101, because he had invited and expected three friends to 3 p.m. supper, Pappas Kristos Alieri, Rabbi James Yeshua and Imam Ahmir Udera. S had known each man of faith, individually, for many years, but he made it a point never to see them all together. This would be the very first time.

At 2:45 p.m., Rabbi James and Pappas Kristos walked together up the cobblestone stairs and opened the huge double doors to enter the villa. Both were surprised to see Imam Ahmir was already in the receiving foyer.

"Good morning, my brothers," said Ahmir.

"Good morning," they said, each bowing to the other.

"I'm so pleased to see you both here," Kristos said with a grin.

"I've never known S to be so insistent about my being here," said Ahmir.

"Nor I," James remarked. "Obviously it's something important."

"Agreed," they nodded.

Then a guard appeared. "Good morning, gentlemen. May I escort you? This way . . . "

The three looked a little confused.

"Sir," Kristos remarked, "we mean no disrespect; but, as for me, I've never seen your uniform type here in Jerusalem. Are you from the Vatican Swiss Guard?"

"I am a private guard, here at the request of my old friend, just as you are, I believe. He asked me to wear the uniform I wore when I met him. I would do anything for him; this request was easy. We are all brothers here, my friends."

They turned a corner and walked down an unfamiliar beautiful corridor. Each man looked at the artifacts, mosaics and paintings representing all three faiths. Finally, the guard slowed and turned to the right. He took a small card out of his pants pocket and waved it over the symbol above the door lock. "S was moved to this special isolation suite, this morning."

The door clicked and opened. They walked in, and couldn't help but notice a comforting feeling from the room's light. The guard led them to three chairs in front of a large fireplace.

"Please, sit; I will see if he is appropriate."

Minutes later, the guard returned. "Gentlemen, you may come this way."

He led them into an oval room, lined with empty bookshelves. Three high back chairsfaced a wide hospital bed. The bed was between two windows, and above it was a masterful fish sculpture, made out of cut stained glass. An elderly, gaunt man looked up from his prone position and smiled at the three fathers. It was S.

"How marvelous you are here. Come, sit, sit . . . here, by me; Kristos . . . Ahmir, James, come, come . . . "

Each cleric bent toward S and kissed his right hand. For years, one of the three would alternate meetings, once a week or so with S; and, he regularly donated large sums of money to each of the local churches, without preferring one over the other. If there was a need, he would fill it, before the question of help even came up.

"O, ye men of the cloth," S grinned. "Thank you for coming on such short notice. Behold, three of the wisest men I know! I am so happy to see you all. Forgive me for not receiving you properly. I am weak today. I longed to speak with you together because this is a very important moment for us all."

"It is good to see you, too," Kristos said. "But, I think I can ask on our behalf, why are we to be here?"

S coughed a bit. "The invitations, my friends, did you bring them, by chance?"

All three dug into their pockets, withdrew their envelopes and then exchanged them, reading each other's.

"They are all handwritten and they all say the same thing," said Ahmir.

"Yes, they do; and for a good reason, my friends." S seemed in distress, so he pushed the call button for the guard. "M; come please . . . "

"Yes, sir?"

"Would you give us all some wine?" S spoke very softly. "And you may bring supper anytime; thank you . . .

. . . I have asked you three here to receive my last confession."

"You are not dying. God would not hear of it." James leaned into S. "Tell us, why the strange words on the invitations?"

"Yes, why have you brought us together?" Ahmir gently squeezed the old man's arm. "You do not need us three to confess anything."

S looked sadly at the three, and then he turned to look out the window at the trees.

"I confess that I have been studying you three of late, behind your backs and without your consent."

The three clergy looked at each other and Kristos replied, "My friend, why would you do that?"

The guard entered, carrying a food tray.

"Ah, the wine is here. Please, let us sip."

M set the tray on the table and gave each man a wineglass, filled with a pearl white liquid.

"I remember, M, when all of you guards wore that puffy uniform."

"Yes, sir, a long time ago . . . you told us it was copied from ancient Roman jesters, to fool everyone into thinking we were not to be feared."

"Yes, quite so. Thank you, M; everything looks tasty."

M closed the door behind him and locked it.

James lifted his glass, studying the drink. "What is this, S? The glasses are exquisite. But the wine, it looks like milky champagne."

"Let us toast," S said. "to the unifying of the faiths."

The three clergy froze, with their glasses raised. They looked at each other, clinking their goblets together, and said in unison, "To the unifying of the faiths."

"Oh, my goodness, I've never tasted anything like this," Ahmir said.

"Nor I," said Kristos.

James closed his eyes. "I can't begin to describe it."

S handed his drink to Kristos. "I wanted you three at your best today. This helps. As for me, it does no good anymore. Whatever its benefits, I receive them no longer. Ah well, such is the way of things . . . James, help me sit up, will you? Now, to my confession, I know what you three have been up to. It is with a sad heart that I say how disappointed I am about your little 'conspiracy of good'."

The three men looked at S with guilty eyes.

"I am to blame," said Kristos. "I, alone, approached the others."

" . . . For the sake of what, my friend?" S put his hand on Kristos' forearm. "And, I know, also, that you were the only one approached, my brother . . . I know this . . . he was the devil himself."

The three fathers sipped the wine again. Then, Ahmir stood up, turned and brought the plate of bread and cheeses, offering it to the others as he spoke, "Do we not love one another? We all believed what he told us. We still believe. If it is true, the world will come together like never before, praise be to Allah. We can be one faith."

"Ah, but alas, my friends, it was not to be. All has fallen sour," Kristos said. "I am so sorry."

"Well," S said as he took another sip, "you boys still have the $16 billion; and, in truth, I confess I know the Brock camp lied to you about the serum."

The three men looked perplexed.

"How do you know all this?" asked James.

"Please, sit. Have one last toast with me, eh?" S raised his glass again. "I solemnly swear to you that, upon my death, I bequeath . . . "

Without warning, S coughed up blood and fell back onto the pillow, spilling the drink on the bed sheets. Kristos picked the glass up and patted the sheets with a clean cloth. Ahmir reached to S and held his hand. "Dearest friend . . . "

"My three wise men," S said.

James squeezed his other hand. "Please let us help you. What can we do?"

"My friends, you can be at peace; and do not let what appears to be my pain or anyone else's euphoric promises cloud your thinking, or deaden your ears and mind to what you must understand . . . Kristos, in the night table next to me, there is a book. Get it, please?"

The priest opened the small door and lifted out a heavy, pearl white book, 20 inches long by 15 inches wide by four inches thick. It had three letters embossed in gold leather, GGM. The three had never seen anything like it. They all touched it and Kristos looked at S.

"What is this, my friend?"

"I have decided to give this to you three. My last wish is that you study it and decide if you should make it public. I trust you with all my heart. It belongs to all of you. It is very old. Protect it. Learn from it. It speaks my truth. Even now, at this moment, I tell you; I will always be with you."

With those last words, Great Grand Master 1-000 Gordon G. Swanson died. The three clergy were spellbound and void of comment. They looked at each other.

"What do we do?" Ahmir asked.

"We should go to the Church of the Holy Sepulchre and read this," said Kristos. "It must be very important."

Then, the three knelt beside the bed. After a moment of prayer, each kissed the GGM on his forehead and stood up. The guard came in, walked to the bed, and with tears, he also kissed S. "Gentlemen, please, it's all right; I will handle this. Everything has been arranged. I will have someone contact each of you regarding ceremony."

The three bowed and shook the guard's hand. They turned and walked out of the room and down the hall.

"What a loss," said Ahmir.

"He was truly a great man," James said. "I wonder how he knew so much about our effort. To my knowledge, we three have never even been in the same room at the same time with him."

Kristos paused in the hallway, "Well, my brothers, let's be honest, our faiths don't have a history or reputation of cooperation, especially here in Jerusalem."

"Yes, I suppose that's true," Ahmir smiled politely but shook his head, " . . . which is why our effort, if successful, would have been so remarkable and important. Can you imagine if we three were the ones to bring all our brothers together, praise be to Allah?"

As they faced each other, Kristos caressed the book.

"I wonder what secrets this holds."

"Yes. I, too, would like to know," said Ahmir. "Let me hold it. I think each of us should read it individually; then, we should study together, at Al Aqsa Mosque, at the Temple on the Mount, where we can tutor all our brothers."

"Kristos, do you think S had something specific in mind, giving this to us?" asked James. "He seemed to know everything we did, everything that happened. My people engaged the strictest security measures."

"The more reason we should each study this gift," Ahmir said. "Please, I will take it first, and then contact each of you." Ahmir bowed before Kristos and extended his arms, expecting the book.

"Here and now is not the time to discuss this, my friends," James interrupted. "I know S was planning on lecturing at my local synagogue. I'm sure he would want us to study it first, along with those related sections of the Talmud."

"Please," Kristos insisted, "let us not forget, my brothers, our combined effort was to prove the resurrection of our Lord and Savior, Jesus Christ. The Church of the Holy Sepulchre was the point of trade, in the first place." Kristos pulled the book tightly to his chest, turned and walked toward the villa's front doors. "We should remember what just happened here, and in respect, let us go in peace."

Ahmir stepped in front of Kristos pleading, "I beg you, my friend. My people trusted you, and you led us through this 'failed effort'. They will not sit still for you to take this gift first. As a gesture of goodwill, give me the book."

James stepped in front of the both of them and opened the villa's front double doors. Kristos looked at the two and said simply, "No, my brothers, I will take the book and pray at the Church of Our Lord for guidance. Then, I will contact you."

The three began arguing in earnest as they walked out onto the stone front stairs. Then they noticed two men getting out of a white stretch limousine at the end of the walkway. As they walked toward the fathers, Kristos was the first to notice.

"Excuse us, please, sirs, we three have been visiting an old dear friend here, who just a moment ago passed away. We couldn't help but notice you two."

One man in front of Kristos replied, "How do you do . . . our apologies . . . you say your friend just died?" They both couldn't help but see the bright book Kristos was holding. The one turned to the other and said, "My God, it couldn't be." He looked at the clergy and spoke, "My name is Dr. Mathew Bellos. We are here to visit an old friend also."

Bellos looked to his right. "May I introduce, Master Gordon G. Swanson?"

"Hello, gentlemen."

They all shook hands. Then, holding the book, Kristos said, "It is an honor to meet you both. Forgive me, please. Are you a relative of our friend? We couldn't help but notice, you have the same name, the same identical look. It is truly remarkable."

Swanson looked at the three men and smiled. "Not exactly, my brothers, if you have that book, you were given a great gift. Read it, and learn that I am he who gave it to you. Be well."

He smiled at all three; and, before anyone could react, Bellos and Swanson walked between the clergy, and into the villa, leaving the three fathers speechless, in a moment of quiet awe.

Chapter 34

Shadows

DIRECTLY ACROSS THE STREET, in a second story room facing the front door of the villa, a dark figure stood looking out the window through binoculars. He watched all five men talk at the front doors.

After Bellos and Swanson entered the building, the three men walked down the stairs along the villa's entry path. They appeared to argue, adamantly, but the man viewing couldn't understand what they were saying. They were obviously bickering, yanking something between them, stopping and going, even shouting at one point.

The man in the room placed the binoculars in his briefcase, along with some personal items. Then, he gathered his belongings, put on his suit coat and walked out and down a narrow staircase to the back entrance. He locked the door behind him, and strolled through a grove of olive trees, which extended about a half-mile or so. The branches shaded his figure as he stopped occasionally to look down at the shallow graves lining each side of the dirt path. Finally, at the last grave on the far right, he knelt down, took an object out of his coat pocket and pushed it into the mound of dirt. It was a small two-inch blue vial.

"Clones," he said to himself. "I never should have invested in clones."

Marion Brock stood back up and walked silently out of sight.

Transmission input Headset 1 complete . . . Andrew 10746-H1

I opened my eyes as Dr. Luanne Rather took off my headset. "There you are, first one done, but you will have to have another session."

"Another? How long was I under?"

"Total transmission time was only two minutes. Amazing, isn't it?"

"I have so many questions about this one. How did I get here? Where am I?"

"Yes, I am sure you do. But it takes time for your mind to accept the information. You are at Time Trust, Ever-Life Post 2."

"Where is that?"

"I have to get back to Arden, New Mexico. You will be in good hands. Try not to worry. Drink this."

I had no idea what that meant or how many headset sessions they would give me; but I had other haunting questions: *Clones...what was Brock saying? Did C.P.T. change everything? What happened to the three fathers and that book? What happened to Brock when the Carrier took him?*

As Dr LuAnne walked to the door, she turned to me and said, "I enjoyed meeting you. You'll be fine. Just be patient. Someone will be here soon. I hope you enjoy Time Trust . . . goodbye for now, Andrew."

Andrew Sarkady

APPENDIX

Ever-Life Subterranean Posts: The following describes the Ever-Life's populated subterranean regions-Posts, worldwide. There are many transport stations within each Post. Some Carrier stations are within one mile below Earth's surface, but heavily populated colonies are a minimum of five miles below the surface.

Post 1: Includes upper East Asian Continent, Mongolia and the China Basin, stretching east and south through the Himalayas, Tibet, India and Pakistan, population: 600,000 . . . There are 250 major Transport Stations throughout the region.

Post 2: Europe, the Netherlands, England and Northern Africa . . . population: 300,000 . . . there are 320 major Transport Stations throughout the region

Post 3: North American Continent-Canada and the United States and across Alaska including the Bering straits, population: 700,000 . . . there are 230 major Transport Stations throughout the region.

Post 4: The Middle East, Turkey and the Baltic, north including Russia and west bounded by Afghanistan and Kazakhstan, population: 400,000 . . . there are 140 major Transport Stations throughout the region.

Post 5: Australia and the Pacific Seas including Japanese Isles and east including South America, population: 500,000 . . . there are 170 major Transport Stations throughout the region.

Post 6: Mid and Southern Africa and Madagascar, population: 300,000 . . . there are 100 major Transport Stations throughout the region.

Post 7: South Pole, North Pole, Atlantic Sea and all major planet fresh waterways, population: 200,000 . . . there are 150 major Transport Stations throughout the region.

Post 8: The deepest most remote living quarters 800 miles below Earth's surface and directly below the post station at the Judah Villa in Jerusalem . . . population: 25,000 . . . there are 25 Transport Stations in the colony.

ഏ൫൰ൟ

C.P.T.—Chemical Personality Transfer: The procedure of withdrawing a persons' coagulated memory/personality and re-injecting it back into that patient or another, who has a compatible genetic code.

Knofer: A singular communication device used by the population within Ever-Life colonies. It offers video, audio, 3-D imagery, unlimited download capability and contains records of all knowledge from historical archives of 500,000 years. It also has a defense mode and security protocols, and is time travel compatible.

Anabolic vs. Catabolic: Within Ever-Life's understanding, anabolic processes within the body replace cells-rebuild them; catabolic processes release energy and cells die. As we age, more cells die than are replaced. C.P.T. stimulates the anabolic processes to regenerate more cells than die; thereby the patient/subject becomes healthier than before C.P.T.

Duplication: The process of growing body parts or an entire body, however, unlike clones, each duplicate has complete DNA.

Cloning: The process of growing body parts or an entire body; however, unlike Duplicates, each has incomplete DNA. The results are unstable and volatile.

Transtosis: The Ever-Life process of reanimating all synaptic connections within a body and rejuvenating all cells to perform anabolic growth processes.

TIME TRUST

My story continues in the second book of the Ever-Life series, *Ever-Life: Time Trust*, available from Christopher Matthews Publishing and bookstores worldwide.

About the Author

Andrew Sarkady was born in Trenton, New Jersey. He studied at Washington & Jefferson College, Lake Forest College, and Northwestern University. He began making notes regarding Ever-Life in 1965, but only after fathering 4 children and a 40 year career in industrial sales did he begin to put pen to paper regarding this extraordinary manuscript. He lives in Illinois and continues to write.

CPSIA information can be obtained at www.ICGtesting.com
Printed in the USA
LVOW10s1546021015

456698LV00017B/646/P

DEC 0 1 2015

9 781938 985638